EMILY ANTOINETTE

ESCAPING THE FRIENDZONE

A DADDY DOM MINOTAUR ROMANCE

ISBN 979-8-9883161-5-2 (paperback)

Cover art by Fallnskye

For all my stressed out babes who want a hot minotaur daddy to take care of them. You deserve to be spoiled, cherished, and thoroughly satisfied.

CONTENT NOTES

Escaping the Friendzone is a fluffy and spicy monster romance featuring a plus size human woman and her brother's minotaur best friend.

It has explicit, kinky open-door sex, including sex in an escape room (MCs are the only people present), oral sex, daddy dom/baby girl dynamics (no age play), spanking, praise, light degradation, cumplay, and a very large monster dick.

There are mentions of internalized fatphobia/body shame (FMC), discussion of food shaming, and lots of profanity (both MCs).

1

ARIANA

The alarm on my phone repeats its annoying song as I slam the dryer closed with a little too much force, almost toppling over the laundry basket sitting on top of it. I hit the button to start the drying cycle and scramble into my living room to turn the blasted thing off. It's been going off for at least three minutes, and I could've turned it off sooner, but without the incessant reminder I would've gotten sucked into another task instead of heading out the door.

I look down at the baggy sweatshirt that I'm wearing for the second day in a row, then do a quick pit check. *Eh, smells fine.* My pajama pants aren't suitable for leaving the house in, so I tug them off, heading to my dresser.

Shit. All my panties are currently in the dryer, and I did a purge of all the ancient ones with elastic so worn out that they don't stay up, so those aren't even an option. Guess I'm going commando. I pull on a pair of black leggings and frown down at the hole that's opened up in the inner thigh. This happens with all of my leggings —my thighs are too powerful to be contained. One more outing in them should be okay. I doubt anyone will be looking between my thighs in a dark escape room.

I swish some mouthwash and shove my frizzy faded pink hair up into a bun, mentally putting re-dyeing it on my endless list of tasks. It'll be weeks before I get to it. Life has been a whirlwind of working non-stop, while trying to keep my head above water with chores and basic self-care. The extreme business is a good thing in theory—my shop has never been more in demand since one of my hoodie designs went viral. But I'm starting to fall apart at the seams, just like my leggings.

If I worried about going out into public looking like an unwashed goblin, I'd never leave the house. I don't have time to be cute. My friends won't care what I look like, just that I show up. Kelly's been bugging me for weeks to get together, and wouldn't take no for an answer anymore. Plus, Doug will be there, and I know he'll give me shit if I bail on another plan with him. Why the hell my brother wants to hang out with me instead of his girlfriend on Valentine's Day is beyond me. Maybe things in his love life aren't going well. Damn, now I definitely can't bail in case he needs to talk.

I don't even bother to check how I look in the hall mirror as I sling my purse over my shoulder and head out the door. Doug will probably call out the dark circles under my eyes that make me look like a sickly Victorian child. He's been on my ass about taking time to rest ever since he joined his monster support group. One of their tenants, which he quotes to me all the time, is "rest is crucial to success". Though, for him, it's more about success at not going into a wolfy rage when something makes him upset.

I'm glad he found the group, even if he drives me a bit crazy with his non-stop proselytizing about self-care. When Doug was accidentally bitten by a werewolf a few years ago, he went to a really dark place. Neither of us knew that monsters existed, and in one night his whole life was turned upside down. I've done my best to support him, and in the process have found myself as one of the rare non-paranormals who has more monster friends than human ones.

Tonight, we're meeting up at a fae-owned escape room that Doug heard about through his support group. Once we're in the room, paranormals can let down any glamors or shift to their monster forms. Even better, the rooms are charmed, so magic can't be used to force through the puzzles.

I pull into the parking lot with only one minute to spare, snagging a spot right by the entrance as someone is leaving. Of course I see *him* standing right by the entrance, arms crossed, his absurd biceps straining the fabric of his button-down's sleeves as he stares down at his phone.

Wesley. My brother's minotaur best friend, who I've been harboring a ridiculous crush on since the moment we met, even though he's so far out of my league he might as well be on another planet. His glamor is in place, so right now he looks like a very attractive, fit human—if a little bit douchey with his too-tight pants and enormous gold watch gleaming against his dark brown skin in a way that screams "I have expensive taste". Honestly, in his work clothes, he's not really my type. Far too polished, shoving in my face the fact that he's so much more put together than I'll ever be. I much prefer him sweaty and mussed, like he is when he and Doug hang out post-workout. And the rare times I've seen him without his glamor, in his natural minotaur form... I start to get overheated just thinking about it.

He looks up and gives me a wave and a gleaming white smile as I approach, his gold nose ring glinting in the setting sunlight. God, why does he only ever see me when I look like a mess? My hand reflexively attempts to smooth down any flyaways, but they're the least of my worries. There's no hiding how bedraggled I am.

"What are you doing here?" I ask. Not that I can't deduce the answer. Doug invited him. Ugh, now I'm going to have to spend an hour locked in a room with Wesley. A whole hour of him teasing me and treating me like an annoying little sister. Sure, I'm 30 to his 41, but we're both adults. I guess he'll always see me through that lens because of his friendship with Doug.

"Hello, Ariana. Nice to see you too," he says wryly, his stupid perfect mouth quirking as he looks at me.

I roll my eyes. "I just didn't expect you to be here. Shouldn't you be out with some babe? It's Valentine's Day."

"Oh, you know. I figured hanging out with Doug's rude little sister would be so much more fun than getting laid," he says, his deep voice dripping with sarcasm. "Doug invited me and I was worried that something had happened with Margaret and..."

"You didn't want him to be alone," I finish. I might not be happy Wesley is here, but I can't argue that he's not a wonderful, supportive friend to my brother. "I guess we'll find out soon enough. Is he inside?"

"Nah, I'm the first one here. I haven't seen Kelly either." His phone vibrates, and he glances back down at it. "Great," he says with a sigh.

"What?"

"Doug's not coming. Margaret showed up at his place in some fancy lingerie and—"

"Eww, gross, please don't finish that sentence." I don't need to know what kind of freaky sex my brother is getting up to right now. "Okay, well, Kelly should still be here soon so—"

My phone rings, cutting me off. "It's Kelly." I take a few steps away from Wesley before I pick up.

"Heeeey," she says when I answer. Shit, that sounds like her apology "hey".

"Hey! Where are you?" I ask, dreading her answer.

"Uh, so, I was about to leave work to head over and...you're never going to believe this, but Susan showed up at my office with a bunch of roses."

"Susan, the hot bitch from sales?!" Kelly's been obsessed with her harpy crush for over a year. "Oh my god, that's amazing! What happened?"

"She asked me out tonight. I told her I had plans but—"

"Screw plans! You're going out with her!" There's no way I'm letting her miss that opportunity with Susan.

"Are you sure?" Kelly asks. "I feel so bad. I'm the one who bugged you to come tonight, and I hate bailing."

I laugh. "It's a nice change for you to be the one canceling this time. Seriously, it's not a problem. Go have fun! Just promise to tell me all the juicy details tomorrow."

"I will!" Kelly says, letting out a little squeal of delight before we say goodbye and hang up.

I grin down at my phone, feeling elated that Kelly's romantic fantasies are finally about to come true, and at the fact that I can retreat to my gremlin lair and maybe get some more chores done.

"Well?" Wesley asks when I rejoin him.

"She's not going to make it. You're saved from being trapped with me. Have a good night with whoever you can convince to come over for a last minute V-day hookup." I turn to head back to my car, but a heavy hand clamps onto my shoulder.

"Where are you going?"

"Uh, home?" I say, trying not to freak out at the weight of Wesley's hand on me. I don't think he's ever intentionally touched me before and it's making me feel hot and cold all over, which is silly because it's my damn shoulder, not my tit. Crap, now I'm thinking about what it'd feel like to have him touch my boob.

"Why?" He furrows his brow and narrows his deep brown eyes at me with the same confusion that I'm currently feeling.

"What do you mean, why? Doug and Kelly aren't coming. Which means there's no reason to stay."

Wesley pulls his hand back with a huff. "Wow, harsh."

Why is he acting butthurt about my answer? I'm giving him an easy out for the night! "I didn't mean it like that! I just figured you'd rather not spend your Valentine's Day doing a four-person escape room with me."

"Ariana 'I love a challenge' Sawyer is backing out of an escape room because we don't have the optimal number of people?" He shakes his head with a laugh, obviously goading me.

I wish I could figure out why. Maybe it'll be fun for him to tease me when I inevitably get frustrated at the puzzles? Still, he's right. I can't back down from a direct challenge.

"No! I could do it by myself if I wanted to," I snap back at him.

Wesley grins at me like I just walked into a trap. Dammit, he's definitely planning to tease the shit out of me. What an ass.

"Then let's do it. Come on, before they get mad at us for arriving late." He places a huge palm on my back, guiding me inside before my brain can catch up enough to think of another excuse.

I'm about to be locked in a room for an hour, alone, with the hottest, most unattainable person I've ever met. A person who seems to get off on teasing me—and not in a fun, sexy way. Please god, goddess, or whoever is out there, help me get through this torture without completely embarrassing myself.

2

WESLEY

What the hell am I thinking? I can't spend an hour alone with Ariana! Not when she flushes so prettily when she gets frustrated. Not when every time I see her, I have to force myself to stop staring at her tits and wonder what it'd be like to fuck them.

Gods, I'm such a pervert. She's Doug's sister. His much younger sister. Totally off-limits.

Doug never explicitly told me that, but it's an implied part of being someone's best friend—don't fuck their little sister. Their sister with a lush body that I dream about seeing naked, and a mouth full of sarcasm begging to be shut up by my cock.

Like I said, I'm a pervert.

I definitely shouldn't be doing this, but she looked in need of fun and so worn out that I couldn't let her go home and exhaust herself even more. Though I guess she's not worn out enough for it to dampen her abrasive attitude. She saves her snark just for me, and fuck me, if that doesn't make my dick even harder for her. I like a challenge, and Ariana's the most tempting one I've ever met.

That also makes me sound like a creep. It's not that I like a challenge in a pick-up artist, "won't take no for an answer" way. It's just refreshing to be around a woman who doesn't fawn all over me because of the way I look. Gods, that makes me sound conceited, but it's a fact! I look good—I work out a lot, I dress well, and my face is decent. So I like that Ariana gives me shit instead of simpering.

I like Ariana for many reasons. She's so damn smart and creative, she works her ass off for her business, and she's fucking sexy even when she's kind of a mess. All of those reasons add up to mean that I shouldn't be pushing to get time with her alone. She's never shown even a hint of interest in me, and I'm not interested in making her uncomfortable. Unless it's a consensual kind of discomfort.

Great, now I'm thinking about spanking her luscious ass. *Dude, get a hold of yourself!*

I can't help but savor the feel of her under my hand as I guide her inside, even if it's through the thick fabric of her enormous sweatshirt. I've touched Ariana twice now. I should not be touching her. There must be some kind of horny Valentine's Day energy in the air, because I almost always manage to keep my distance, but it's almost impossible tonight.

She doesn't pull away from my touch when we get up to the check-in desk, which I note with far too much satisfaction before forcing myself to back off. The receptionist is finishing up with another group, allowing me to take stock of the situation. Ariana's pale cheeks are a little flushed and I suppress a grin as I watch her mentally wrestle with how to get out of spending this time with me. If she comes up with something, no matter how flimsy of an excuse it is, I won't force her to stay. Part of me hopes she thinks of something, so I don't spend the next hour trying to solve riddles while half the blood in my body is allocated to my semi-hard dick.

"You're thinking awfully hard there," I say, prompting her to give me her excuse.

"I'm preparing myself to spend an hour locked in a room with you," she says with a dramatic sigh.

She's not leaving. Shit. Hell yeah. But *shit.*

"Hah! Use that as motivation. The faster you solve the puzzles, the faster you can be free from me." That earns a chuckle from her. Gods, I love her laugh.

She opens her mouth for what I'm sure is going to be another witty barb, but the receptionist interrupts, turning to greet us. "Welcome to Fantasy Escapes! Are you here to check-in for a reservation?"

Ariana gives him a weak smile. "Yeah, it should be under 'Sawyer'."

The receptionist nods, his eyes dipping momentarily to give her a once-over before looking at his laptop. Ariana tugs at her sweatshirt self-consciously as she waits for him to look up our reservation.

Why is she acting nervous about her appearance? Is she attracted to him? Sure, he has nice hair and an elegant face typical of a fae, but she could do a lot better. Is he her type? Damn, no wonder she's so indifferent toward me.

A surge of jealousy and indignance rushes through me. She looks great. Sure, that sweatshirt has a small pasta sauce stain on the sleeve and it's at least two sizes too big, but he would be so lucky to get a shot at Ariana. My hand twitches, wanting to wrap a possessive arm around her waist, but I hold myself back.

"Ah, here we go," the receptionist says, finding the reservation. His eyes drop again to Ariana's chest and his lips twist into a small grin. It better be because he's a fan of the adorable cat design on her shirt, not because he's staring at her tits. It's one of the designs she sells in her shop and it's cute as shit. Godsdammit, now I'm staring at her breasts. Look away from the kitty titties!

"Just the two of you?" he asks, smiling at my girl in a way that's far too friendly for my liking.

"Yeah," I say, my voice coming out deeper than usual. Any restraint I had a moment ago evaporates, and I drape an arm over her shoulder.

Ariana tenses and looks up at me, her cute eyebrows scrunching together at my weird behavior. I squeeze her shoulder and try to play it off as an innocent brotherly gesture, but she still looks perplexed. I don't blame her. That's the third time I've touched her tonight. Doug is usually around when I see her, so it's easier to keep my distance. Now that he's absent, my hands seem to want to make up for lost time.

The receptionist gives me a knowing look. "Nice, man. We have a lot of couples here tonight. You've picked the perfect time slot, too. Last booking of the night means we can let you stay in the room longer than an hour if you need more time to..." He trails off with a smirk.

"We're not! We won't need more time!" Ariana sputters at the receptionist's insinuation.

"Oh? Well, I'll still give you privacy. Just in case the close quarters inspire you to change your mind and have some extra...fun." He winks at Ariana and she flushes bright red.

While the thought of having some fun with Ariana in the escape room makes my dick perk up, this dude needs to back the fuck off. She's clearly uncomfortable.

"We won't need the time. She's really good at puzzles," I say, patting her on the shoulder before releasing my hold on her.

"Y-yeah." She gives me an appreciative nod.

The fucker has the audacity to grin like it's some kind of innuendo. "I bet." I scowl at him and he sobers immediately.

"Follow me," he says, heading down a narrow hall with no further comments other than to give us a quick synopsis of the rules of the escape room and to let me know that my glamor won't work inside the room because of the anti-magic enchantment on the space.

He opens the door to a small room styled to look like an abandoned Victorian parlor—peeling damask wallpaper, flickering candlelight, and creepy portraits all working to create an effectively spooky atmosphere. The vibe is broken a bit when we step inside, and he gives us a rehearsed speech about the people that lived in this house, their mysterious deaths, and some nonsense about how their vengeful spirits have trapped us inside and we have an hour to put them to rest and escape or be doomed to an eternity of haunting the manor with them. I honestly wish this jerk would shut up and leave us alone, because Ariana still looks embarrassed by his earlier comments.

"Great, cool, doomed for eternity. Thanks, man. We've got it," I say, cutting him off and gesturing for him to leave.

Now that my glamor is down, and he can see my full, hulking

minotaur self, he gives me a nervous look and nods before scurrying out of the room. Good riddance.

As soon as the door closes and "locks" behind him, I let out a sigh. "Man, that dude was such an ass."

Ariana grimaces. "Yeah. Sorry."

"Why are *you* sorry?" Please tell me she doesn't think she deserved for him to perv on her like that.

She shrugs, looking down at her feet. "I feel bad that he thought we're, uh, on a date. I'm sure it's a repulsive thought to you, what with me being Doug's little sister and all of *this*." She gestures down at herself with a strained laugh, still not meeting my eyes.

"All of what, Ari?" I ask in a rough tone. Is she kidding me? I want to tell her that the thought of this being a date and getting to have my way with her while we're trapped in this room is making it hard for me not to pop a boner.

She glares back at me like I'm the biggest moron in the world. "God, you're such an ass. You really want me to enumerate the reasons why it'd be embarrassing for someone like you to be on a date with me?"

She thinks I was upset with that guy because he thought we were on a date? "Ari, what the hell—"

"Forget it. Let's just get started," she says dismissively, turning away from me to start scanning the room.

Everything in me wants to grab her and confess how godsdamn wrong she is, but I can feel her bristling with anger even with her back turned. She'd probably think I'm messing with her and it'd piss her off even more.

I'm pissed, too. She thinks I'm that much of an egotistical asshole? Even if I wasn't attracted to her, I sure as fuck wouldn't give a shit if people thought we were dating. I almost say that, but hold myself back. Focus on the room, and let her cool off. Let us both cool off.

I move to inspect the other side of the room, rummaging through a beat-up desk for any potential clues. This is going to be a long hour.

3

ARIANA

"Hmm, that's not right... Maybe try turning it the other way?" Wesley's voice rumbles in my ear as he leans over my shoulder to look at the torn letter pieces we've found searching the room. Shivers skitter down my spine at the feel of his breath against my neck. I simultaneously want to turn around and shove him away and pull him closer so I can feel his mouth on my skin.

I settle for acting annoyed. "Stop hovering, I've got it! Go try to figure out what the marks on the portraits mean."

Another puff of breath hits me as he lets out a small laugh and steps back. Goddammit, why does even his breath turn me on? It smells like apples and cinnamon, and I bet his mouth tastes like apple pie, my favorite dessert. What would kissing him in his minotaur form feel like? Would he lick inside my mouth with that wide tongue? Heat pulses between my legs. Better yet, what would that tongue feel like on my clit?

"So bossy, Ari. Who made you in charge of this escape room?" Wesley asks, his low, teasing tone doing nothing to stop my horny train of thought.

"I'm not bossy! I just can't focus with you...breathing on me like that!"

"Fine, I'll stop *breathing* on you," he says, rolling his eyes like I'm being absurd. Even though he's the one that's been plastered to my side for the last ten minutes, not giving me room to think because he's fogging my mind with his stupid, perfect beefy body that I want to climb like a tree.

I don't know why he's so clingy tonight. He keeps touching me, even before we got into the room. Nothing inappropriate, just brushes against my arm, or a steadying hand on my lower back. Maybe it's some weird protective brother's-best-friend BS because of the weird receptionist? I wish he'd stop. Or do a whole lot more.

Fuck, I need to get out of here so I can go home and furiously masturbate to the thought of his casual touches like the sex-starved hermit I am.

Now that he's not standing directly next to me, my mind clears enough to figure out the puzzle I'd been struggling with. Reading through the message on the assembled paper, I find that it's a hastily scribbled note about revealing hidden truths through diligent study.

"The bookcase!" I exclaim, a little too loudly judging by the way Wesley startles and knocks into the desk he's rummaging through for the tenth time.

I scramble over to the bookcase covered in fake dust and scan through the tomes. Some of the words in the note were capitalized oddly, and put together they spell out "grimoire". Ugh, I could've figured out that a book with the word "grimoire" on the spine would be important without the note if Wesley hadn't been distracting me. I tug on the book and there's a loud click.

"Hell yeah, great job!" Wesley says, startling me with how close he is again. I stumble backwards in surprise and right into his solid chest. He grabs my arms to steady me against him. "Careful, baby girl," he rumbles, trailing off in a low chuckle.

Baby girl? Is he trying to torture me? I sputter and pull away, moving so he can push the hinged bookcase open to reveal a tunnel into another room.

"Oh wow!" I can't help my excitement at the reveal. This escape room is a lot cooler than I'd anticipated.

"Shit, I don't know if I'll fit," Wesley says with a groan.

My perverted mind immediately imagines him saying that as he tries to fit his undoubtedly enormous cock inside me. "Shut up, Wesley. You're not that big. Y-you'll fit," I say, ducking my head so he doesn't catch the way my face flames from my dirty thoughts.

"If you insist. Ladies first." He gestures for me to go into the tunnel.

The passage is wide, but not tall enough for me to walk through, so I crouch down. As I do, I hear a ripping sound and realize in horror that the small hole in the thigh of my leggings is now a full tear going further up into the crotch. I let out a little squeak of alarm and stand back up.

Wesley gives me a perplexed frown. "What's wrong?"

"Y-you should go first!" I say, backing away from the passage.

"You scared of the dark, princess?" Wesley asks in a teasing drawl.

"No, I, uh, I just don't want you to get stuck behind me and then have no way to get out. If you go first and get stuck, then I'll still be okay."

He rolls his eyes at me. "You're such a brat, you know that? You tell me that I can fit, but now you're making me go through first in case I get stuck. Which is it?"

The image of him bending me over his knee and punishing me for being bratty comes to mind unbidden, and I clench my thighs together with a groan that I disguise as frustration. "Ugh, you'll fit! I'm trying to save you from getting a face full of my ass while I'm crawling in front of you."

Wesley snorts. "You say that like it's a bad thing."

Isn't it? I've been told by plenty of guys that I'd be much more attractive if I'd "take better care of my body," aka lose weight. I told them to go fuck themselves, but you can't fully undo the mental damage that kind of shit leaves on you. The idea of a gym fanatic like Wesley watching my wobbly ass as I crawl makes me want to die. As if him getting weirded out that the attendant thought I was his girlfriend wasn't bad enough.

"Please, just go. We're wasting time!"

"Fine, fine." Wesley drops to his knees and pokes his head into the passage, testing to make sure he'll fit. He pulls back out and looks at me over his shoulder. "If I get stuck, promise you won't leave me here to die?"

"I might if you don't stop talking!" I snap.

He laughs and starts to crawl. His bulk fits through, but just barely.

Before I join him, I feel around on my inner thigh to assess the damage. The hole has spread enough that it's precariously close to my crotch. *Dammit.*

"You coming?" Wesley calls back to me and him saying that

while my fingertips are so close to my pussy sends an absurd pulse of excitement to my clit.

"Y-yeah!"

The hole in my leggings expands even more as I crouch again and I curse, but crawl after him. As soon as I'm inside, I have to suppress a sharp inhale at the sight of Wesley's round, tight ass in front of my face, his tail only drawing my attention to his backside more. It's just so *juicy*.

I'm so distracted thinking about biting one of his firm cheeks that I almost collide headfirst into said ass when he stops abruptly.

"Damn, you gotta see this," Wesley says with a low whistle.

His tufted tail smacks my face and I shove it away with a disgruntled huff. "If you'd get your ass out of the way, I will," I mutter under my breath.

He chuckles and keeps crawling. I forgot how good his hearing is. "You're going through first next time, if you hate looking at my fine butt so much. Fair is fair."

He pulls himself up to standing and reaches into the tunnel to help me up. I take his hand, marveling at how much bigger it is than mine. Is *everything* about Wesley so big?

"Whoa," I say softly, when I stop thinking about how huge Wesley is and take in our surroundings.

The walls are made of a stone-like material, covered with fake spider webs and dust. There's a large fake stone pillar carved with runic symbols in the center of the small room. Three passages lead from the chamber into narrow corridors. I peek my head down one of the passages to find that it takes a sharp turn and then forks in two directions.

"It's a maze!" I exclaim. Scanning over the pillar, my brain starts to go into analytical mode. "I wonder if the symbols on the pillar correspond with things we'll find in there. Or maybe they're guides to what direction to go... This is so cool!"

I look up and grin at Wesley, expecting to see amusement at my nerdy excitement, but he's got a strange, intense look in his eyes.

His wide tongue darts out to licks his snout as he stares down at me. A moment later, he shakes his head, the weird expression dissipating into his usual cocky smile as he rubs the base of one of his horns. "Think you can find your way through it, puzzle master?" he asks.

I scoff at him, secretly thrilling in the challenge. "Uh, yeah. Do you even have to ask?"

"Dammit, why isn't this working?" I resist the urge to kick the stupid faux stone pillar after I press the symbols in what *should* be the right order. After wandering through the small maze for the last ten minutes, collecting clues, I thought I'd figured out the puzzle. With no help from Wesley, who seems to think his job is to crowd me in the small passageways and keep giving me these weird, intense stares whenever I stop to think.

Feeling overheated from frustration and his ceaseless closeness, I tug my sweatshirt off over my head. Wesley lets out a low huff as I do, no doubt trying to stifle a laugh as I get it momentarily stuck on my bun. I glare at him as I rip it off and tie it around my waist, but he stares back with that odd gleam in his eyes.

"What?" I ask, looking down to check the shirt I have on. It's nothing weird, just a plain camisole, but it clings to my body and shows off a good portion of my cleavage. "God, stop looking at me like that. I'm sorry if my boobs offend you, but it's fucking hot in here and someone keeps standing right next to me and breathing their cow breath on me and I can't think!"

He blinks slowly at me, then runs a hand over his face with a groan. "Ari, you have no clue what you're talking about."

What kind of answer is that? Ugh, he's impossible. I turn back to the puzzle and try pressing the runes yet again, hoping somehow the tenth time's a charm. He steps up behind me, and I can practically feel the heat radiating off of his bulky body. Warm, spicy breath hits me again as he leans over my shoulder.

That's it. I turn back to face Wesley and level my most withering glare at him. It's not as effective as I'd like because I have to tilt my head up a lot to meet his eyes and he's making my head fuzzy as he looms over me. "Please stop," I say sharply.

He frowns down at me. "Stop what?"

"Stop being so close! I can't think."

"In case you hadn't noticed, this space is fucking tiny and I'm big. I'm just trying to help. I get that you don't like me being close to you, but I can't do anything about that." He looks hurt that I'm not delighted by the idea of his body close to mine.

It's ridiculous. Of course I like him being close. It's all I've wanted for almost a year.

I scoff. "Don't get butthurt. I didn't say that I don't want you close to me. It just makes it hard to think!"

"Because of my 'cow breath'?" Wesley asks, making my frustrated rant sound a lot more insulting than I meant it.

"No! Because I—" I cut myself off before I do something horrible like confess how wet I am and how every time I feel his breath on my skin it makes me want to tear open the hole in my leggings and finger myself until I get some relief from how much I want him.

"Because what, Ari?" he asks, his voice coming out in a low rumble that makes my breath hitch.

"It doesn't matter. I'm sorry for being a jerk. I'll move so you can look at the puzzle."

I sigh and wait for him to let me pass, but he stays where he is. I reach up to shove against his chest to prompt him to move out of the way, but he grabs my wrist.

"Because *what?*" His voice is even deeper now, and it makes my nipples harden.

"Because I want you!" I blurt. I don't mean to say it, but I'm so frustrated and turned on. I can't take it anymore.

Wesley's eyes go wide with shock.

Fuck, I'm such a moron.

"There. Are you happy? I want you and I know that there's no universe in which you'd want me back, so can we please move on and finish this damn escape room so I can go home and hide in shame until you forget how pathetic I am?"

I try to pull my hand away, but his grip on my wrist tightens. "You're so damn wrong, baby girl."

"Quit making fun of me and let me go. And s-stop calling me 'baby girl'. It's weird!" I know my face is beet red and all I want to do is go crawl in a hole and die.

"*No*," Wesley says, enunciating the word in a rough growl.

"What do you mean, 'no'?" I scowl at him, and the bastard is cruel enough to laugh in reply.

"I said 'no' because I need you to know how wrong you are. Because every time you glare at me, it makes me want to bend you over and spank your bratty ass. Because every time I've called you 'baby girl' you flushed so prettily, and it's made my dick hard as steel."

My mouth falls open and my whole body suffuses with heat. This isn't happening. There's no way. "Y-you can't be serious."

"You really want me to stop, finish this escape room, and pretend this never happened, I'll do that. But say the word and I'll show you just how serious I am." Wesley's thumb strokes the inside of my wrist as he waits for me to reply.

It still seems like some kind of prank, but fuck, I want him so badly. Even that little touch feels incredible, and he's so close, and big, and smells so good.

I meet his eyes in a challenge. "Okay, fine. If you're not being a cruel ass, then show me."

4

WESLEY

This is a spectacularly bad idea. When I got into this maze, my resolve snapped. Why did it have to be a godsdamn labyrinth? There's something primal inside me that tells me Ariana's my sacrifice, demanding that I claim her. The more we've wandered around in the tight corridors, where there's no room for me to keep my distance, the harder it's gotten to keep my control.

Now that Ariana told me she wants me, the need for her buzzes through me like a live wire. Still, I'm not only a beast driven by instinct, so I have to double-check that she truly wants this. "You sure, Ari?" I murmur, drawing her trapped hand down my chest in a slow drag. Her thick eyelashes flutter as she gazes up at me with wide eyes, waiting to see what I do next. "I don't want to make you uncomfortable."

I want to lean in and kiss her, but don't know how she'd react to my bull snout mashing against her face. As much as I prefer being without my glamor, I wish it were back up so I could kiss her pouty frown away. My tongue darts out to wet my lips at the thought. "You matter to me…this isn't a—"

"For fuck's sake, Wes!" she says, cutting me off with an exasperated huff. "Just show me or shut up and let me finish this damn puzzle."

Well, that answers that question.

I laugh, the sound coming out tinged with my need for her. "Someone needs to teach you some manners. Say 'please'."

Red splotches cover her pale cheeks, and I can't help how much it turns me on. I want to see that same red on her thick ass as I spank her.

"I'm not going to say that!" she says in an indignant squeak. She bites her lip, refusing to break eye contact even though I can tell she's squirming at the heat in my gaze. It's fucking delicious. I want her to fight me so I can discipline her, then soothe away the pain and make her beg in other ways.

I grab her waist with my free hand and pull her in closer. "You're right. Say 'please, *daddy*'." Being Ariana's daddy is my deepest fantasy, and I can't help testing to see how she reacts to the idea.

The way her breath hitches and the hint of her arousal in the air between us makes my cock threaten to burst out of my pants. I swear I feel the inseam start to tear.

She scoffs at me, which I expected. I wanted her to. It'll make her obedience that much hotter. "Next you'll be asking me for a safeword," she says, like the thought is ridiculous.

It's not. My fingers knead into her waist, and fuck, she feels so good. She's all thick curves and softness underneath my massive hand. I need to be careful with her. I'm so much bigger and stronger than her, and as much as I want to torture her sexy body, the idea of hurting her beyond some consensual pain play terrifies me. If I want her to call me daddy, I need to keep her safe.

I nod. "Good thinking. Seeing as you're in a maze with a minotaur, how about yarn?" I chuckle at my own dumb joke. "Or you can tap my thigh three times if you can't speak."

"W-why wouldn't I be able to speak?" Ariana asks, her voice trembling slightly. I hope that it's from excitement rather than discomfort.

"Oh sweetheart, I think you know why." I savor the look on her face as understanding dawns in her eyes. I don't say anything else, just hold still and wait. It's a test to see if she wants the same things I do. I won't push her if she doesn't like it, but gods, I hope she does.

A tense few seconds pass in silence before she breaks. "Please...I want you to show me. Please, d-daddy." She stumbles over the word a little, but that only makes it sound more incredible.

"Good girl," I rasp, and bring her hand down from my chest to rest on top of my clothed cock.

"Holy shit, y-you're...you aren't joking about..." Ariana blinks up at me rapidly, her insistent disbelief of my attraction to her melting into hesitant hope.

My cock throbs at the feel of her hand resting atop me. "Yeah," I finish for her, my voice rough. "Been wanting you for so long, Ari." Some of my deep affection for my stubborn, clueless crush bleeds into my voice, despite my best efforts to keep it restrained.

Her brow furrows. "Why?" she asks, and there's no defensive

huff or combativeness to her tone now. Just pure, heartbreaking confusion. Who made her think she wasn't desirable?

I release the hand holding hers over my cock, and bring it up to stroke her cheek. "The better question is, why wouldn't I want you? Can you really not see how great you are? I'm not talking about your looks—though gods, the thought of you letting me see you naked is making it hard for me to control myself. I'm talking about *you*, Ari. You're tough, talented, hardworking, funny, and caring. Even when you pretend that I drive you crazy, I always know you have my back. Not just because I'm Doug's best friend, but because you've got an amazing heart." I clear my throat after my confession, feeling shy as her mouth falls open in surprise. I give her a wink, adding, "and an amazing rack."

"Dammit Wes," she says softly, and to my horror, tears well in her eyes. "You're going to make me cry in a damn escape room because you're being so sweet to me and my brain can't keep up."

I swipe one of her tears away and grin down at her. "The only tears I wanted to see from you were when you're choking on my cock, baby girl."

She lets out a strained laugh and shoves at my chest, though she's not strong enough to move me. "It'd be impossible not to. That thing is absurd!"

"I bet you could handle it," I say, using the hand on her waist to pull her flush with my body. Her stomach presses into my cock, the height difference a stark reminder of how much smaller she is than me.

Am I too big for her? Does it even matter? I'll take Ariana any way she'll let me. If my cock won't fit inside her, I'll fuck her with my fingers and tongue, and then maybe she'll let me stroke myself until I come on her tits. My cock throbs at the thought.

She squirms and I fight not to grind myself against her. "I...I want to try. To handle it."

I raise a brow at her, my impatient dick rejoicing at her words. "That's my girl. Take out daddy's cock and show him how eager you are to try."

There's a flicker of hesitation, but then she nods. She brings her hands down and her fingers shake a little as she fumbles with my belt. When she gets it undone and eases the fly down, I stroke her hair. "Good girl."

Her breath hitches and she bites her lip, still keeping her eyes locked with mine as she slips her fingers into my boxer briefs and wraps them around my swollen cock. I hold back a hiss of relief as she eases my cock out into her waiting palm, which can barely hold my girth.

My fingers slip under the elastic that's holding her hair in place and I tug it off, letting her faded pink tresses fall loose. The way it cascades down makes her look adorably messy, and my heart flutters at the sight.

"Fuck, you're huge," she says, hands exploring my length. Her eyes go even wider when she feels the metal barbell piercing at the tip, and she finally drops her gaze to glance down at my dick.

"Like what you see?" I ask as calmly as possible, aching for her to tighten her grip on me and give me some relief.

"It's alright, I guess," she says, mouth twisting into a teasing frown.

I grip her hair at the nape of her neck and force her to look back up at me. "So rude. Rude girls don't get daddy's cock. They get punished."

"How would you punish me?" she asks, eyes wide with aroused interest.

"I'd bend you over and spank that pretty ass of yours until you learned to be a good girl. Then, if you're lucky and if you've shown me you can behave, I'll give you my cock." The thought makes my balls ache with the need for release.

"I'll be good," she says, her voice saccharine.

"Hah, sure you will." I give her an assessing look, her hair still in my grip to keep her eyes locked on mine. "Ari, you gotta promise me you'll use the safeword or signal if I do anything you don't want or you need to stop. I'm not going to do anything crazy tonight, but I need to make sure you're okay if we're doing this."

Her tongue darts out to wet her lips and once again I wish I were in my glamor so I could kiss her.

"Y-yeah. I promise. Yarn or three taps to stop." A wicked grin crosses her lips when I nod in approval. "Can I suck your cock now, *daddy*?"

Fuck, I shouldn't have told her to call me that. I'm going to nut all over her face the second her mouth gets near my dick at this rate. Still, I can't say no to her.

"Go ahead, baby girl. Make me nice and slick for when I fuck your pretty little human pussy."

I release her hair and she sinks down to kneel in front of me. I groan at the sight of one of my favorite dirty fantasies brought to life. Though my imagination couldn't compare with how incredible she looks, her green eyes sparkling with mischief and nerves, her cheeks flushed, and her breasts rising and falling in shallow, excited breaths. I need to bend my knees some to be the right height for her to take me in her mouth, but it's worth it. I'm just glad I don't skip leg day.

My cock bobs as she stares at it, but I don't rush her. I hope she likes what she sees, because I certainly like her looking at me. I let out a relieved sigh when she finally takes me in hand again, her dainty fingers doing their best to grip my length while her other hand reaches up to cup my balls, testing the weight of them in her palm.

I hold myself perfectly still, anticipation making my thighs clench as she brings her mouth to the head of my cock, her tongue darting out to lick off a bead of pre-cum. She makes a pleased humming sound before swirling her tongue around the head, then teases around my piercing and frenulum.

"Fuck, sweetheart. That's it," I groan, threading my fingers back through her hair to hold it out of her face. Her eyes rise to meet mine as she takes the whole head of my cock into her mouth, her lips stretching wide to accommodate even that much of me. It's an image that will be burned in my brain for the rest of my life—Ariana looking so eager and willing as I fill her mouth to the brim.

I reach down with my free hand to stroke her cheek, and her eyelashes flutter shut at the intimate touch. She tries to take me down further but doesn't get far before she gags, and I gently tug her off of me with the hand in her hair.

She gasps and looks up at me in confusion, a trail of spit connecting her mouth to my cock.

"You don't have to choke yourself on me, baby. I know I'm too big for you to take much. Whatever you can give me is perfect," I murmur. Sure, I'd be lying if the thought of her gagging on my dick as she sucks me off didn't have any appeal, but I don't want her doing it just because she thinks she has to.

She rolls her eyes at me. "Did I use the signal? It's not like you were forcing me to do it. I...I want to do the best job I can. I want to please you...daddy."

Fucking hell, I'm going to come all over her pretty face.

"You are, baby." I stroke her cheek again, then tug her lower lip down with my thumb. "But if you roll your eyes at me again, I'm going to put you over my knee."

She inhales sharply at the threat.

"Put my cock back in your mouth and don't take me any deeper than you comfortably can." I guide her mouth back to my dick and she eagerly sucks me back inside. She brings both hands up to wrap around my cock, stroking me in tandem with what her mouth can't reach.

"Mmm, that's perfect. You're perfect. So pretty on your knees for me, working daddy's cock like you were born to do it. Do you like making daddy feel good?"

Ariana moans against me, pulling off for a moment to lick a long stripe from the base of my cock to the tip. The length of my cock is bigger than her face, and I groan as she drops down to lick along the seam of my balls. "Fuck yes. Look at you, baby girl. You're gonna make daddy nut all over your pretty face."

"I want that. Please," she says, looking up at me with wide eyes as she works my dick with both hands and then takes it back inside her warm, wet mouth.

It's too much. As much as I'd love to coat her in my cum right now, I want to be inside her even more. But first, I want her gasping my name as she comes.

I ease her off of me. "Enough."

She pouts. "But I want to make you come."

"I said enough," I rasp, but she glares at me and darts her tongue out to lick the tip.

I tighten the fist in her hair, and she gasps as I yank her away. "That's it. I've warned you multiple times, but you keep disobeying me. Stand up and put your hands on the wall."

"Wh-what? No! I didn't—" Ariana says.

My cock throbs at the defiant excitement in her voice, but I cut her off. "You heard me. Do it before I decide to make your punishment worse."

Fuck, I can't wait to see how she takes my discipline.

5

ARIANA

I just had Wesley's dick in my mouth. His enormous, *pierced* dick. I'm tempted to pinch myself because my secret crush confessing to wanting me back, telling me to call him daddy, and punishing me when I disobey him is something from my dirtiest dreams. But it's real, and it's happening.

Holy shit.

I never thought I'd be the kind of girl to suck someone off in an escape room, but these are extenuating circumstances. He's saying everything I've desperately wanted to hear from him, he looks so damn good, and it's Valentine's Day! Can you really blame me for going for it?

Part of me worries that the moment we leave this place, Wesley will come to his senses and realize it was *me* he's doing all these things with, and not some hot fitness model from his gym. I need to seize the opportunity while I have it, because it's probably the only chance I'll get.

That depressing thought doesn't linger for long when I see how ragged Wesley's breaths are as I stand. I want to tear his tight shirt off to run my hands along the broad expanse of his chest and stomach, but I doubt he'd let me. The dark, hungry look in his eyes makes my clit throb as I turn away from him and press my hands against the wall, bending at the waist so my ass is pointed back at him.

"Good girl," he rasps, stepping behind me. His delicious heat radiates across my back and I wish he'd press his whole body against mine so I could soak it in even more. My traitorous mind wanders to thoughts of him snuggled up next to me in bed on a cold morning, his tail twined around my leg as he holds me cradled against his chest. But he didn't say anything about wanting me beyond sex, so I should focus on that and stop getting ahead of myself.

I return to the present when he starts to take off the sweatshirt I have wrapped around my waist and I remember the giant hole in my leggings. "W-wait!" I squeak, face flaming.

"That's not your safeword, Ari." Wesley tugs it the rest of the way off and tosses it to the side. He grabs my hips and yanks them back further so my ass is presented even more to him. I inhale sharply as I feel cool air on my inner thighs, and I know he'll be able to see the giant hole.

"What's this?" he asks, hands sliding across my ass to grab the backs of my thighs and spread them wider. I gasp as he runs a finger across the bare skin exposed by the tear. "My naughty girl isn't even wearing any panties. Did you wear this, hoping you could tease me with a flash of your pretty pussy?"

"N-no! It's laundry day and I-I didn't have any clean ones!"

Wesley's finger dips in further until he's just shy of touching me where I ache for him. "Hmm, sounds like you need someone to help take care of you. If I were your daddy, I wouldn't let you leave the house in ripped leggings and no panties. Only dirty sluts who want to get fucked go out like that, baby girl."

If I were your daddy. God, why does that sound so good? I don't need a man to take care of me. I can do it on my own...but fuck, it would be so nice to let him help me. To know that someone else has things under control. To know that I don't have to do everything on my own and I can just relax for a bit.

He laughs darkly as I whimper and feel myself grow even wetter. "You like the sound of that, don't you? You need daddy to take care of you?"

My hips rock back as I beg him to touch me. "Yes. Please, daddy."

"If you're good for me and take your punishment, I will. I'm going to give you ten, and I want you to count them for me."

"Ten what—ah!" My question is cut off when Wesley's palm collides with my ass in a stinging crack. "Ow, that hurts!"

"That's the point, baby girl. Otherwise, how are you going to learn? Count it."

"One," I say quietly, tensing up as he removes his hand and I try to prepare for another strike.

He waits for what feels like an eternity, leaving me squirming with anticipation. Like lightning, his hand collides with my other ass cheek and I cry out. The pain shocks me, but what shocks me even more is how turned on it makes me. "T-two," I remember to say after Wesley makes an agitated huff behind me. Three more strikes come in quick succession, and I count them, my breaths coming out in shuddering exhales.

"You're doing so well. Need to see how pink that pretty ass is getting," he murmurs. I flinch as I feel him move, but instead of another spank, he hooks his fingers under the waistband of my leggings and tugs them off.

"Fuck," he says in a low curse, gliding a hand down to knead my tender backside. "Been dreaming of marking this bratty ass."

"W-Wes, I-I..." I feel shaky and like I'm going to combust as he grabs my ass cheeks and spreads me open, knowing how exposed I am to him.

"Shh baby, I know what you need. Take your last five and I'll give you your reward."

I nod and he spanks me again, the blow landing so close to my pussy it makes me want to cry with unfulfilled need. The last four strikes bleed together as the pain and pleasure swell inside me. I barely recognize myself as I beg for more after I count. When I reach ten, tears prick my eyes and I feel like I could come in an instant if he'd just *touch* me.

"Good girl. Fuck, such a good girl," Wesley groans behind me. Without warning, he drops down to his knees and buries his face between my legs, giving my pussy a swipe with his wide, textured tongue.

I almost collapse forward, and he wraps an arm around my waist to steady me. There's a flicker of worry about the bush I'm rocking after almost a year of not dating, but he doesn't seem to give a shit. "Mmm, knew I was gonna get addicted to this pussy. You taste so good. I want you dripping all over my face until all I can smell for days is your cunt."

"W-Wesley!" I moan his name as he eats me out like he's starving. He alternates between fucking his tongue inside me and lapping at my clit until I'm a shaking, mewling mess.

It takes him embarrassingly little time to make me come, but I'm so worked up that I can't fight the cascade of pleasure when it hits. He has to hold me steady as stars dance behind my eyes and I tumble over the edge with a deep moan.

He doesn't give me time to come down all the way, standing almost immediately and turning me around to face him. He's wild-eyed and his cock looks almost painfully engorged, dripping copious amounts of pre-cum. "Ari, I...we don't have to—"

"Fuck me, daddy," I say, cutting him off from whatever concerned, gentlemanly thing he was about to say. I know I'll be feeling it for days, but I want him inside me so bad I could scream.

His nostrils flare, and it's the only warning I have before his massive arms grab under my ass and lift me into the air. I wrap my legs around his waist and throw my arms around his neck with a startled squeal.

"What are you doing?!" I ask, wide-eyed.

"What do you think I'm doing? I'm going to fuck you."

"But I'm too heavy!" The protest falls from my lips before I can think better of it. Decades of conditioning have made me worry about the size of my body, self-love and body positivity be damned.

His stern dom demeanor breaks for a moment. "You've got to be shitting me, Ari. I'm twice your size. I can deadlift over a thousand pounds. So shut up and let me fuck you."

"O-okay, fine. Sorry for doubting your gym bro credentials!" I snap back at him.

He laughs, and the sound causes my own giggle to erupt out of me. Wesley dips his head to nuzzle against my neck and my heart surges with how right this feels.

At least mentally. The beast of a dick currently trapped against my belly may prove otherwise, but I want to try.

Wesley presses my back against the wall, pinning me there so he can free a hand to yank down my top and bare my tits. "Godsdamn, that's a pretty sight," he murmurs, roughly palming one of my breasts. I arch my back into his touch and he laughs. "Gonna fuck these tits some day. But I need your pussy right now."

He hoists me further up his waist to position his cock at my entrance. I gasp as he lines himself up and I feel the blunt tip press inside a fraction. Fuck, he's so big.

He lifts me up and presses me back down on just the head of his cock again, groaning into my neck as he restrains himself from thrusting inside any further.

It's already a stretch, but I want more. "Please, daddy. Please put it inside me. I'm so empty."

"Fuck, baby girl. I don't know if you're ready for my cock," he says in a deep growl. I can't tell if he's just playing the game or if he's genuinely worried he won't fit.

Screw that. I want to do this. I've wanted him for years. "I can take it. I want to be good for you, daddy. I want you to stretch me open and fill me up until I feel hollow without your cock inside me."

"Dammit, I can't say no when you ask so sweetly." His hips thrust more insistently, and he presses inside me another inch.

It burns, but I don't care. "More," I beg in a half sob, half moan.

He lifts me up and plunges me back down onto him with a rough grunt. "That better, baby girl?"

I'm stretched so wide and the pain is melting together with my delirious desire. I wish he could fit all the way inside, but even I know my limits. He's so thick and long, and he'll hit my cervix if he goes deeper.

"Ahh, oh god!" I cry out as he starts working me up and down on his cock like I'm nothing more than a toy for his pleasure.

"You're taking daddy's cock so well. Such a good girl. You were made to take me, baby girl. Gonna fuck this pussy every day for the rest of my godsdamn life."

I keen at the sensation of him working inside me, and at the thought that this isn't just a one-time thing for him. The piercing on his cock rubs against my g-spot with each thrust. I want this to last forever. I never want to stop feeling Wes's cock inside me, never want him to stop whispering dirty praise, never want to stop being his baby girl.

I usually need to touch my clit to get off, so I'm shocked when my orgasm tears through me. "F-fuck, oh my god, Wes, fuck, I'm coming!" I cry in disbelief, my pussy clamping hard around him as I shake with my release, a gush of wetness escaping me. Did he just make me squirt?!

"That's it, soak my cock," he says, voice rough and breath heavy as he continues to work me over his length. I go limp in his arms as he thrusts inside me, unable to do anything but cling onto him as I ride out my pleasure.

He grunts and curses. "I'm not gonna last. You're too good. Where do you want me to come?"

I want to beg him to come inside me, but don't know if that'd freak him out. We haven't talked about contraception, though Kelly helped me with a ward against pregnancy and disease. Telling him to fuck his cum into me is probably too much for a quickie in an escape room, no matter how hot it would be.

"On my tits," I gasp.

He groans and nods, then pulls out of me, setting me down on the floor. I watch him give his cock a few rough tugs as I press my breasts together. "Fuck, baby girl, here it comes. You ready for it?"

God, I'm so ready. "Yes, daddy."

He tugs his cock one more time before it erupts, hot cum jetting out to coat my neck and breasts. I bring a hand up to squeeze his balls gently, coaxing him to give me everything he has. His eyes flare and he lets out a low moan as he shoots even more of his load onto my tits. I'm a mess by the time he finally stops, cum dripping down my chest and stomach, but I wouldn't have it any other way.

I feel claimed and cherished by him as he looks down at me in a daze and threads a hand through my hair. "Gods, Ari. You're incredible. Such a perfect girl."

As absurd as it sounds, with him looking at me like that, I do feel perfect.

6

WESLEY

My spent cock twitches with interest as Ariana drags a finger through the cum coating her tits. Her tank top is ruined, and I'm thankful that her sweatshirt and leggings were tossed far enough away to not be in the splash zone.

I hold still, not wanting this moment to end. I want to lay her down and feast on her cunt again as she holds my horns, then stroke inside her until she's so well-fucked that I have to carry her out of here. I'd drive her back to my place and dote on her like I promised. A vision of her soaking in my tub while I massage her scalp floats through my mind. It'd end with me massaging other parts of her as well, but it'd all be part of how I want to spoil her.

"Uh, you okay there?" Ariana asks, and I shake myself out of my reverie.

"I'm great," I say in a husky croak, then clear my throat and try again. "I'm great. Should probably get you cleaned up though, if you don't want to get stuck here with a horny minotaur all night."

She chuckles. "That doesn't sound too bad. Teach that receptionist a lesson for being a creep." Her teasing expression drops and she scrambles to pull her top back up to cover her breasts, despite the mess covering them. "Oh fuck, do you think he watched us?!"

A rumbling growl builds in my chest at the thought. "If he did, I'll rip his balls off and feed them to him," I say loudly to the room in case there's hidden monitoring. Fuck, I should have thought of that. I don't give a shit about some loser seeing my cock, but Ariana's sweet body is only for those who she deems worthy of looking at it.

I reach out a hand to help her up from the floor and keep her steady as she slips her leggings back on. She's tugging her sweatshirt over her head when the dim lights in the room flash, giving us a five minute warning. I could've sworn we'd been fucking for hours with how lost I got in her, but I guess not. Shit, I'm going to have to work on my stamina for next time.

If there even is a next time. I don't know what Ariana wants. Maybe this was just a moment of pleasure and forbidden fun. I can't say it'd be the first time that happened to me. Gods, I hope she wants more. Even if she just wants to be fuck buddies, I'd take it. Anything to have more of the bliss I experienced tonight, knowing that she wanted me and having the chance to touch her.

"Oh damn, we still could win this thing!" Ariana exclaims excitedly. She rushes over to the pillar and presses the symbols and this time they work, causing the pillar to glow. "Ahh, yes!!"

I frown at the pillar. I'd bet money that the receptionist kept it from activating properly, because that's exactly what she'd been doing before. He either really wanted to play matchmaker or he's a pervert who wanted to jerk off watching us fuck. For my sanity, I'll pretend it's the former. It is Valentine's Day—maybe he has some kind of cupid complex?

The glowing coalesces at the base of the pillar and a hatch slides open to reveal a key. A lump rises in my throat at the thought of leaving this space. When we open that door, will reality come crashing back in?

"Come on!" Ari shouts, swiping the key and grabbing my hand to tug me back to the passage we crawled through.

She dives inside and I suppress a groan as my cock twitches at the sight of the hole in her leggings and her cute ass in front of my face as I follow. She offers me a hand up when we get back to the first room, and the sweet gesture makes butterflies kick up in my stomach.

I laugh as she rushes to the exit, letting out a string of expletives as she fumbles with the key in her hurry. I join her and place my hand over hers to steady it. She smiles up at me over her shoulder and together we put the key into the lock and it turns.

The door swings open to reveal the plain hallway. "We did it!" Ariana exclaims.

"*You* did it, baby girl," I say, smiling down at her.

She startles me as she reaches up to tug me down, pressing her lips to mine. She pulls back, face flushed. "Sorry! I don't know if that's weird for you, but I've been wanting to kiss you for so long."

"If it's not weird for you to kiss me without my glamor, it sure as fuck isn't weird for me. Kiss me again," I say in a deep command.

"O-okay." Her eyes flutter closed as she raises up onto her toes, and I bend to meet her halfway. Her plush lips feel perfect and I press against the seam of her mouth with my tongue. She sighs and opens for me, our tongues tangling together for a divine moment before she breaks the kiss.

"Too weird?" I ask.

"Not at all! Just weird enough," she says with a giggle. "I just realized that there may be people around who don't know minotaurs exist, so we should either close the door or you should come out here so your glamor can work."

I nod and step out into the hallway with her, a tingling wave of magic washing over me as my glamor reappears. I tug Ariana to my chest and kiss her hard, now that I have more lips to work with. She gasps, then returns the kiss with equal fervor.

Someone nearby clears their throat. "Uh, sorry to interrupt, but I'd like to close up."

I reluctantly pull away from the kiss to glare at the reedy blond receptionist, who braces like I'm going to hit him.

Ariana wraps her arms around herself self-consciously and I step in front of her to shield her from view of the creep. "We'll leave when we're ready to." I say as calmly as possible.

The receptionist winces. "Of course, uh, yeah. I was just hoping to get home before midnight..."

I dig out my phone to check the time. *11:45*. Holy shit, we were in there for almost three hours. I mentally pat myself on the back that my stamina *is* as good as I thought.

I place a hand on Ariana's back and we head out of the building into the chilly night air. Our cars are the only ones left in the parking lot, lending to the tension between us as she turns to look at me.

She gives me an awkward smile and my heart sinks. "Uh, that was an...interesting night, wasn't it?" She forces a laugh and looks down.

"Right. Interesting," I reply, internally warring with myself about what to say. Should I pretend that it didn't mean anything? Does she *want* me to pretend it didn't even happen? Gods, how could I even do that? I can't do that.

"Well, goodnight," she says with forced cheer. Fuck, I have to do something. If I let her get in her car without saying something, I'll never have another chance with her. I know Ariana. She won't let me in again. I might embarrass myself by hoping for more, but that's better than not trying.

"Go to dinner with me!" I say, my too loud voice ringing out in the silent night air.

She laughs dismissively. "It's a little late for dinner."

"Not tonight. Tomorrow. Or any night that works for you. Please, Ari. I want to take you out."

She doesn't say anything for a moment, and all my hopes and dreams for us plummet to their fiery death. But then her lips twist into a wry smile. "Okay, daddy. But you have to promise you won't spank me at the table if I misbehave."

My heart feels like it's going to explode out of my chest with elation, and I laugh. "I can do that. But you have to promise that you'll come back to my place for your punishment if you're bad, baby girl."

She beams back up at me, emerald eyes sparkling with mischief. "Deal."

7

ARIANA

The drive back to my place is a blur. It's good that it's late and the streets leading to my tiny house on the outskirts of Moonvale are empty, because I end up almost running a red light. Twice. My brain has vacated my body in the aftermath of what happened tonight. It's only when I pull into the garage and turn off the engine that my ability to think comes back online—with a vengeance.

Panic and confusion spike inside me, and I clutch onto the steering wheel instead of getting out of the car.

I had sex with Wesley. *Wesley*. In an escape room! What. The. Actual. Fuck.

My phone buzzes inside my purse lying on the seat beside me, and I startle, scrambling out of the car and away from it so fast you'd think it was a grenade. I wince and let out a hiss of pain, the soreness between my legs making its presence known now that I'm no longer sitting. It feels like I tried to shove a coke can inside my pussy. Which isn't far off from how big he was.

I still can't believe it. I saw Wes' dick. I sucked Wes' dick and let him fuck me with that monster. I'm wobbly and lightheaded, the events of the evening hitting me like I've had one too many drinks. My breathing starts to speed up as I replay what happened in the escape room.

Oh *god*. I fucked my brother's best friend, who I thought saw me as nothing more than an annoying mess. I called him *daddy*.

I bring my hand up to my chest and force myself to take a deep breath before I let panic take over. It's okay. People have casual sex all the time. Right now, I feel like my whole world has been turned upside down, but I'm sure once I get some sleep and distance from what happened, I'll feel normal again.

I register the stickiness on my skin and grimace. Okay, once I've washed the remnants of Wesley's jizz off of my tits, *then* I'll feel normal. Who knew minotaurs come like a firehose? The way he groaned as he coated me in his cum...would he make an even better sound if he came inside me?

My cheeks heat and my heart speeds up again at the thought, but I quickly shove it aside. Sure, Wes was fine with having sex with me tonight, but that doesn't mean I should picture us together again. I've fallen into the trap of reading too much into interactions with men in the past, me imagining our next date and them thinking it was a one-night stand with an "easy fat chick"—one particularly nasty jerk's words, not mine.

I take another deep breath and try to let realism wash away

my foolish excitement, then grab my purse out of the car and head inside. I have to flick the kitchen's light switch a few times before the fluorescent light turns on with a dull buzz. Shit, I really need to replace that. Yet another thing to add to the list that I probably won't get around to for at least another month. Which reminds me, I need to change the air filters. And clean out the vacuum.

Just as thoughts of all the home maintenance I'm neglecting start to drown out tonight's events, my phone vibrates again. My stomach clenches hard at the thought that it's Wesley texting me to tell me what we did was a mistake. I debate leaving it in my purse and pretending like it doesn't exist until the morning, but I should get this over with. I dig around in my purse and grab my phone, heart racing as I pull it out and unlock the screen.

I was right. It's Wesley.

Meathead: Hope you got home okay, baby girl.

Meathead: Does tomorrow night work for dinner?

A tense bubble of laughter comes out of me, seeing Wesley's nickname in my contacts after calling him daddy earlier. It's absurd. This entire night is completely and utterly absurd.

Ariana: It was only a ten-minute drive from the escape place. Of course I got home okay. Your dick was good, but it didn't make me suddenly forget how to drive.

That's a lie, but I'm not about to tell him how dazed I was by our encounter.

Meathead: Just good? Hmm, I'll have to work on that for next time.

Next time? He said a lot of things in the heat of the moment, but that was just dirty talk, right? He wants to have dinner, but I figured that's him trying to be a nice guy and not immediately tell me it was just a one time thing.

I don't know why he's still flirting, so I use humor to deflect his comment.

Ariana: You want me so dazed from your dick that I become a danger on the road?

Meathead: Don't worry, I'll drive. You won't need to worry about that.

Meathead: So...dinner tomorrow? Or are you going to keep ignoring my question?

My stomach flutters as I imagine him saying that with the same expression on his face that he had before he spanked me. I've always argued with Wesley, but it usually made me frustrated, not breathless and excited to push him until he loses his composure.

It's hot, but fucking weird. I'm so used to shoving down my crush on Wesley that letting myself acknowledge that attraction seems wrong. Like I'm letting my guard down and asking for reality to come slap me in the face and tell me how stupid I am for thinking that someone like Wesley would want me.

Yes, I know his dick was inside me. That shouldn't leave room for doubt about him desiring me at least a little, but the cognitive dissonance and past trauma remains, seeping into my reply before I can stop it.

Ariana: I'm not ignoring your question. I have to check my schedule and see if I even have any time tomorrow. I know it's shocking, but I don't sit around like a lonely spinster ready to leap at the chance for a pity date.

There's an odd twist of grim validation in my stomach when he doesn't reply right away to deny that it's a pity date. It hurts that the mean voice inside me is right, but it's a pain I'm familiar with. Much easier to manage than the anxious, excited hope that was floating inside me like a balloon waiting to burst.

Deflated, but calmer, I accept that dinner was his way of giving us a chance to talk about what happened and then move on. But I don't need that. In fact, I don't *want* that. It would be so much worse to sit there and listen to him tell me how I'm a great girl, but not what he's looking for. Screw that awkwardness. Let's get this over now.

> Ariana: You don't need to take me to dinner, by the way. We can just move on and pretend it didn't happen.

There. Problem solved. A minute passes with no reply. Unable to leave it alone, I message again to make things crystal clear.

> Ariana: I don't even think I have time for dinner. So you're off the hook. We're good.

Another minute passes and I start to get pissed. What the hell? Now he's ignoring me? I gave him an out. I was trying to be nice and save him the weirdness of letting his best friend's sister down. The least he can do is reply! Why isn't he—

My phone rings. It's Wesley. Who the hell calls someone in the middle of texting, with no warning? I scowl at my phone and consider letting it go to voicemail, but pick up after a few more rings.

"What do you want?" I snap.

"You done?" His voice is threaded with amusement, making me want to reach through the phone and strangle him.

"What the hell is that supposed to mean? Done with what?"

He exhales dramatically. "Being a dumbass."

"*Excuse me*?" My face heats with anger. I know he likes to tease me, but calling to insult me is extreme, even for him. I can't believe I let him inside me. God, maybe I *am* a dumbass.

He laughs. The fucker laughs! "You're excused, baby girl."

"Screw you, Wes. You're such a dick. I'm hanging up."

I go to end the call, but a commanding "wait" from his end freezes me. I hate that I listen to him. "You have ten seconds to explain to me why you're being such an ass."

His throaty thinking sound makes my damn nipples harden even though I'm upset. "You asked for time to think about dinner. So I was giving you time. And then you were texting nonsense about how it was a pity dinner and that we didn't need to talk. I wanted to let you get that out of your system before I replied. Because you're wrong. I'm the one that'll be waiting around for you to deign to go out with me. I'll give you all the time you need, Ari. But I won't let you convince yourself that I don't want you. So, I'll ask again: Are you done?"

My frustration evaporates and I'm left with a strange fluttering mix of embarrassment and hesitant excitement that finally drowns out the doubt. He wants me. Even my pessimistic ass can't argue when told so blatantly.

I let out a shaky exhale. "Y-yeah. I'm done."

"Good girl." Hearing him say that makes me feel squirmy and hot, and the deep rumble of his voice when he replies lets me know he can tell how it affects me. "Take a look at your schedule and text me in the morning about dinner."

"Wes." I pause, swallowing down the remnants of my embarrassment at him calling me out. "It's going to take me a while to...

accept what you're saying. That you... ugh, I never thought you'd be into me and it's fucking with my head!"

"Well, I am, and I'm happy to keep telling you. And showing you. I'm so godsdamn into you that I got hard just from hearing your indignant voice when you answered the phone."

I snort. "Pervert. Leave it to you to be turned on by making me mad."

"And leave it to you to love me pissing you off," he chuckles. "You're telling me you're not wet right now, baby girl?"

"You wish!" The flippant reply is instinctive, but my pussy clenches, knowing he's right. Which elicits a hiss of pain from me. Shit, I'm sore.

"You okay?" Wesley's voice goes soft in concern.

"Yeah, just a bit wrecked from your monster cock."

"Mmm, poor baby. Need me to come kiss it better?"

The idea makes my breath hitch, and for a moment I consider it. He could come over and lick me again with that wide tongue of his until I have no brainpower left for doubt or worry. But a glance over at the microwave clock tells me it's almost 12:30. Shit. I need to sleep so I can tackle shop orders in the morning. I can't afford to be impulsive, even if I wanted to.

Wesley seems to understand my hesitation. "Let's save that for another night. Get some rest, sweetheart."

My chest squeezes at the endearment. "Goodnight, Wes."

I stare at my phone, dumbfounded for a minute in the aftermath of our call. After a dazed shower and a haphazard version of my nighttime routine, I slip into bed and try my best to fall asleep. But all I can think about is that in the course of an evening, everything I thought I knew about Wesley has been turned upside down. I can't decide if that terrifies or exhilarates me.

8

WESLEY

For the first time in months, I don't hit snooze on my alarm when it goes off at the ungodsly hour of 5am. I pop out of bed, thrumming with energy like I've already had two cups of coffee. Guess that's the power of experiencing the pussy of the woman I've been low-key obsessed with for a year. Still can't believe *that* happened. It's no surprise I'm elated this morning.

There's an enormous grin plastered on my snout as I practically skip into the bathroom to take a leak, which is tricky given my morning wood. It doesn't go down after—my dick is far too excited by even the tiniest thought of the escape room encounter to be chill.

I wrap my palm around it, wishing that the hand on me was a much smaller, softer one.

Godsdamn, she was so perfect. I give my cock a stroke, letting my thumb brush against my piercing and groaning at how worked up I am already. I pump my shaft as I remember her cries and the jiggle of her luscious ass as I spanked her. Fuck, I love her ass. I could write a poem about how pretty it looked all tender and red from my hand. Seeing how wet it made her, her thighs practically coated with her arousal. *Fuck.*

I speed up my strokes as I think about the determined line between her brows when she fought to take my cock inside her. She was such a good girl, taking it even though it barely fit. Gods, the way she called me daddy as she begged to come...

My balls draw up and then I'm shooting off ropes of cum all over my hand and stomach with a rough groan. Shit, I don't think I've come that fast since I was a horny teen. *Godsdamn, baby girl, even when you're not here, you make me lose control.* I let out a hoarse chuckle as I clean myself up, feeling lightheaded from the force of my orgasm.

I finish up my morning routine, still floating on cloud nine at the thought that I might get to see Ariana again tonight. It's hard to resist the urge to text her good morning before I head out the door to go to the gym, but I don't know if she's up yet. She needs rest, if the dark circles under her eyes last night are any indication. We're going to have to work on that. My urge to take care of Ariana rumbles to life inside me, potent and protective. I want to make sure she gets what she needs. I want to spoil her.

Crap, my dick is firming up again at the thought. Now that the chains on my desire for her are off, it's like my cock wants to make up for lost time. Getting through my workout and work today is going to be hard—literally.

When I get to the gym, I do my usual warmup and then head over to the weights, grinding out my first few sets with ease. I wonder if I can convince Ari to come with me to my next out-of-town weightlifting competition. I bet I'd smash my record if I had a night with her beforehand.

I know I should chill and not make future plans with Ari in my head. She's more skittish than I would've guessed. It's clear after our call last night that I need to take things slow and steady if I want more with her. Probably should find out if she even wants a relationship, for starters. I tend to charge headfirst into things when I want them. My determination and fast action are the source of my greatest successes, but also my worst failures. The stakes are too high to be bull-headed.

As expected, the weights feel like nothing this morning. Damn, I wish Doug were here to see this. We meet up most mornings to help keep each other accountable, but I'll give him some slack the morning after Valentine's Day. He'd be stoked to see my improvement. Then again, he'd ask what has me so amped and I doubt he'd like my answer. *Yeah bro, I banged your little sister and now I feel like a god.*

Guilt worms its way into my high. How the hell am I going to explain this to him without getting punched in the face? Doug's come a long way with his anger management, but even that has its limits. He knows all about my fuckboy tendencies. He'll assume I was only thinking with my dick, and that I'll hurt his sister.

Why wouldn't he? My relationship track record over the time he's known me is non-existent—I have casual sex and move on. He doesn't know that my lack of commitment is due to the fact that I knew who I wanted, but thought I couldn't have her.

Ugh, should I even tell him anything? I hate the idea of keeping it a secret, but maybe it'd be better to wait until things are more established with Ariana. Then he'd see I'm not just looking to get my dick wet. Besides, Ari would murder me if I told Doug before we discuss what to say to him.

Okay. Not telling Doug yet. I'm not great at keeping secrets, but I convinced Ari I wasn't thinking about how much I wanted to bend her over the nearest object every time we talked over the past year, so hopefully I'll be able to manage. Though stray thoughts about her sweet tits covered in my cum are going to be harder to suppress now that I actually know what that looks like.

Damn, she has the best tits.

My cock starts to harden in my gym shorts. *Calm down, dude.* This is not the place to get a chub. I surreptitiously rearrange myself as best I can, then get back to my reps. Hopefully, burning off some of this energy will make it so that I don't have a semi-hard dick all day.

Unfortunately, it doesn't help. My arms and back ache from how hard I pushed myself at the gym, but I can't stop thinking about Ariana. It doesn't help that it's almost 1pm, and she still hasn't texted me to let me know about dinner. I check my phone between every meeting, getting progressively more frustrated as time ticks by. She hasn't agreed to let me be her daddy yet, but that doesn't stop me from getting excited about how I could punish her for not doing what I asked. I'm fighting the increasing urge to go jack off in the bathroom just to be able to focus on my work, when she finally messages.

🩶Ari 🩶: I don't know if I can do dinner tonight.

My heart sinks. That's it? After waiting all morning to hear from her, it stings to get such a curt message. I make myself pause before replying, practicing one of the breathing techniques we use in the monster support group to level my emotions.

She's allowed to be busy tonight. I'm allowed to feel disappointed. I need more information before I get all doom and gloom.

Wesley: Is there anything I can help you with? I could grab some takeout and swing by your place after work.

🩶Ari 🩶: You don't have to do that. I'm sure you don't want to spend your night packing up shop orders.

I can't tell if she's saying that because she's not used to letting someone help her or if she's using it as an excuse to avoid seeing me. I'm 99% sure it's the former, because Ari's the kind of person who doesn't want to look incompetent or come off as a burden.

Wesley: I want to spend my evening with you. I don't care what we do. It's okay if you don't want that, Ari. Tell me if you aren't interested in more with me and I'll drop it. I'll always be your friend, no matter what happens.

I hope she can tell how true that last part is. Whether or not she knows it, she's just as much my friend as her brother. It didn't start out that way, but now I can't imagine my life without her sass and laughter. Setting aside my attraction to her, she's important to me. Too important to let my potential crushed feelings get in the way of keeping her friendship. If she tells me that she doesn't want anything beyond what we did last night, I can deal.

Wesley: I'd rather know now before I get too far into planning our wedding.

My second message is meant as a joke, but I cringe seeing the word "wedding" sitting in our conversation as I wait for a reply. It gets worse when I see the three dots of her typing out an answer appear and disappear at least five times.

Finally, she settles on a reply.

🩶Ari 🩶: Doug would be my maid of honor, just so we're clear. I know he's your best friend, but he's my brother.

A relieved laugh bursts out of me, so loud that Craig passing my office door raises an inquisitive brow at me. I wave him off, and he reluctantly leaves with a bemused expression. I guess laughter isn't typical for me at the office. It's not that I'm rude or unfriendly, but I focus on getting my job done at the expense of joviality.

🩶Ari 🩶: If you really don't mind, I'd like to see you. I want to try this. I'm sorry I made you worry that I didn't.

Wesley: Hah, I was only 1% worried. So no apologies needed.

🩶Ari 🩶: You're too cocky for your own good.

Wesley: You like it.

🩶Ari 🩶: 🙄🙄🙄

Wesley: Careful, baby girl. You're asking for a punishment after we get your work done.

🩶Ari 🩶: Are we going to keep doing that whole... thing?

I frown down at my phone. Does she not want to? Gods, this is a bad conversation to have via text.

Wesley: It's definitely still on the table for me, if you want it. Let's talk about that tonight.

🩶Ari 🩶: Ugh, we're not going to get anything done, are we?

Wesley: Of course we will. Never doubt my ability to multitask. Now, what do you want to eat? Other than my dick, that is.

🩶Ari 🩶: I'm a vegan.

Wesley: Since when? I thought you liked eating hot meat?

🩶Ari 🩶: Since just now, when you called your dick "hot meat".

I laugh again, and Craig pops his head in my door again. You'd think his job was sticking his nose into other people's business. The stocky human smiles at me. "What's so funny? Is it that video of the chihuahua riding on the back of a pit bull?"

"Uh, no. Just a friend." He seems disappointed at my boring reply. "Send that one to me, though. That sounds cute as shit."

Craig looks taken aback for a moment, but then grins like I made his day. "Sure, man!" His snooping sorted, he heads off, no doubt to inundate me with videos for the rest of the day.

Once he's out of sight, I reply to Ariana.

Wesley: If meat is off the menu, how about a nice tossed salad?

🩶Ari 🩶: You're the worst.

I can vividly imagine the wry tone she'd use to say that, and it makes my dick twitch. Definitely no rubbing one out in the office bathroom though, since apparently Craig is lurking around waiting for a chance to catch me doing something out of character.

Wesley: Sushi?

That's one of her favorite foods. I've collected little facts about Ari over the time I've known her, hoarding them like precious treasures every time she revealed something new. I hope she doesn't think that's creepy. I can't help it. She's my favorite subject.

🩶Ari 🩶: That's perfect.

Wesley: Just like me.

🩶Ari 🩶: 🙄

Wesley: Just like you!

🩶Ari 🩶: Go back to work.

Wesley: Fine fine. See you later, Ari.

I set my phone down reluctantly. Godsdamn, I can't wait to see her later.

9

ARIANA

Between catching up on admin tasks, working on a new design for my shop, and attempting to stay on top of my socials, the day flies by way too fast. I have some stray thoughts and pangs of nerves about Wesley coming over, but I can't afford to let them sidetrack me for long. It's almost 5pm when my back and bladder start screaming at me loud enough that I can't ignore them anymore.

As soon as I stop working, all the anxiety I pushed aside comes crashing in. *Shit, Wes is going to be here in an hour!* My stomach clenches as I take in the wreckage that is my kitchen table. There's no space to sit down and eat a meal with all the merch and packing supplies I've piled on it. I've been eating at my desk or shoving random food in my mouth while standing in front of the fridge for at least the past few weeks. When faced with someone else coming over to have dinner, that habit seems less reasonable and far more embarrassing.

I'm a mess. I speed pee, then scowl at my appearance in the bathroom mirror as I wash my hands. Ugh, more than a mess. My dull pink hair is a frizzy cloud, the dark circles under my eyes are reminiscent of a ghoul, and there's a giant zit on my chin. I should've redyed my hair, or at least washed it. I should've shaved my legs and tried to tame my bush. It's been forever since I've had a guy over to my place and rather than enticing, I look feral. Wes is going to take one look at the state of my place and appearance, and turn right around.

Glancing at the clock on my phone, I mentally calculate what I have time for. Shave my legs, put product in my hair to reset my curls, slap on some makeup, run the vacuum, shove some of the crap in the living room into a closet, clear away a spot on the coffee table for food, and light some candles. I can do that in 50 minutes.

Wait, what about my bedroom? My bed is covered in laundry that needs to be folded. He's going to want to go in there, right? Why else would he be coming over? He said he'll help me pack orders, but there's no way that's happening. All it will take is him calling me "baby girl" in that rumbling tone of his and I'll do whatever he wants, orders be damned.

I re-prioritize. Sort out the bedroom, find something that resembles sexy underwear, shave my legs, fix my hair, put on makeup, shove the mess in the living room into a closet, and light candles. And find my lube. And take out the trash. Shit, I forgot it's trash day!

I should cancel. It's already 5:15. I've wasted fifteen minutes freaking out about what I need to do. I unlock my phone to message Wes, but find that he's already messaged me.

Wes: I'm getting spicy tuna, salmon, dragon, and cucumber rolls, and some sashimi. They have a bunch of flavors of mochi, so I'll get one of each. Wait, no, two of each, so you don't have to share if you don't want to. And some of that fluffy cheesecake! I think I'll also get some katsudon because it's really good from this place. What else?

The pangs of panic in my stomach morph into amusement. He's ridiculous. More importantly, he's still Wes. Yes, he's gorgeous and a sex god that's way out of my league, but he's a goof at his core.

Ariana: That's enough. Leave some food for the rest of their customers.

Wes: Hmm, you're right. I'll see if I can grab some other stuff while I'm out. See you in a bit! Oh, wait. Do you need me to be late?

Ariana: What?

Wes: Do you need extra time to hide the bodies? I know today was busy for you, so I can come later if you need me to.

Warmth spreads in my chest, and I grin at my phone like a fool. I'm nervous about him coming over, but I don't want to delay seeing him.

Ariana: I'm good, if you don't mind my place being a little messy.

Wes: I've been to your place before, and it's never as bad as you say it is. Unless you've recently become a hoarder. In which case, we'll meet at my place next time.

Ariana: No, not a hoarder. Just haven't had much time to keep up with things.

That's embarrassing to admit to someone as neat and organized as Wesley. I've been inside his place once before, and it was immaculate—just like he is in his fancy work clothes. I'm sure he's just as busy as I am, yet he manages not to be a walking disaster.

Wes: I know, baby girl. I promise, none of my attention will be on whatever mess there is when your fine ass is in the room.

My skin tingles at him calling me baby girl again. It's strange how much that turns me on. It feels dirty and a little taboo, and I must be a freak, because that makes me like it even more.

Ariana: Okay. See you in a bit.

I want to add "daddy" to the end of my message, but I chicken out. It's too weird to see typed out, even though it makes my stomach dip in excitement thinking about him asking me to call him that.

Wes: Can't wait.

I'm swiping on some mascara after my mad dash to make myself and my place as presentable as possible, when the doorbell rings. I startle and accidentally smudge onto my eyelid. Attempting to wipe it away with my fingertip just makes it worse. *Dammit!*

I scramble out of the bathroom and down the hallway, the doorbell ringing again. "I'm coming! Hold on!" My leg bumps hard into the edge of my couch and I grab it with a yelp, hobbling over to the front door as pain throbs in the spot where I'll no doubt get a huge bruise.

Yanking open the door, I'm greeted by a mountain of takeout bags and boxes so high they almost completely obscure Wesley's face.

"Wes!" I'm glad he can't see most of me past the ridiculous amount of stuff in his arms, because I know I'm beet red from my race to answer the door.

"Hey Ari." Just those two words have my cheeks burning even more. Has his voice always been that sexy?

"Why do you have so much stuff?" I ask, surveying what he's holding.

He lets out a soft chuckle and steps through the door, making his way to the kitchen and setting his packages down on the kitchen island with casual ease. No "can I come in?" or "where should I put this?". He acts like this is his own place, which both annoys me and makes my heart flutter.

"Whew!" Wes exhales dramatically after setting down his burdens, his eyes widening when he takes me in.

Crap, I thought maybe he wouldn't notice my botched makeup.

"Not what I was expecting when I said I'd come over to help you, but I don't mind." He licks his lips and his eyes drop shamelessly to my breasts.

My brow furrows at his weird statement. "What do you—" I look down at my chest. Oh god, I didn't put my top back on.

He flashes his perfect bright smile at me and raises a salacious brow.

"That's not...I forgot to...I'll be right back!" I turn to run away, but the way his smile widens freezes me in place. My legs go wobbly as his dexterous fingers make quick work of his tie and the top few buttons of his crisp white shirt.

Are we seriously doing this right now? No preamble, no discussion, just clothes off less than a minute after he gets here?

I cling onto the counter to steady myself. "W-what are you doing?"

"Getting more comfortable." He winks at me and my heart races as his human glamor dissipates. He rolls his shoulders and groans softly. "Much better. If you wanna grab a top, I'll get out some plates. Unless you have a no shirt policy in your home. In which case, I can take mine off too."

My face heats and a trickle of sweat runs down the back of my neck, despite my lack of clothing, but I do my best to push my embarrassment down. "No policy. I'm just a mess. Give me a minute and we can start over, okay?"

I don't give Wesley a chance to reply, needing to get away from him to regroup. I hurry to my bedroom and tug on my top. After taking a moment to fix the mascara mishap, I stare myself down in the mirror. "He's already seen you naked and totally disheveled. Get a grip." I repeat that to myself three more times, then let out a deep sigh and force myself to go back into the kitchen, even though my legs still feel shaky.

While I was gone, Wesley set out and arranged everything. The amount of food is truly mind-boggling, helping to push away some of my churning nerves and embarrassment.

Wesley lights up when I rejoin him. "Gorgeous," he murmurs before closing the space between us and gently tugging me against his chest. I blink up at him rapidly, unsure of what to do. Should I hug him? Maybe a kiss on the cheek? I feel as bumbling as I did before my first kiss.

He bends his head down toward mine, his snout hovering a few inches from my lips. "I'm going to kiss you," he says in a low drawl that has my palms tingling with anticipation. "I've been thinking about it all day, and I can't wait any longer."

"O-okay," I reply softly, even though it wasn't really a question.

He closes the distance, and the kiss takes me off-guard despite his warning. My brain still can't seem to compute that he's the one kissing me. Never mind that he's a freaking minotaur. Though, kissing him without the glamor is a little easier the second time around. His mouth parts, his wide tongue seeking entrance into mine, and my breath hitches as I let him in. It's languid, like he wants to savor every second of the kiss. I cling onto his arms as my body floods with arousal, and his hands on my waist dig in to hold me tighter.

When he pulls away, I take in a shaky breath as I look up into his dark eyes and recognize *yearning* in their depths. The intensity makes me squirm, and I take a nervous step back, turning my attention to the food before I do something stupid. Like profess the depths of my infatuation with him.

"Uh, what the heck is all this? I thought you were getting sushi." I cross my arms over my chest, hiding how hard my nipples are after that kiss.

Wesley shrugs, his wide shoulders straining against his shirt. I momentarily get distracted, wondering about what would happen if he took off his shirt while using his human glamor. Would it grow to minotaur size or does the glamor extend even when it's not on his body? Where does he even buy shirts in his size?

"I did, but the Japanese restaurant is right by Cupcake Fairy, so I went in and grabbed some of those lemon meringue cupcakes. Those are your favorites, right?"

His question draws my focus away from stray thoughts of how magic and clothes interact. "Huh? Yeah, they are, but you didn't need—"

"Oh, and the coffee place next to Cupcake Fairy has that vanilla hazelnut cold brew you were obsessed with last year back on the menu!" Wesley interrupts me, excitedly gesturing to a plastic to-go cup.

I stare back at him, dumbfounded. Not at the absurd amount of food—though it's ridiculous—but at his off-hand mentions of picking up things I love. My brow furrows. "How do you even remember that I like those things? You've forgotten where you parked your car almost every time I've gone somewhere with you."

He shrugs again, a small smile forming on his face. "I pay attention to things that are important to me."

The words sizzle through me, lighting me up. My heart skips a beat and I grab the coffee and take a sip to conceal my shock. I'm important to him?

Wes moves closer and brushes a thumb against my flaming cheek. "And I only pretended to forget where I parked so I could spend more time with you."

I shake my head in disbelief and scoff, trying to hide how fast my heart is racing. "You've got to be kidding me." I recall him leading me around for blocks after we went to a concert in the city. Doug went off with some girl he met, so it was just the two of us on the way home. I was so frustrated that he got us lost and was about to chew him out when his hand accidentally brushed against mine as we searched down the narrow sidewalks. I can still feel a ghost of the electric pulse it sent through me, as well as the furious blush that spread across my face and chest. I told myself I was being ridiculous. It was an insignificant touch. But now... Did it mean something to him too?

His hand slides down to brush my hair off my shoulder. "Nope. I actually have an excellent sense of direction and memory for that kind of thing. I think it's from my minotaur blood."

I attempt to glare up at him, but I doubt I'm doing a good job of it. "You're such an ass," I say weakly.

He bends down and brings his snout to my neck, inhaling with a soft groan. "I'll make it up to you."

"Oh?" My voice is rough and breathy as I wait for what he'll do next, but he just steps back and smiles.

"Yeah. Let's get some food in you, and then I'll help you tackle your orders."

"R-right. Yeah. Great."

He smirks at my flustered response. "Did you think I came here for something else?"

Of course I did! Why else would he be here? I hold my hands out in exasperation at his teasing. "I don't know! I didn't think you'd really want to help me with that."

His eyes darken, and I catch the gleam of his inner beast observing me with blatant hunger. It makes me lightheaded. Or maybe that's from only eating handfuls of goldfish and a couple of almonds for "lunch" today. My stomach growls, agreeing with the second theory.

Wesley chuckles and hands a plate to me, gesturing for me to pick what I want first. "Helping and taking care of you is my pleasure. And once we're done with dinner and work, we'll explore *your* pleasure."

10

WESLEY

Ari places a few pieces of sushi on her plate, then backs away from the spread I brought. I watch her with a frown as she turns toward her living room. As she takes a step in that direction, I grab her arm gently.

"You're kidding me, right?" I raise an eyebrow pointedly at her meager selection. "All this food and that's all you're having?"

"I didn't tell you to get so much!" she snaps, frowning back at me. "I know I'm fat, but I don't eat my weight in food every meal."

I suppress a wince and release her arm. *Shit.* I knew I was going overboard, but I thought it would make dinner special. Getting all this food was meant to be a sign of how much I want to spoil and provide for her, not a commentary on her body size or eating habits.

Rubbing the back of my neck, I shoot her what I hope comes off as an apologetic smile. "That's not what I meant. I was worried you weren't eating enough, but it's none of my business what you choose to eat or not eat, so I'll shut up."

The tension on her face eases slightly, and she lets out a weary sigh. "I know. Sorry. It's just... a man talking about what I eat is triggering. I try to avoid eating on dates—one too many judgmental looks or 'helpful' tips about my diet."

The beast inside me seethes at how she's been treated. "Fuck those guys. Insecure dickwads who couldn't handle you. You don't have to worry with me."

"Why? Because this isn't a date?" Ari asks, crossing her arms over her chest.

"Nope, this is totally a date. Because I'm a monster, not a man," I say, stroking one of my horns and letting my tail smack playfully against her leg. "Also, I'll probably eat most of what I brought. Just wanted to make sure you got everything you wanted before I demolished it. You're not the only one who fucking loves those cupcakes." I grab one and give the frosting a lascivious lick while maintaining eye contact.

She laughs and shoves my tail away as I go to twine it around her waist. "Okay, okay. I'll eat more. I'm pretty hungry..."

Pride swells inside my chest, knowing she's letting herself relax around me. "Good. I want to take care of you, Ari. I won't bring up what you eat again. But I hope you learn that you're safe with me," I say, stroking her leg again with my tail.

She looks up at me, eyes glassy as she nods.

Fucking hell, the world is so cruel to women. That this goddess worries that even I'll judge her food choices makes me see red.

I push the anger away, not wanting her to misinterpret it. "Alright, let's eat! I'm starving," I say, dragging my eyes up and down her body and savoring the way she blushes and averts her eyes.

We eat around her coffee table, with her insisting on sitting on the floor while my bulky ass takes up the majority of her couch. I tried to convince her to squeeze in next to me, or better yet, sit on my lap. I could've casually touched and teased her until she was squirming her ass on my cock. But she scoffed and rolled her eyes before plopping down on the floor.

We'll work on that. At least I hope we will. I want her sitting on her daddy's lap when he offers, like a good girl should. Fuck, I want her sweet submission and hint of brattiness so bad I can taste it lingering in the air between us. I groan and attempt to adjust my hard dick to a more comfortable position without making it obvious.

Ariana sets her plate aside and moves on to her cold brew, taking a sip with a pleased hum that makes me stare at her mouth. I'm too turned on and eager that I can't wait any longer to bring up the elephant in the room. I'll stay and help her with her orders no matter what, but my mind is buzzing with the need to define what we're doing together.

"We should talk," I say as evenly as possible.

Her eyes widen. "You know that's the worst way to start a conversation with an anxious person. Can you be more specific? Because we've been talking for the last half hour."

Gods, she's so snarky. It makes my cock twitch. "We should talk about our dynamic. Set some...parameters. Is that better?"

She huffs out a wry laugh and shakes her head. "Not really. Just tell me what you want from this. I can't handle beating around the bush or vagueness."

I resist the urge to make a bush joke and nod. "I can respect that." I take a moment to consider my words, more than a little worried about scaring her away even after the conversations we've had in the past 24 hours. Bluntness wins out, since that's what she asked for.

"I want to be your daddy."

Ariana chokes a little on her drink, obviously not expecting me to be so forthright. "W-what does that even mean? You... you want me to be your kinky fuck buddy?" Her tone holds a mixture of arousal and disdain at the idea.

I run a hand through my hair, trying to find the right words. "It means I want you to be my baby girl. Like we were last night, but more, and on a long-term basis."

I almost say a permanent basis, but that isn't a reasonable request with a kink like this. She always needs to be able to give or withdraw her consent from that kind of arrangement and not feel pressured to keep it going if she stops enjoying it.

"For as long as we both feel like it's right," I add. "Me being your daddy means me taking care of you, both in and out of the bedroom. Spoiling you like a princess. Rewarding you when you're good and disciplining you when you're naughty. That's what I want. Now, what do *you* want?"

Ariana blinks back at me, her chest rising and falling with her rapid breaths. I give her a moment to process while I fight back the urge to haul her up into my lap and whisper every dirty thing I want to do with her while I grind her on my cock until she's begging for it all.

"I…I don't…" She struggles with her answer, and my stomach sinks as I watch the conflict on her face settle into a frown. "I liked what we did last night. A lot. But I'm not a little girl, Wes. I don't want to pretend I am. I can't see myself playing with toys, wearing kid's clothes…having you cut my food and wipe my ass. That's not for me."

Ah, so that's what's tripping her up. My worry eases and I give her a reassuring smile. "I know you're not a child, and I'm not interested in age play. I enjoy the caretaking and discipline. I want the exchange of power and control. I know it's unconventional, but I can't help what turns me on. Being your daddy like that is what I crave. I have since I met you."

I shouldn't admit that, but fuck it. I want her to know. "I think you want that, too. I think you want someone to take care of you. Someone to set rules and enforce them so you can give up always being in control. Someone who uses your sexy body because it belongs to them—making you theirs to discipline, fuck, and cherish."

Yep, now I'm officially hard as steel, especially as I watch her pupils dilate while I talk. My baby girl wants this. She just needs to feel safe enough to embrace it.

She laughs weakly. "You think you have me so figured out, don't you?"

"Don't I?" I ask, letting my voice drop lower. "Say the word and I'll drop this. I want a relationship with you, whether or not there's kink involved. I don't need to be your daddy to make my dick hard for you or to want to spend time together."

"Really?" She looks a little taken aback.

"Fuck yeah. I'd give my left nut for you to be my girlfriend."

Ariana laughs, her face softening in a way that makes my heart clench. She's so damn perfect. "Wow, your left nut? How could a girl say no to an offer like that?"

"I know. It's a great deal!" I get up from the couch and offer her a hand. She takes it and I tug her up and into my arms. She fits so well against me, her plush breasts and stomach melding against my bulk. I lock eyes with her and squeeze her tighter. "I'd give you anything your heart desires, if it meant I could call you mine."

Her mouth falls open in a soft gasp, but then her brow furrows. "You've gotta stop saying romantic shit like that."

My eyes drop to her lips, eager to feel them against mine again. "Why?"

"Because you're going to make me fall for you!" she says, sounding almost annoyed by the thought.

Good. Then I won't be the only one head over heels. "I don't see a problem with that. After all, you're my girlfriend now."

She sighs dramatically, but her eyes light up. "Fine. I'm your girlfriend."

My lips are on hers as soon as she says it, and she lets out a little squeak in surprise that melts into a soft moan. I soak her in, letting my hands roam up and down her body as our tongues slide together. My dick begs me to throw her over my shoulder and take her to the bedroom, but I pull back, needing to know the answer to my earlier question.

"Do you want me to be your daddy, too?"

11

ARIANA

The question hangs in the air between us, so thick and heavy it feels like I'm drowning in it. Everything Wesley has said tonight makes it hard for me to breathe properly. He wants me as his girlfriend. He wants to be my daddy. He wants *me*.

And what do I want?

Everything.

I crave Wesley. I've spent so long fighting my attraction and affection for him. It's time to surrender and take whatever he wants to give me.

"Fuck it. Yeah."

Wesley's entire face lights up. I don't think he expected that answer. "Yeah? You sure?"

"Yes, daddy." Now that I've decided, I don't feel as shy saying the word.

I'm rewarded with Wesley's mouth on mine again, his hot tongue forcing my lips open as he squeezes my ass with both of his enormous hands. An embarrassing whimper escapes me as his cock grinds against my belly, and he pulls back with a heated chuckle. "Shit, baby girl. Daddy wants to fuck you so bad."

I rock myself against his massive thigh, desperate for some kind of relief from the pressure building between my legs. I'm still pretty damn sore, but right now I couldn't care less. "Then why don't you?"

His grip on me tightens, holding me still. "We've got work to do, remember? What kind of daddy would I be if I let you neglect that?"

"A fun one?" I bat my eyelashes at him, though I doubt it will work.

He shakes his head, meeting my rebuttal with a soft warning smack on my ass. "Nope. Now, show me what needs to get done."

With Wes' help, packing up my shop orders goes much faster than usual. He listens to my instructions with such a serious look of focus on his face that it makes my heart melt that much more. Things would go even faster if I didn't keep distracting myself by glancing up at him to check that he's not just some figment of my imagination. But he's real, and he's here, and he's surprisingly dextrous packaging up the delicate earrings and necklaces despite his thick fingers. He takes extreme care to make sure everything is wrapped up as nicely as possible. My heart flutters with amused affection whenever his tongue sticks out the side of his snout in concentration as he works with the delicate tissue paper.

Each time I pass him a new stack of items to wrap up, he makes little exclamations about how my art is “cute as shit” and that I’m “super fucking talented”. The off-hand compliments feel strange from a man who, for most of our time knowing each other, has taken great pleasure in teasing me. That is until I realize that Wesley’s never once said anything teasing about my art or shop. Even Doug was a little dismissive when I told him I was going to focus on my shop full time. Most people take one look at my cutesy, weird art style and dismiss me as being as unserious as my designs. But not Wes. In fact, he told Doug off in that very same conversation we had about me making my art the main source of income.

God, how did I not see how much he cared?

“Oh, hell yeah. This one is amazing! I haven’t seen it before. Is it new?” Wesley asks, holding up a tank top with a technicolor raccoon in a birth of Venus pose. It’s nothing groundbreaking, but I’m still proud of the mix of cute and feral vibes I put into the art.

“You keep track of all my designs?” I ask, raising an incredulous brow.

“I follow you,” he says with a shrug, like it’s a given. Which I guess shouldn’t surprise me since he’s apparently been obsessed with me for a year. Affection and arousal warm my insides at the thought.

Wesley smiles as he continues. “I see your stuff in my feed all the time—it’s hard not to with how many people are sharing it. You’re killing it, Ari. It makes me so fucking proud every time I see one of your designs.”

The honeyed warmth building inside me cools, and my cheeks heat as I struggle against the urge to wave off his compliment. I’m not good at handling praise. I know I've worked my ass off to get my shop to where it is, but a lot of my success lately comes down to luck and good timing. If I accept his praise, and therefore accept that my shop's success was my doing, then I also open myself up to feeling like a failure when my surge of popularity wanes.

"Don't give me that look," Wes says, tossing a stray piece of tissue paper at me. It bounces off my chin and lands in my cleavage, which makes him cackle in delight.

I glare back at him as I fish the paper out of my boobs and throw it back. It falls short, landing feebly in front of him. "What look?" I ask, with an indignant huff.

He rolls his eyes at me. "The look that says 'it's no big deal'. Don't you dare minimize what you've done, Ari. You're the hardest working person I know. You're talented and determined and can do anything you set your mind to."

I blink at him, taken aback by his vehemence. As much as it embarrasses me to be called out like that, his pride in my achievements makes me melt. "I am pretty great, aren't I?" My tone is playful, still not fully able to accept his blatant praise.

He nods emphatically. "The best. Now, do you have any of these in my size?" He holds the tank top up to his massive chest.

I giggle at the thought of the cute raccoon stretched across his bulk. "Sorry, I don't have much of a minotaur client base so I didn't order any in your size. I mean, you could probably squeeze into one, but it would fit more like a crop top."

"Sold!" he exclaims, snatching a shirt from a box nearby. "All the bros at the gym are going to be so jealous."

I laugh and shake my head at him. "You're ridiculous. But if that's what you want as payment for helping me tonight, be my guest."

"No way, I'm not taking it for free. I don't need any payment for helping you, Ari." His expression sobers. "You know that, right? I'm here because spending time with you like this makes me happy."

"I know. Gosh, it was just a joke. Let me give you the damn shirt." The flush from earlier is back on my face. I know it's silly, but I still feel guilty having him help me out instead of doing what a normal date would do.

"Needed to check. Thank you for the shirt, sweetheart." His tail snakes under the table to brush against my calf. "You're such a good girl, letting daddy help you," he says, voice lowering into a deep rumble.

My breath hitches at his sudden energy shift. He has a hungry look in his eyes that signals that fun, friendly Wesley is taking a backseat to his daddy persona.

"I think I can finish these last few orders in the morning," I say breathily, unable to look away from him as he slides his tail up my leg in a slow drag.

He crosses his arms over his chest, giving me an appraising look that makes my skin tingle with excitement. "You sure? I don't want to encourage you to be irresponsible."

"I'm sure." I squirm at his authoritative tone, arousal pooling in my belly. "I need you, daddy."

Wesley stands from his chair and crosses to my side of the table in a heartbeat. He reaches down and scoops me into his arms with ease. I let out a squeal of surprise and he shushes me. "Don't worry. I've got you. Daddy's going to take care of you now."

He strides down the hallway and into my bedroom, then sets me down on the edge of the bed with surprising gentleness, given the intensity of his energy. His hands slip under the hem of my shirt, and I inhale sharply as his fingers touch the bare skin of my stomach. I barely resist the urge to suck my belly in as he runs his hands across my stomach with a pleased hum. He clearly likes my body, and he's already seen me mostly naked, but the impulse to pretend it's smaller is a holdover from past relationships. With Wesley, maybe I'll finally be safe enough to accept my body without fear of being torn down by the person who's supposed to love me.

Unaware of my internal struggle, Wesley strokes my stomach a few more times before pulling my top up. I raise my arms to aid the removal of my shirt and he murmurs a soft "good girl" as tugs it off carefully.

"Look at you," he rasps, his gaze raking over my exposed skin. "Take your bra off, sweetheart."

A wave of shyness courses through me, and I hesitate, the urge to cover myself with my arms too strong to resist.

Wesley's eyes narrow. "Don't hide from me. I've been waiting all day to see you again. Show daddy those perfect tits."

My breath hitches at his words, and something shifts inside me. I realize that in this moment, I don't have to be the Ari burdened with relationship trauma and body hangups. I can just be Wes' baby girl—untethered to anything but trust in his gentle, but firm guidance and the knowledge that he'll keep me safe.

I nod. "O-okay, daddy." My skin prickles with excited nerves as he watches me unhook my bra and push the straps off my shoulders with faintly trembling fingers. When I'm bare to him, his eyes darken.

"Perfect." He sinks to his knees in front of me, and coasts his hands up my sides to cup my breasts, his huge palms engulfing them and reminding me just how much *bigger* he is than me. That unfamiliar sensation of being small is emphasized by the fact that I still need to look up to meet his eyes, even when he's kneeling.

"Daddy," I whisper, my voice hoarse even though he's barely touched me.

He groans softly and his head dips to press his face into my neck, taking a deep inhale as his thumbs swirl teasingly over my nipples. "You make it hard for me to go slow when you say that so sweetly, baby girl. It makes the beast inside me want to come out and make you scream it."

"You can use me how you want, daddy. I want to make you feel good." I don't recognize the blend of meek vulnerability and arousal filling my voice, but the thought of him being so undone that he can't hold himself back from taking what he needs from me makes me burn with desire.

Wesley raises his head from my neck and meets my eyes, pupils blown wide. "Sweet, perfect girl. I'm not sure you're ready for that."

"I am! I promise. Please," I say, my voice almost a whine from how much I want him to keep going.

He chuckles, the dark warning threaded into his laugh making my stomach clench in anticipation. "We'll see about that." He hooks his fingers under the waistband of my skirt, tugging it off with deft ease, then stands back up. I want to cry out in protest, pull him back down to my level, and kiss him until we're both breathless, but I know that's not how this game works.

Wesley towers over me, his chest rising and falling with heavy breaths as he unbuckles his belt. I take in the outline of his cock, absurdly thick and erotic with how it strains against his pants. When I'm able to tear my eyes away, he's grinning at me.

"You like what you see?" he asks as he strips off his shirt, then toys with the zipper of his pants. I'd roll my eyes at his cocky confidence, but I'm too turned on to give him shit right now.

Instead, I continue to sink into my role. "It's so big, daddy." The momentary embarrassment from the silliness of the words quickly fades when his nostrils flare and his expression grows even more heated.

Wes reaches down and grabs his length through the fabric with a low groan. "Mmm, it's all for you. Been hard all day thinking about your sweet pussy."

"I thought about you, too," I murmur.

He reaches out and strokes my cheek, and my eyes flutter closed at the tenderness. "Naughty girl. Did you touch yourself thinking about your daddy's cock?"

As hot as it would be to say yes, I tell him the truth. "No..."

He frowns. "No? Why not, sweetheart? I don't like the thought of you being needy all day."

"I didn't have time and..." My cheeks grow hot and I hesitate, not wanting to ruin the mood.

He tilts my chin to guide me to look at his face, which holds a mixture of sternness and concern. "And what? Tell me, baby. No secrets between us."

"I... I'm still a little sore." My pussy throbs and I feel the dull ache between my thighs from how much he stretched me last night.

His grip on my chin tightens, and he lets out a low, displeased sound. "You're still hurting? Why didn't you tell me?"

"It's okay. It's not that bad. I still want to do this." I'm so turned on and part of me likes the thought of feeling the pleasure-pain of him stretching me again.

He lets out a disbelieving huff. "I'll see for myself. Spread your legs for me, baby girl. Let daddy help make you feel better."

12

WESLEY

Gods, I'm such an idiot. Of course Ari is still sore. Our bodies weren't made to fit together—at least not without a lot of practice and a fuckton of lube. But no, I just *had* to shove my dick inside her with zero prep like a mindless beast. Sure, she begged me to, and yes, I thought it was my only chance to feel her come undone around my cock, but that's no excuse.

Guilt makes my stomach clench. I asked to be her daddy, and yet I failed the fundamentals from the start. No more. If we're doing this, we're doing it right. Which starts with taking care of her tonight.

A low rumble of frustration at myself escapes me, and Ariana inhales sharply, but she follows my command, spreading her legs wider. I forgo undressing the rest of the way, afraid that my fragile control over my desire for her will become even weaker if my dick isn't trapped in my pants. Instead, I sink to my knees before her, supplicating myself at the altar of her sumptuous body.

She's opened her legs, but not enough to keep her thick thighs from hiding her pussy from my view. I stroke my fingers up the sides of her legs, then dip in to her inner thighs and press her open wide enough that I can fit between them.

"That's better," I murmur, trailing my hands up to tease the edge of her flowery pink panties. The center of the delicate fabric is already wet and she whimpers as I idly trace the tip of my finger around the damp spot. "Mmm, this for me, baby girl?"

"Y-yeah. Just for you. Please touch me. I want to feel you inside me again."

Fucking hell, she's going to be the death of me. Flushed and breathless and already begging for my cock. The hot bar of my dick throbs in my pants, just as eager for what she's asking for.

I press a kiss to her inner thigh and use the intoxicating scent of her arousal to drown out my own need. *Focus on her.* She's what's important. "You sound so good when you beg, angel. But I need to make sure I'm not going to hurt you."

"I told you. I'm okay!" she whines, but I shake my head in warning to let her know she's not winning this fight.

She squirms as I trail my mouth up her leg to the source of her heady scent. I indulge myself in this moment, letting myself savor how she fills my senses as I lick across the damp patch of her panties. Her taste explodes across my tongue—tart and ambrosial. Minotaurs don't have fated mates or mate bonds like some other monsters, but we're still possessive and covetous. We know when we've found something worth keeping for our own. And Ariana tastes like she's *mine*.

Needing more, I quickly tug down her panties. My instinct is to rip them off, but they're too cute to destroy.

Her cheeks redden with more than arousal as I take a moment to gaze at her. "I should've shaved. Sorry! I'll do it before next time," she says, hands falling to cover herself in embarrassment.

I grab her wrists and ease them out of the way with a frown. "No."

"No?" Her brow furrows in confusion, and I want to reach up and smooth her worries away. Gods, she's just as clueless as I am sometimes.

"Ari, I'm a fucking minotaur with fur on most of my body. You think I give a shit about the cute patch of hair between your legs? Unless you enjoy being bare, leave it."

"Oh. Duh." Her mouth twists into a cheeky smile. "What if I want *you* bare?"

I laugh and gesture down at my furred torso. "I don't think there's enough body wax in the world to take on this job. Though, if it bothers you for real, I can always put my human glamor back up."

She scowls at me. "No! Your human form is hot, but like this you're...you."

My heart flutters in delight at her words, and I grin at her like a lovesick fool. "Hmm, if you insist. Now, where was I before you interrupted me?"

"You were going to lick my—ah!"

Ari's words cut off with a gasp as I waste no time in burying my face between her legs. With a tongue as broad as mine, there's no room for finesse or precise teasing. I don't lick her pussy—I *devour* her.

She's so wet and warm, and I seek out as much of her honeyed arousal as I can get as she moans and brings a hand down to one of my horns to brace against my onslaught. "W-Wes...daddy, oh fuck."

"That's it. Hold onto my horns and take what you need from me," I rasp in between my insistent strokes against her clit.

She holds them hesitantly at first, but her grip tightens as she gets closer to her release. My dick is harder than steel at her taste, and the way her hips start to rock against my tongue is driving me to the edge.

"Oh! Just like that. Oh god, I'm gonna come, daddy," she gasps, her thighs trembling beneath my grip with the tension of her pending release.

I let out a muffled groan of approval against her pussy, unwilling to stop what I'm doing and risk her losing her orgasm. She bucks and cries out, and I feel her clit pulse against my tongue as she crashes over the edge. It's so fucking delicious and perfect, I feel like I could come from even the smallest touch.

I lick her through her orgasm, only letting up when she tugs at my horns with a whimper of protest. She beams down at me, face and chest washed with a pretty pink as she tries to catch her breath.

Now that she's more relaxed from her release, I place a finger against her entrance and slide it in slowly. "How does that feel, baby?" I ask, watching her expression for any sign of pain.

"Mmm, good. I want you inside me, daddy."

I'm not convinced yet, even though by cock is screaming at me to listen to the woman begging for my dick. I remove my finger and circle her clit, then add another. When I press inside her wet channel, she winces.

"Tell me again how you're fine?" I ask with a frown, removing my fingers as gently as possible so I don't cause her more pain.

She frowns back at me, her legs falling closed as I ease back. 'Okay, *fine*. It hurts. But I want to do this. I can handle some pain."

"This isn't the kind of pain you mess around with, baby girl. I tore you by shoving my dick inside you without the proper prep, and that needs to heal." I swallow down the lump of shame building in my throat. "I'm sorry I hurt you. I was irresponsible and I won't do that again."

She shoves against my shoulder. "Dude, I begged you to fuck me. If anyone is at fault, it's me. I couldn't give up the chance, and I..." Her voice lowers into a whisper, like she's confessing a secret. "I thought it'd never happen again, so it'd be worth the pain."

It's a miracle we were able to get past our mutual insistence that our attraction was one-sided. I hate that our skewed perceptions ended in her getting hurt.

I stroke her thighs in reassurance. "I was scared it was only that once, too, which is why I gave in. But now we know that it'll happen many, *many* more times. There's no need to rush."

Now that we've confessed our feelings, now that she's here spread before me like the most sumptuous dessert, I make an oath to myself that I'll do everything in my power to never hurt her again—physically or emotionally. Barring any mutually agreed upon pain play. Speaking of which...

"Do you want me to fuck you tonight because you're into the pain, baby?"

Ariana shakes her head slightly and sighs. "No. God, why do you always have to be right? I was being a horny idiot. I like when you spank me, and I think I might like other things along those lines, but stretching out my pussy after last night's abuse isn't my kind of pain." She pauses and gives me an assessing look. "Why? Are you into pain?"

I can't help the grin that spreads across my face. I know she asked the question flippantly, but it makes my cock pulse with unfulfilled need. "I don't mind pain. Anyone who gets their dick pierced has got to be at least a little masochistic. Do you want to hurt me, angel?"

Her eyes grow comically wide. "No!" As the shock of my question fades, her surprised expression shifts into a smirk. "Though sometimes when you're being a turd, I imagine smacking you. But that's from sheer frustration, not horniness."

"Hah, noted. If you ever get curious, let me know. Not just about that. Anything that goes through that kinky brain of yours, we can discuss it. I want you to get whatever you need."

She bats her eyelashes at me, and I get lost in the sparkling jade of her eyes. She's so damn beautiful. "*Whatever* I need?"

I'll give her the world if she'll let me. She already has my heart, even if I can't tell her that yet. "Yeah, Ari." My voice sounds hoarse as I answer her. "Anything you need—*sincerely* need and aren't just doing because you're anxious or you think you 'should'."

She takes a few seconds to process my answer, opening and closing her mouth multiple times before speaking. Shit, I hope I'm not coming on too strong.

When she finally gets her words out, all my fears crumble to dust. "What if... what if I just need *you*?"

My heart swells, threatening to explode from joy. Precious, adorable, amazing Ari. How did I get so lucky to have her say something like that to me?

Needing an outlet for my overwhelming emotion, I surge forward, grabbing her under her legs, and lift her up. She gasps into my kiss as I claim her lips, desperate to show her that she has me. I hold her in my arms, relishing the way she clings to me with equal fervor.

Gods, if only I'd known she felt the same way. We could've been doing this for months already. I need to claim every kiss, every touch, every orgasm that I missed out on giving her.

"Wes," Ari pants between frantic kisses, rocking her hot, wet core against my stomach.

"I've got you," I rasp, setting her down on the bed, and making quick work of my pants and underwear, before joining her. I kiss my way up her lush stomach, loving the give of her hips as I knead my fingers into them possessively. When I settle my hips over hers, caging her in with my arms as I hold my weight up from crushing her, she lets out a shuddering exhale that I'll hear in my dreams.

"I'm okay, you can—"

I cut her off with a forceful kiss. "Hush, baby girl. That's not happening until you're healed. I'm gonna tease your little clit with my cock until you can't stand it any longer. Then, when you're begging for me to let you come, I'll use my mouth on you."

She gasps as I punctuate my words with a rock of my hips, sliding my cock against her. "What about you? I can suck you off, daddy."

I groan into her neck, my cock weeping pre-cum at the thought. "No need. I love your perfect mouth, but I'm going to bust as soon as I get a taste of you again. Just lie back and let me give you what you need."

13

ARIANA

How is this real?

I've asked myself that question over and over in the last 24 hours, yet I'm still baffled. In all the times I got myself off in this very bed to the thought of Wesley's body above mine, pressing me into the mattress, it never felt like something that would actually happen. And damn, my imagination was lacking because the Wesley in my mind couldn't hold a candle to the solid bulk of the minotaur currently teasing me with a cock the size of my forearm.

I also never imagined him having a dick piercing. I gasp softly as the metal brushes against my clit and Wesley lets out a pleased chuckle. "You like that, sweetheart?"

I nod, eager for more. "Yeah...feels good." It only brushes against me a little in this position, but it still sends a thrill through me knowing he's hard and so close to sliding inside me, even though we agreed not to do that.

"Hmm, good isn't amazing." He looks down at where our bodies press together, lips downturning slightly.

Does he not like how I look from this angle? The arousal he's been kindling threatens to extinguish as my body issues rear their ugly head.

It only gets worse when he reaches down and grabs my lower belly with one hand and pushes it upward. His fingers sink into my ample flesh there and my face burns in shame.

"W-what are you doing? Stop it!" I squeak, reaching down and grab his wrist in an attempt to yank it away, but he doesn't let go.

His eyes meet mine with a stern glare that makes my breath stutter. "Behave."

"But—"

He releases his hold on me, grabbing both my wrists and pinning them above my head with staggering speed and ease. "Do you want me to let you come?" he asks, voice a low growl of warning.

My desire wars with my embarrassment. "Y-yes. I do. It's just—"

"Your body belongs to me, baby girl. It's mine to do what I want with. If I want to grab your cute belly, then I'm going to. No arguing."

He pauses, waiting to see if I continue to protest. I can't help squirming against his hold, even though it's futile. I'm so exposed and vulnerable, and when he talks about my stomach and using my body I can't decide if I want to fight or beg him to keep going.

"Yes, daddy," I whisper, unable to meet his eyes because I'm afraid he'll see my frustrating shame about my stomach in them.

He huffs, switching his grip on my wrists to one hand so he can use the other to turn my face to look at him. His eyes burn with command and wicked heat as he speaks. "Use your safeword if you need to. Otherwise, you complain again and I'll leave you on the edge and come all over that sweet softness you're so adamant about keeping me from touching."

The idea is so filthy and strange, I can't help the whine that escapes me.

Wesley laughs darkly. "You'd like that, wouldn't you? You like knowing how hard your pretty, perfect body makes daddy. How he can't help but jerk his cock every time he thinks about you. Dirty girl." He grinds his erection against me with a rumble of pleasure, emphasizing his point. "Keep your hands above your head while I show you just how much I love it."

His words leave me reeling and speechless, the harmful noise in my mind fading away as I let what he's said take over. He *loves* my body.

I cry out as he grabs my belly again, taking a moment to knead it with a deep groan. His manhandling feels exciting rather than embarrassing with the new context, though still taboo. All my life, I've been taught to hate my fupa. When I was a pre-teen, the boy I had a crush on asked me if I was pregnant. My mom only bought me swimsuits that had an attached skirt or wrap so the cut of the leg wouldn't reveal the roll where my stomach meets my thighs. Magazines provided infinite exercises and diets to target a stubborn low belly. It's a part of me that's supposed to be pointedly ignored, not appreciated.

Wes watches my face as he touches me, searching for a sign that I want him to stop. "Such a good girl," he rumbles, gentling his touch to a soft caress. He strokes me with reverence, dragging his gaze down my body to focus on where his hand glides against my stomach. "You're beautiful, Ari."

A feeble laugh escapes me. "You must have a fat fetish."

His eyes dart back to meet mine, and he shakes his head. "Not really. Yes, I find fat women attractive, but it's not an exclusive preference. I love your softness because it's *yours*. Touching your stomach turns me on because it's a part of *you*."

Tears pour from me as something deep inside me releases. "How is this real?" I don't mean to ask the question that's been on loop in my mind aloud, but it tumbles out anyway.

He reaches up to brush away some of the moisture with his thumb, then cups my cheek. "Good question, angel. I've got no clue how I got to be so damn lucky, but I'm sure as hell going to embrace it." The hand on my belly presses the flesh gently upwards, and I gasp as the pierced head of his cock slides through my labia and bumps against clit, now more exposed to him.

Jesus, he was just trying to make it easier to get me off. "O-oh. That's why..."

He smiles softly. "I told you. It's my job to make you feel good, baby girl. It's your job to trust me to take care of you."

"I trust you," I whisper, the bone-deep understanding of that truth finally apparent now that I've been given a reprieve from the morass of my anxieties and shame.

Wesley grins at me, hunger and pride filling his expression. Bringing the hand not on my stomach down to press his cock more firmly against my pussy, he begins to rock against me in a steady drag. "Fuck, you're soaking my cock. Feel how easy it is for me to slide against you? You're so godsdamned good."

"More," I gasp, tilting my hips to try to meet his. I want to reach down and grab his hips to grind him against me harder, but I don't want to risk him stopping because I didn't keep my hands above my head.

He rearranges the hand holding my stomach so that his thumb presses against my clit, and the added stimulation has me shaking with the need to come. "Ah, yes. Please, daddy. Please, Wes." I'm babbling as he speeds up his strokes, his weight pinning me down to the bed as he grinds and grinds against me until I'm ready to shatter.

"Gods, shit, I'm gonna come," Wes gasps suddenly, his hips stuttering against me. He releases a rumbling, primal groan as hot jets of his cum splatter against my stomach and labia. He keeps moving, the thumb on my clit circling insistently, and the thought of his release so close to being inside me pushes me over the edge.

"Daddy!" I buck against his touch as I come, senses overloaded with pleasure.

"That's it, baby. Such a good girl," he rasps, stroking me through my orgasm until I let out a shuddering sigh.

I have the urge to do something tremendously foolish, like tell him I love him, but thankfully he tugs me up into his arms and kisses me before the words can escape. He strokes my back as he holds me against him, drugging me with slow kisses until I'm languid and drowsy in his arms. He's so solid and warm and *wonderful.*

"How do you feel, sweetheart?" he asks as he eases his mouth from mine.

"*Amazing.*" I nestle in against his shoulder and close my eyes, savoring the comfort his strong hold provides.

He strokes my hair, sending pleasant prickles down my spine.

"Mmm, good. Don't fall asleep yet, though. I gotta get you cleaned up before I tuck you in bed."

I sigh, not liking the idea of getting up but recognizing the need. "You love making a mess of me, don't you?"

Wesley chuckles. "I fucking love it. But I love the idea of cleaning you off, too. Now, shower or bath?"

"Shower. I don't have a bathtub."

He looks down at me, aghast. "You're kidding me. What kind of house doesn't have a bathtub?"

I shrug. "Uh, one that was owned by an elderly lady who converted all the tubs to showers for accessibility? It sucks, but it's one of the reasons I was able to afford the place."

He frowns, giving me a look of deep concern. "So you never get to take a bath? Doug told stories about how you used to hog your bathroom for hours as a kid, filling and refilling the bathtub so you could read as long as you wanted. That's awful."

"It's not some great tragedy. I'm used to it," I say, confused why he cares so much.

"That's it."

"That's what?" This whole conversation is so strange.

He grabs my shoulders and looks me in the eyes with determination. "You're moving in with me."

My heart skips a beat. "What?!"

"How the hell am I supposed to spoil you, the queen of baths, without a tub? Come live with me—I have an enormous one that will fit both of us."

"Wes, what are you talking about? I can't move in with you! We literally just started dating. That would be insane."

He gives me a cocky grin."Would it?"

"Yes, it would!" I shove his shoulder with a scowl that makes him laugh.

"Hmm, would you change your mind if I told you it was a minotaur thing? That once we find a partner, we need to keep them in our lair?"

I roll my eyes. "Maybe, if you weren't completely full of shit."

"Hah, fair! Alright, if you're not moving in, then you're at least going to spend the weekend at my place." He pushes a lock of my hair behind my ear with a devastatingly seductive smile.

"I..." The thought of spending the whole weekend with him is incredibly tempting, but weekends are always so busy for me. There's no way I can afford to take off two days. I can barely take a few hours for myself.

He sighs dramatically, but the sound doesn't hold any real frustration. "Saturday night and Sunday morning at my place? I can cook you dinner while you read in the tub. Let me spoil you a little, sweetheart. Otherwise, I'll spend the whole weekend pining for you."

I should say no. How the fuck am I supposed to be his girlfriend when I can't even make time for myself. The responsible thing to do is tell him I can't. But when he presses a kiss to my shoulder, I crumble. "Okay, okay. But only if you make your lasagna."

"Your wish is my command." His delighted smile makes my chest ache with affection. "Now, get your butt in the shower. It's late and you have a busy day tomorrow."

"You're not going to join me, daddy?" I ask, batting my eyelashes at him.

"If I go with you, you'll just get dirty again," he says, voice threaded with a touch of heat.

"I promise I'll be good," I whisper, brushing my lips against the column of his throat.

His cock twitches against my ass, and he groans. "I'm trying to be responsible, sweetheart. Plus, I doubt we'll both fit."

I let out a long sigh and slide off his lap. "Fine."

He grabs my hip as I go to walk toward the bathroom. "Before you go, where's your linen closet?"

My brow furrows. "My linen closet? Why?"

"I'll change the sheets while you shower." He gestures down to the large damp spot on my bed.

Yikes, I didn't realize he came that much.

"Oh, you don't have to do that. It's late and you're probably tired." My stubborn anxiety creeps back in. Does he want to spend the night? "You can go home if you want. Or stay. Whatever is fine."

He squeezes my hip. "You say the most ridiculous things sometimes, baby girl. Of course I'm spending the night. Go wash up and then I'm snuggling the shit out of you."

I head off to the shower with a giggle. When I shut the door behind me, I lean against it and close my eyes. The question that's been burning inside me fades to blissful, befuddled acceptance.

Holy shit, this is real.

14

WESLEY

Waking up with Ariana curled against me, her face pressed against my chest and legs threaded with mine, is the best feeling in the world. Hmm, well, tied for the best with her coming on my cock. But honestly, I think this might win, even with the small spot of dampness on my fur from where she's drooled a little in her sleep. She's so warm and soft, and the gentle florals of her shampoo combined with the subtle notes of her natural scent create a soothing, soporific effect. I wish I could spend all day together in bed holding her like this, savoring that she's finally mine.

Unfortunately, that's not an option. A glance at the clock on her bedside table shows it's almost 7:30. *Damn.* I hate to wake her up and ruin this perfect moment, but she said she needed an early start today to get everything on her task list done, and I've got to get to work.

With a sigh, I stroke her back, gently at first, relishing the glide of her silky soft skin against my palm. My cock twitches eagerly when she lets out a little groan of protest and nestles in against me even more. *Sorry bud, I know you're excited that she's naked and in your arms, but there's no time to dick around this morning.*

I increase the pressure of my touch. "Time to get up, baby girl."

She groans more emphatically and shakes her head as best she can while pressed between my pecs.

I chuckle at her adorable resistance. "As much as I love a little morning motorboating, you gotta wake up." I reach down and squeeze her ass. Not the best idea for keeping my lust under control, because my cock jerks at the feel of her lusciousness in my hand.

"Mmm, but this feels so nice. Don't make me," she mumbles against my skin. Her hips rock forward onto the thigh she's wrapped her legs around, and she lets out a breathy sigh that threatens to crush my resolve.

With my own groan, I push down the urge to indulge in a morning quickie. I don't think I'd be able to make it quick—not with how much I love seeing Ariana come undone. The next thing I know, I'll be face deep in her pussy, making her come for the fourth time and an hour late to work. Fuck, that sounds good. My dick agrees, firming up even more against her belly.

Ariana rubs herself against my thigh again, making a needy humming sound.

A low curse escapes my lips. She's too tempting. Only through sheer willpower am I able to resist pulling her on top of me and letting her grind her way to orgasm against my cock while I play with her tits.

"Ari." I grab her hip to hold her still. "Before we fell asleep, I promised you that I'd get you up early. I don't intend to break any of my promises to you, sweetheart."

She sighs and her eyes blink open, then blearily look up at me. My heart skips a beat as they focus on my face and a sleepy, unguarded smile spreads across her lips. "Even if I beg you to?" she asks, voice taking on a breathy tone meant for seduction.

This woman. Gods give me strength to not give in to her. I shake my head in an attempt to clear away her beguiling presence. "Nope. Now quit humping my leg and get your ass out of bed." I give her a light spank to emphasize my words.

She lets out an indignant squawk of protest and shoves against my chest. "Fine! I was going to offer to blow you, but never mind. I'll get up."

She moves to roll away, but I tangle my hand in her hair and hold her still. "Keep being a brat and see what happens. Trust me, you won't like it," I say, lowering my voice in warning.

Like the submissive she is, Ariana melts at the combination of my hand in her hair and my command, pupils widening and breath stuttering.

My breath becomes just as ragged. She's *stunning*. Her reaction calls to all the dominant urges in me. My beast tells me to haul her back to my place and never let her out of my sight again.

I watch her expression flicker, obviously warring between needing to please me and wanting to push back. Eventually, her submission wins out. "Okay, daddy," she says with a soft sigh. "I'll get up."

Her compliance intoxicates me, and for a moment I forget why I'm trying to make her get out of bed. My snout lingers against her hair, breathing her in as I allow myself one more moment of bliss. Reluctantly, I give her hair a kiss and pull back. "That's a good girl. Let's get dressed and then I'll make us some coffee and breakfast."

She sits up and stretches out her arms with a yawn, treating me to a view of her heavy breasts tipped with dusky pink-brown nipples that beg to be sucked. I wonder if she'd be into nipple clamps...

"I'm not really a breakfast person," she says, face flushing as she notices my perusal of her tits.

Her reply draws me away from my heated thoughts, and I frown. "What? Ari, breakfast is the most important meal—"

She scowls at me and smacks me in the chest with her pillow. "Don't lecture me! It's not sexy."

"Liar," I retort, leaning forward to kiss the little line that forms between her brows when she gives me that pissy look. She half-heartedly shoves me away, but I catch the breathy little sigh she makes at the contact. "Sorry, Ari." I say as I pull back. "I know you don't need a lecture, and I'm not judging your choices. The care-taker in me wants to make sure you have everything you need to feel your best."

"Food before 10 makes me nauseous." Her lips twist into a cheeky grin. "But if you want me to feel my best, an orgasm is a good way to perk me up in the morning."

"Ari..." I groan, my need to make her feel good in direct conflict with my need to be responsible and take care of her.

"I know, I know. Had to try though," she says with a soft chuckle and an adorable smile that fills my chest with tender affection.

This right here, this easy banter, is my new favorite thing. I want to spend every morning with her, joking and flirting. Oh, and fucking. I make a mental note to wake her up earlier next time.

The best part about this new thing with Ariana is that I can text her whenever I want, with no need for an excuse. The worst part is waiting for the chance to see her again—which won't be until Saturday. I offer to stop by each morning and grab any packages she needs taken to the post office, but she doesn't take me up on it. I suggest that I swing by with an afternoon coffee during my lunch breaks, but she says it'd be "too distracting".

She's probably right on that account, even though I hate it. Just the thought of being near her is enough to get me hard. It makes texting at work awkward as hell since Craig seems to have developed dickdar, popping his head into my office as if on cue any time I'm turned on by Ariana's messages. But I can only go for a few hours before I'm messaging her again about something that reminded me of her or to make a dumb joke.

Texts aren't enough. It's driving me crazy, having to stay away and not being allowed to help her out. If I didn't know better, I'd think she was avoiding me, but I can viscerally feel how stressed and overwhelmed she is through her messages. I believe her when she tells me she'd much rather be together than doing admin work, so I'm giving her space even though I hate it.

To make matters worse, my usual outlet for venting my frustrations isn't an option, because he's Ari's brother. I attempted to broach the subject of telling Doug about our relationship, but it didn't go well. She told me she wanted to make sure we were solid before freaking him out. Which upset me, because in my mind, us being together is set in stone. But I couldn't think of a way to tell her that without freaking her out, so I've had to stew in my own frustrations and hurt feelings.

Every morning we've worked out together, I've had to pretend that nothing is different or new. I'm not a good liar, and I can tell that Doug knows something is up. Part of me wants to tell him and get it over with. Sure, he'll freak out and Ariana will be pissed that I didn't wait for her permission, but it's torture keeping the best thing to happen to me from my best friend. The only thing holding me back is that I'm not sure what level of anger the revelation will provoke. Fucking your friend's little sister isn't usually met with pats on the back and congratulations. Doug has worked hard to get a leash on his rage, but for all I know, he might get so mad that he'll shift and try to claw the shit out of me in the middle of the gym.

By the time our monster support group meeting rolls around on Thursday night, I'm about to crawl out of my skin from the combination of yearning to be near Ariana and guilt from lying to Doug. I resolve to tell him at the meeting, since doing it in our sharing circle is probably the safest option for both of us. I hope Tomas won't be too upset if his backyard gets destroyed in the fray.

But it ends up being a moot point. When I arrive at our mothman host's house, Doug isn't there, and I get a text a few minutes later saying something came up with his girlfriend. My body sags in defeat as I take my seat around the firepit.

"Whoa, are you alright?" Sage, the changeling next to me, asks, their browless forehead wrinkling in concern.

"It's that obvious?" I let out a weak laugh.

Sage nods and reaches out to place a cool, gray hand on my arm. "Sorry buddy, but yeah. I don't think I've ever seen you come here looking so frazzled."

"It's true, you look like shit," Susan says from across the circle, in her typical blunt harpy fashion.

Nik crosses his burly arms over his chest and frowns at her. "This is a safe space, Susie. We don't tell people they look like shit."

She rolls her eyes, her feathered wings puffing up a bit behind her in a challenge to our shifter leader's admonishment. "I'll be more polite if you stop calling me Susie. You know I hate that."

"Shit, sorry, Susi—Susan," Nik corrects himself as she narrows her eyes at his blunder. "It's hard to change what I've called you since you were a cub, but I'll do better."

Her expression softens a fraction. "Good. I'm not a child anymore. Anyway, back to Wesley looking like shit."

Nik lets out a soft growl of exasperation, but her bluntness doesn't bother me, so I wave his protectiveness off. He's the leader and founder of our little group and thinks of us all as his "cubs", even though I think Sage and Ren are older than him. "It's fine. Guess I'm sharing first tonight."

"That's my cue to go inside. If you need more snacks, let me know." Tomas' human mate gives us a wave, and goes to head into their house, but the mothman snags him by the waist to plant a quick kiss on his cheek. A furious blush spreads across the pale human's cheeks, and he scurries away.

"Such a sweet human," Ren sighs, sounding wistful. We all know how much the soft-spoken cyclops yearns to find his own mate, and when he found out that Tomas had mated a human, his hopes of finding one in Moonvale have increased tenfold. He's even started going on human dating apps, though he's yet to work up the courage to actually go on a date with anyone. Poor guy. He'll get there when he's ready.

When everyone settles in their seats, I cast a worried glance over at the empty chair where Doug normally sits. It feels wrong to divulge my relationship with Ariana to the group before he finds out, but I need to tell *someone* or I'm going to explode.

"I was really hoping to talk about this with Doug here, but oh well. So—"

"Are you guys fighting? Is that why he's not here?" Susan interrupts, leveling her hawkish gaze at me.

"*Susan*. Don't interrupt," Nik says with a long-suffering sigh.

"We're not fighting now, but I know he's going to be pissed." My stomach clenches with dread at the thought.

"Oh shit," Max says under his breath. Of course the handsome part-succubus would immediately know what's going on. Not only is he a private investigator, but he can sense the emotions of those around him. Honestly, I'm not sure how he's able to handle the miasma of emotions of this group, but he's come back every week since he joined a few months ago.

"Oh shit?" Tomas cocks a brow at Max's reaction, his feathery antennae fluttering with intrigue. "Is it really that bad, Wes?"

I scrub a hand across my snout and let out a hard exhale. "Yeah. It is. I, uh... I slept with Doug's sister."

The chatter of speculation stops in an instant as every monster in the circle focuses on me. Tomas and Sage's brows furrow, Nik's mouth hangs open, Ren's singular eye widens comically, Susan mutters something that sounds like "horny idiot", and Max smiles with weak sympathy.

Guess I'm even more fucked than I thought.

15

WESLEY

"He's never going to speak to me again, is he?" I mumble, the snacks I shoveled into my mouth before the meeting threatening to stage a violent coup in my stomach.

Sage reaches out and squeezes my arm, always the one to give a comforting touch during our meetings. "I don't know about that. He loves you. He loves Ariana. Maybe he'll be... happy?" Their voice lilts up in a question that's not particularly reassuring.

Susan snorts derisively. "I doubt that. He's more likely to rip your throat out with his fangs."

"Don't listen to her," Nik says, shaking his head in dismissal.

"It'll be fine. Doug has come a long way with controlling his wolf's temper. You'll find a way to work through this." He runs a hand through his bristly salt and pepper beard, expression thoughtful. "A sincere apology is always a good place to start. Let Doug know that you made a mistake and it won't happen again. He knows that sometimes our inner beasts push us to do things we're not proud of."

I know the kind bear shifter's advice is meant to soothe me, but it only serves to spark my temper. I hate that the automatic assumption is that I was thinking with my dick, and that I didn't have good intentions. If that's sweet, empathetic Nik's initial conclusion, then there's no way Doug will be any more understanding. I love my best friend, but he's the type to react first, and ask question later.

"It wasn't a mistake," I reply through gritted teeth, unable to keep my frustration out of my tone.

Nik's bushy brows raise, taken aback by the bite in my voice. "Oh!" He waits a moment, then hesitantly continues. "Then what, may I ask, was it?"

I don't have to think at all about my reply. "The best gods-damned thing that's ever happened to me."

Ren lets out a dreamy sigh that contrasts almost comically with his intimidating appearance. "You're in *love*."

My heart flutters at the mention of love. "I'm not..."

Max quirks a brow at my denial. Of course the damn succubus empath can tell that's a lie.

I shake my head, my face heating at being caught about to lie in our circle of trust. "I care about Ariana. I've been into her for a really long time, so when she gave me a shot, I took it."

"And it's not just a fling? You want more with her?" Sage prompts, their spindly gray fingers giving my forearm another reassuring squeeze. I appreciate the grounding calm their touch provides.

"Gods, yes. I want *everything* with her."

"Oh, that's so romantic!" Ren gasps, clasping a hand to his chest as his large eye practically fills with hearts.

"If you care about her, then what's the issue?" Tomas asked with a soft smile. "You're one of the kindest people I've ever met. Everyone loves you. Why wouldn't Doug approve of someone so good dating his sister?"

"Because he knows about Wesley's shit dating history," Susan volunteers, though her voice lacks its usual bite. She almost sounds sympathetic, which makes sense given her own romantic track record. The harpy has broken more hearts than the numbers of feathers in her wings.

"Forget about Doug's reaction for a moment. How does Ariana feel?" Max asks, his black eyes boring into me as if he can see into my soul.

No doubt he feels the surge of affection and frustration coming off of me in waves as I reply. "She agreed to be my girlfriend, but wants to wait to tell Doug. I don't think she believes me when I tell her I want something long-term with her. And I... I get it. Like Susan said, I have an awful dating track record. But that's because she's the one I've wanted! She...she's it for me."

Tomas nods, his antennae fluttering in sympathy. "I felt the same way when I met Caleb." His eyes grow soft with obvious love for his mate. "I couldn't stay away and I certainly couldn't hide my feelings. How the hell did you wait so long to make a move?"

I shrug. "I didn't think she was into me, and I didn't want to be her brother's creepy friend who made a pass at her. Minotaurs don't have mate bonds, so I could handle wanting her without acting on it. Yeah, it sucked, but it wasn't as bad as it would've been if you'd tried to stay away from Caleb."

"How many times do we have to talk about this in our group?" Nik asks with a rueful shake of his head.

Susan and Sage exchange a quick look of amusement as Nik dives into one of his signature lectures, but I don't mind his pontificating. His guidance and care is why this group has been so successful.

The shifter reaches his hands out to gesture around the circle. "We all have urges and challenges unique to being a monster—none of us are immune to our instincts. Just because you don't have an official mate bond doesn't mean that keeping your feelings to yourself wouldn't be hard. Minotaurs still have a strong urge to claim a partner when they find someone they think is 'theirs', right?"

"Well... yeah." When he puts it like that, it makes my pining and near constant fantasizing about Ariana seem a bit more reasonable. I never consciously allowed myself to think of her as mine, but that knowledge must have been there despite my best efforts.

Nik's chest puffs up as he continues, clearly pleased at my reaction to his words. "Having a human partner adds another layer of complexity to a relationship as a monster. Ariana knows about monsters because of Doug, but she doesn't know the ins and outs of minotaur behavior. You have to explain it to her like you would with any non-minotaur partner. I know we all tend to shy away from discussing our monstrous nature with humans to protect them from our 'strangeness.' But our needs are just as natural as a human's."

A few people around the circle nod in agreement. It's tough to accept that I'm not strange when I spend most of my life hiding behind a glamor so I don't terrify humans that are unaware of paranormal creatures' existence. But Nik is right. Our differences don't make our needs any less valid.

"Don't assume she won't understand or that she won't want to accommodate your needs," Nik continues. "Openness and honesty are key to any paranormal pairing—we all know what happens when you assume—"

Susan groans and rolls her eyes. "Please don't say it."

"Hah, fine. But you get it," Nik says with a gruff laugh.

There's a moment of silence as I process his words. I think we're going to move on to talking about something else after Nik's sage advice, but Max speaks up. "I almost lost my partner because I wasn't open about my nature. Learn from my mistakes. Tell Ariana how you feel."

His serious tone sinks into my chest, and I take his words to heart. "Okay. I will. I'll talk to her. Thanks for listening, everyone."

"That's what we're here for," Sage says, finally letting go of my arm now that I'm not actively panicking.

Susan swipes a taloned finger toward me in an accusatory gesture. "Wait, wait, wait. We're ignoring the elephant in the room. Or the minotaur. Whatever. How the fuck did you have sex with a human? How did *it* fit?" She visibly shudders at the thought.

"Susan!" Nik exclaims, aghast.

"I mean... we were all thinking it though, right?" Sage says, giving me a sheepish grin that shows off their razor-sharp teeth.

"Wesley, you absolutely do not have to share the details of your sex life." Nik gives everyone in the circle a stern, disappointed look.

I laugh, unbothered. If there's one thing I've never been shy about discussing, it's sex. It's an important part of a lot of monsters' lives, especially those with mating imperatives, so it's not like we haven't talked about sex in our group before. Plus, maybe someone will have advice on how to handle the size difference. As much as

I've slept around, I've only slept with humans while using my glamor. I've stuck to other monster species when in my true form. Most other monsters have magic that aids in being physically compatible, so I've never had to think much about it.

"Well, she wanted me as I am naturally, so... it was definitely a stretch," I say with a sheepish laugh.

Susan winces. "Gods, poor woman."

Someone clears their throat, and I look away from Susan's horrified expression to see Tomas' mate standing beside him with a tray of cookies. "Sorry to interrupt. Just wanted to bring these out while they're hot. What's that about a poor woman?"

"Wesley is dating a human who wants to be with him. As a minotaur," Tomas says, winking at Caleb before snagging a cookie from the tray.

"*Oh.*" Caleb's cheeks flood with color. He looks at me, eyes widening. "Yeah, that would be a lot to, uh, take in."

Sage snorts, almost choking on a cookie.

Looking at the blushing human man and his mothman mate, a thought occurs to me. "Do you two have any advice? Not to pry, it's just, I dated a mothperson, so I know how shockingly enormous their dicks can be."

Caleb sputters, face turning an even deeper red. "I don't—It, uh..."

"Shit, sorry! I shouldn't have assumed you'd be the one taking... you know what? Forget I even said anything," I blurt, realizing how inappropriate it is to ask Tomas' mate how he's able to get railed by moth cock.

Tomas grins adoringly at Caleb, clearly unbothered by the discussion of their sex life. In fact, he looks proud. "My perfect mate is able to take me. It just takes time and careful preparation."

Caleb looks like he doesn't know if he should preen at being called perfect or run away in embarrassment. He settles for mumbling something and looking down at his tray of cookies as his blush deepens.

Ren's enormous eye focuses on Tomas with intense interest. "This is good to know. I was worried that if I found a human mate like yours, I would destroy them with my cock."

"I'm going to go back inside," Caleb says, his voice a high-pitched squeak as the cyclops eyes him as if mentally assessing his capacity for taking monster dick.

"Thank you for the cookies, my love." Tomas kisses his hand. "I'll make this up to you later," he says, lowering his voice to a whisper.

"I'm really sorry, Caleb!" I call out, feeling terrible for turning my question into an awkward conversation for the shy human.

"Okay, enough about cocks," Susan says, mouth half full of cookie. "I have something to share with the group!"

"Is there anything else you wanted to, um, share before we move on, Wesley?" Nik asks, looking almost as flustered as Caleb was by the raunchy turn our conversation took.

I shake my head. The pressure in my chest that I came here with tonight has eased significantly, and now I have a plan of action. Talk to Ariana and tell her why letting Doug know about our relationship is important. Mutually agree on how to break the news to him. Spend the rest of our time together this weekend doting on her and working on stretching her so she can take my cock again.

The rest of the meeting passes quickly, with Susan sharing some coworker drama, and Max confessing his struggles with forming friendships because of negative experiences in the past. I invite him to come work out with me and Doug, but he seemed reticent to join us. I realize belatedly that my offer probably sounded like it came from pity, so I don't push it. I'll bring it up again in a few weeks and bug him until he gives in to my charms.

As I head to my car after we wrap up our meeting, a hesitant voice calls my name. I turn over my shoulder and see Caleb approaching with something in his hand.

"Dude, I'm so, so sorry," I say preemptively. "That was not okay for me to ask such a personal question. Sometimes I can be an insensitive jerk. My head is all mixed up with this stuff with my girlfriend. I'm worried about hurting her and want to do things right, and shit, I'm being inappropriate again by telling you this."

"Oh, uh, it's okay!" Caleb says, looking taken aback by my rambling mess of an apology. "I forget sometimes that monsters are a lot more open about sex. I know you weren't trying to be weird. Honestly, I'm a little glad you asked."

"Oh?" That's not what I was expecting at all.

"Not because I want to talk about my sex life!" he exclaims, shaking his head. "I have something that can help you. Here!" He shoves something into my hand.

It's a... jar? "What is this?"

"Lube. Magic lube! Tomas knows a witch who makes it and I can give you her contact info if you want more. It helps with stretching and, um, healing. We had an unopen jar, so I figured..."

Of course there's magic lube. Witches come up with shit for everything. "Damn, you're amazing!" I reach out to give the much smaller man a hug, but stop myself before I crush him to my chest in my excitement, transitioning it to an awkward pat on the back instead. "Thank you, Caleb. Magic lube... this is perfect. I'll definitely take that contact info."

He writes it down for me, then retreats to the safety of his house before I can make things weird again. The entire drive home, I'm buzzing with a sense of relief and excitement. This weekend with Ariana is going to be amazing.

16

ARIANA

Sometimes, when I find myself drowning in emails or trying to tackle my mile long to-do list that never seems to get any shorter, I think back on my life six months ago. I try to remember the person I was back then, even though she feels like a complete stranger. That Ariana struggled daily with worries about her decision to quit her soul-crushing receptionist job, wondering if it was the biggest mistake of her life. She had the bandwidth to do things like visualize her goals and journal her plans. She fit working out and meditation into her schedule with ease. Hell, she even had enough free time to get bored and feel lonely. Ariana of the past would've killed to be where I am now, and yet, when faced with the mountain of work on my plate and the prospect of a relationship, part of me yearns to go back to my past self. Her life may have been lackluster, but it was easier.

That probably makes me sound like an ungrateful jerk. I'm very aware of how lucky I am that my leap of faith has worked out so far. I'm living the dream of having a successful business and making art as my livelihood. But what people don't tell you is that when you start to achieve your dreams, it doesn't stop there. You don't get a gold star and then spend your days basking in your accomplishments. No, you have to keep working. You certainly don't have time to celebrate. Instead, the bar moves higher and the pressure to maintain success becomes a weight that threatens to crush you if you lose focus.

I realize now how foolish it was that the implicit motivation behind my goals was that if I met them, I'd be happy. That if I proved I could make something of my shop and my art, that would prove that *I* was something. Instead, I'm still me—flawed, stubborn, self-deprecating me. Only now I'm fucking exhausted on top of all that.

Oh, and somehow I've ended up with my dream boyfriend. I hate that Wesley, the man I've been obsessed with for a year, is relegated to my mental back burner because there are more pressing things to focus on. Every time he texts me, the fluttering excitement is swiftly followed by a surge of guilt, especially when he tries to find ways to spend time with me.

I feel like such an asshole telling him no. Both my heart and my body yearn to say "fuck it" to my schedule and be irresponsible, but my mind has a firm grip on the reins. I can't let myself be reckless. Not when my shop is finally doing well. Not after all my hard work.

Wesley is what I wanted—what I still want. But this week has proven that just like my business, the dreams of a relationship are not the same as actually living them. Being with someone means you have to have time for them, and I can't figure out how the hell that's going to work when I'm already drowning. What kind of person starts a new relationship knowing they have nothing left to give?

It doesn't help that I can't talk to my best friend about my predicament. Kelly is amazing, but she's terrible at keeping secrets. One mention of what's going on with Wes, and Doug would be calling me to demand an explanation. The last thing I need right now is to add the pressure of Doug's judgment and temper to my uncertainty about things with Wesley. So I'm left trying to deal with the mess of my frazzled mind and emotions on my own, which is never good. I vacillate all day long between convincing myself that I need to call things off since I can't give Wesley the time and energy he deserves, and being unable to fathom letting the opportunity to be with him slip through my fingers.

By the time Saturday afternoon arrives, I'm no closer to knowing what to do, and terrified of what will happen when I see Wesley again tonight. My mind is a complete disaster, my worried thoughts amplified to the extreme after a week with no outlet or time to work through them. To make matters worse, Wesley's not texting as much as he was earlier in the week. Being the terrible new girlfriend I am, I didn't even notice the lack of messages until I'd pulled myself away from my desk to shove some food in my mouth and check my socials.

Fuck, I bet I won't even have to make the choice to call things off. He's probably already sick of my shit and is planning on breaking up with me.

Dread roils in my gut all day, enough of a distraction that I barely make a dent in my workload. It doesn't help that I spend the morning fighting off a full-blown panic attack when I get an email from my manufacturer saying that my order is delayed, and they have no estimate for when it will arrive. No stock means lost income, as well as losing momentum with my shop's success.

I make a bloody mess of my legs as I attempt to shave them during my hasty shower, my whole body seeming to vibrate with stress and anxiety. As I'm heading out the door, I realize that I've forgotten to pack half the things I need for an overnight stay, and then trip in my haste to rush back inside, scraping my palms raw on the gravel path as I attempt to brace my fall. I abandon collecting my toothbrush and cute pajamas in favor of hoping to at least arrive on time for our date. Who knows if I'll even spend the night if I turn up bloodied and wild-eyed? Wes will probably take one look at me and tell me he made a mistake asking me to be his girlfriend.

The cherry on top of the shit sundae that is my day happens when I start my car up. It takes three tries before the engine turns over, and there's a concerning thunk when it finally gets going.

Don't cry. Don't cry. Don't cry. I chant the words to myself the whole drive over to Wesley's house, taking deep breaths to try to even myself out. Through sheer willpower, I'm able to hang on to my composure despite the churning anxiety and pain throbbing in my hands. When I pull into Wesley's driveway, my resolve to be calm wavers.

It feels like a metaphor for me and Wesley when I park my beat up, dirty station wagon next to his pristine, sleek sports car. My car doesn't belong here at his gorgeous house with its immaculately manicured lawn, and neither do I.

This will never work. I'm too pathetic and damaged, and I certainly don't fit in this picture-perfect place with a man so far out of my league he should be dating models. I should turn around and go home. Text him I can't make it. Break things off before he comes to his senses.

I put my keys back in the ignition, cursing as it once again fails to start. I try again and it makes a pathetic high-pitched whine, but still doesn't work.

I slam my hands against the steering wheel. "Shit!"

A knock on my window startles a scream out of me, and I look up to see Wesley in his human glamor, watching me in bemusement.

My heart races, my instincts urging me to flee from the pain that's headed my way, but it's no use. He knows I'm here and my fucking car won't start.

I give him a weak wave and unbuckle my seatbelt, shoving my car keys in my purse as he opens the door for me. "H-hey," I say as I get out of my car, legs trembling with nerves. My lip wobbles as the tears I'd pushed back come rushing back to the surface. I'm only able to hold my composure for a second before they come flooding out, along with a choked sob.

A moment later, I'm crushed against Wesley's chest as his thick arms band around me. "Baby girl, what's wrong?!" He sounds bewildered by my tears, but I can't do anything but sob into his chest. I cling to him tighter, not wanting to face the pain that's coming my way.

His hands smooth up and down my back. "Shh, it's okay. I've got you, Ari."

"I-I-I can't d-do this." I manage to get the broken words out. God, this hurts too much.

"Do what, sweetheart?" he asks, his voice heartachingly tender.

I want to be a coward. Selfishly, my heart begs me to stop talking. As much as don't want to bring it up, I can't stand the thought of stringing Wesley along when he deserves someone who has time for him and fits into his lifestyle. I care for him too damn much to trap him in a shitty relationship with me.

I shudder against him and steel myself as best as possible, but my voice still cracks pathetically as I speak. "B-break up."

The arms around me tense for a few long breaths, like time has frozen in the aftermath of my words. He releases me and pulls back to look into my face, heavy hands clasping onto my shoulders like he's worried I'm going to flee.

"Who the fuck said anything about breaking up? What's going on?" The rough edge to his voice makes the painful clenching in my chest even worse. His gaze darts over me in panic, before landing on my scraped up palms. "And why are you *bleeding*?"

My chest shudders with each of my stilted breaths. I'm already regretting saying anything, because his worry slices through me like a knife. This is going even worse than I could've imagined. I reach up to swipe away some of my stubborn tears, and wince as the scrapes on my palms touch my cheek. "I fell. I'm sorry. God, I didn't want to cry." Dammit, I'm just making this whole thing worse. I don't deserve to cry when I'm the one that's ruining things.

He pulls my hand away from my face gingerly, avoiding my injuries. "Baby, it's okay to cry when you get hurt—"

I shake my head. "I c-can't do this, Wes. I can't be the person you n-need. Look at me." I hold my palms out to emphasize my point. "I'm a fucking mess. I'm constantly on the verge of a mental breakdown and this whole week I was guilty because I didn't have time for you. It's only been a week and I'm already f-failing." The ache in my chest threatens to push me back into an incoherent, sobbing mess again. "W-we should just e-end things."

An endless silence stretches out between us and it's all I can do to not crumple to the ground with grief for the relationship I'll never have with him. He drags in ragged breaths, and his face contorts into an expression I can't read through my tear-blurred vision. Is he angry? Relieved? My gaze drops to the ground, unable to bear finding out.

Finally, he speaks.

"No."

No? My heart lurches and my eyes snap back up to his. "But—"

"No." He doesn't elaborate after cutting me off, radiating dominance and finality.

We stare at each other in a bizarre emotional standoff, my tears dried up in shock. It doesn't take me long to give up my fight. I should be upset that he's dismissing my concerns, but all I feel is overwhelming relief.

The tension that was keeping me from collapsing releases, and my body sags. My legs buckle, but Wesley's there to catch me. He scoops me up into his arms, and I cling to him, wrapping my arms around his neck despite the pain in my hands as I do so. Hot tears slide down my cheeks and I press my face into his chest.

"Let's get you inside and cleaned up," he says in a soothing murmur as he carries me into his house. "Are you hungry? I can put the lasagna in the oven now, so it'll be ready sooner."

I don't understand what's happening. How is he so chill after I just tried to break up with him? "A-a-are we not going to talk about my f-freakout?" I ask, directing my words into his chest since I'm too embarrassed to look him in the eyes.

He pauses, and I feel his body grow larger as he lets his human glamor fall away now that we're inside. A heavy exhale flutters my hair, and his cinnamon-apple scent washes over me. "Oh, we will. I need to make sure you're alright first."

I force myself to remove my face from where I've pressed it into his worn t-shirt, needing to see his expression. His voice is placid, but his eyes are burning with hurt and frustration.

Shit, what have I done? I can't just pretend that things are fine when they're not. "We can talk n-now. I'm okay."

"Like hell you are. You showed up here bleeding and distraught. Do you have any idea how that—what that..." Wesley huffs in exasperation, emotion bleeding through his calm veneer. He shakes his head. "Stop being ridiculous and let me take care of you!"

"Fine!" I snap back at him. His raised voice shifts something in my brain, and my despair gives way to a much more comfortable feeling—irritation.

The weirdo *smiles* at my bratty tone, eyes warm with affection.

God knows why, but the combination of his bossiness and smirking makes me feel safe. I release a heavy exhale. "I'll do whatever you want. I'm sorry, Wes. I—I didn't mean to hurt you... I'm a mess."

He strokes my cheek, then pushes a stray lock of hair behind my ear. "Good girl. Apology accepted."

Anyone else saying that to me would feel patronizing, but when Wesley praises me, the sincerity in his voice makes me melt.

"Now, about the lasagna—should I put it in the oven before or after I give you a bath?"

My brow raises. "Later is fine. A bath is excessive. I need to clean out my scrapes and maybe put on some antibiotic cream, but I took a shower before I got here. Do I smell bad?"

"You smell incredible. That's not the point, Ari. I need to do this." His voice is clipped and rough, like the thought of not bathing me pains him. "Didn't you just say you'd do whatever I want? I want to give you a damn bath, and you're going to be good and let me."

I blink up at him, eyes widening at his intensity. "O-okay. You wanna give me a bath, then give me a bath."

He carries me up a set of stairs and into his bedroom, but I don't have time to register much more than dark gray wallpaper and an enormous bed before he heads into the connected bathroom. Flicking on the lights with his elbow, he brings me inside a bathroom that's almost as big as my bedroom, and sets me down on a marble countertop between two raised glass bowl sinks.

"Wait here," he says, placing a kiss on my head before stepping over to a bathtub that looks more like a small swimming pool.

Wesley tugs his shirt over his head and unceremoniously tosses it to the side before bending down to turn on the tap. Now that I'm not crying into his chest, I can see that he's wearing a pair of light gray sweatpants. Because of course he is. I watch his rounded, tight ass flex, and his tail twitches like he knows exactly what I'm doing.

When he turns around, I'm treated to the sight of the obscene outline of his cock against the thin material of his pants. Even when he's not hard, he's enormous.

I blush and look away. I shouldn't ogle him right now. I lost the right to do that after I tried to break up with him five minutes ago. My fingers fiddle with the tie of my wrap dress, unsure if I should take it off.

"Allow me," Wes says, shaking his head. He closes the distance between us and takes hold of the tie at my waist, undoing the bow with ease. He doesn't look down at my body as he skims his hand up my arms and inward to push the fabric of my dress off my shoulders, his eyes intensely focused on my face, watching me.

Is he worried I'll tell him to stop?

My stomach quivers as the fabric slides off and pools beneath my hips on the counter, but I can't look away from him either. He makes quick work of my bra and panties, and steps back, only then allowing himself to look away from my face.

It takes everything in me not to shy away from his assessment. His nostrils flare as I shift in place, and molten heat pools between my thighs. When he moves closer, his powerful body caging me against the counter, my breath hitches. He reaches out and I wait breathlessly for his touch, but his hand goes to a drawer beside my leg instead, retrieving a tube of antibiotic ointment and an alcohol wipe.

"Give me your hands," he murmurs.

It's ridiculous how I shake as I obey. There's nothing sexy about him tending to my minor injuries, and yet I feel hot and needy.

With extreme care, he cleans my scrapes, the sting of the alcohol making me hiss softly. He rumbles in displeasure, like my pain hurts him too. He spreads the ointment on my palms with a thick finger, and I sway toward him, needing him to keep touching me in any way I can get.

When he's finished, he releases a deep exhale, then looks back up at me. The longing and hunger shining behind his eyes takes my breath away. It doesn't make any sense. I've shown Wes the most pathetic, vulnerable parts of myself and instead of running away, he weathers the storm and looks at me like *that* in the aftermath.

One thing becomes crystal clear as he lifts me again and then gently lowers me into the warm bathwater. I'd have to be an absolute idiot to let a man like this go without even trying to make it work. I don't want to let him go. He's my favorite person—the *best* person. I have to find a way to carve out space in my life for him, because losing him would destroy me.

17

WESLEY

Stay calm. She's okay. You've taken care of her injuries. You're soothing her pain. She's here, and she's safe.

Worry and instinct have my nerves so tightly wound that I have to play those thoughts on repeat in order to function. It's in my nature to protect what's mine, and I've *failed*. Why else would Ari have gotten to the point that she broke down the moment she saw me? Why would she have thought the solution to her worries was not to lean on me, but to push me away?

My hands tremble from the adrenaline coursing through my system, and I pull them out of the warm water and away from her body before Ariana can feel how rattled I am. When I pictured how our date tonight might go, her showing up at my door bloody and weeping, telling me that we need to break up, was the last thing I could have imagined. Gods, I'm a moron. She's been struggling, and I was too busy worrying about how to explain my minotaur side and get my cock inside her, that I didn't see it.

Guilt sits like a stone in my stomach. The signs of her stress have been there for months. Dark circles under her eyes, fading hair that she kept putting off re-dyeing, canceled plans with Doug. She's told me multiple times how busy she is. I just didn't realize *how* busy.

My mind screams at me to find a way to help her. To shoulder some of the burden so she can breathe again and prove that I'm a worthy partner who can take care of her. The small rational voice attempting to tell me that Ari's struggle goes far beyond me gets drowned out by my instinct, which demands that I make things right.

She looks so small in my bathtub, barely taking up a third of the space that's built to accommodate my bulk. Staring up at me with wide, watery eyes, she searches my face for a moment, then reaches out a hand to me. "Will you come in with me?"

Her hesitant question snaps me out of my spiraling thoughts. "Yes, if you want me to."

Her lip wobbles, and she nods. "I want you," she whispers.

I don't know if she means she wants the comfort my body can provide, or if she truly wants *me*. There's a not insignificant, terrified part of me that wonders if she's changed her mind about being together, and that I'm forcing things because I'm desperate to have her in my life. But I can't deny her anything, and right now, I need to be near her as much as I need air.

"You have me."

She scoots forward to make room for me as I remove my sweatpants, and I ease in behind her, more grateful than ever for the size of my tub. I coax her to lean back against my chest, and she lets out a shuddering exhale as I wrap my arms around her. She fits against me like she was made to be there, and my damn cock loves the contact of her lush ass pressed against my groin, but it's going to have to chill the fuck out. Now is not the time.

Neither of us says anything for a minute, as I stroke her stomach and hips, carefully avoiding the heavy swell of her breasts and the tempting curls between her thighs. She's tense at first, like she's trying to hold her weight off of me, but with time, she lets herself sink against me. Lying here with Ariana in my arms, the coiled tension in my chest bleeds out into the steaming water.

When the haze of my need to protect her fades into a manageable ache, I kiss her shoulder, careful not to gore her scalp with my horn. "Alright. Tell me what's going on."

She tenses against me, and I caress her hip to encourage her to relax. "I'm sorry," she says, her voice trembling and soft.

It breaks my heart to hear her sound so worn down. "I didn't ask for an apology. I need to know what's going on in that pretty head of yours and why you said we should break up." I hesitate for a moment, but make myself ask the question. "Is that really what you want?

"No! I don't!" She sputters, trying to turn to look at me, but I hold her still, pressing my palm against the pillowed curve of her stomach possessively. Letting out a deep sigh, she reluctantly lies back on me again and continues. "But I told you... I'm a total mess. I don't know how I'm going to manage being your girlfriend, and I don't want to be selfish." Her hand squeezes my thigh like she's trying to anchor herself to me. "I can't string you along with no plan for fitting you into my life."

Even though I hate her answer, it makes an annoying amount of sense that she'd feel that way. Ariana is so giving that she'd rather be in pain than let anyone else suffer. She gave up her entire life in another state—a boyfriend, a decent job, and a circle of close friends—to move to Moonvale and take care of Doug when he was bitten. She'd never take credit for it, but she's the reason he made it through that terrible time. Of course she'd think that because she couldn't give me everything or be the "perfect" girlfriend, she shouldn't be with me at all.

Ariana deserves to have someone show her the same care she pours into others. The only thing stopping me from being the one to do that is her fear of asking for help.

"So let's make a plan." I run my hand down her arm, then place my hand on top of the one holding onto my leg.

"You make it sound so easy." She lets out a weak laugh. "I spent a week thinking about it and came up with nothing."

I'm glad she's facing away and missing my exasperated expression. I release a frustrated huff. "That's because you were trying to do it alone. And I would bet anything that you weren't thinking about finding actual solutions. You were freaking out and telling yourself you aren't enough. You're the smartest woman I know, but you need someone to help ground you when you freak out." I nuzzle her shoulder, lowering my voice to a mock whisper. "In case it wasn't clear, I'm that someone."

"Wes... I can't ask you to do that. It's not—"

"Good thing you're not asking," I interrupt, unwilling to let her guilt or toxic self-sufficiency keep us from figuring this out. Ariana needs a firm hand, both in and out of the bedroom. She agreed to let me be her daddy, and I'm done tiptoeing around it. I want her in my life, and I want her to be happy. The only path I can see to get there is taking some of the control out of her hands. "I'm telling you I'm going to help you. If you don't let me, you'll only make both of us miserable. Do you want that?"

She shakes her head as best she can in this position. "No, of course I don't."

"Good. It's settled. I'm helping you." I can sense the argument building inside her as her arms stiffen. "And before you tell me it's unfair or not my responsibility, just listen. I'm not human. It's easy to assume we're the same because monsters put a lot of effort into not standing out. But as a minotaur, there are certain instincts that you need to understand if we're together. The most important one being the need to protect and provide for my partner, followed closely by the need to stake my claim on you so that everyone knows you're mine." My hand on her belly squeezes her closer, and I have to suppress a groan when she gasps softly at the feel of my hard cock pressing insistently against her lower back. "So what would be unfair is if you didn't respect those instincts. The danger to our relationship isn't you not having enough time to devote to me, it's you not letting me devote time to you. I want to give you so much, baby girl. But I can't do that if you don't let me."

"Well... shit." My stomach clenches with anticipation, unsure of what her reaction means, but it melts into relief and arousal when she twists to look back at me. She's smiling. Not an appeasing, nervous smile, but her genuine, lopsided Ari smile that makes my breath stutter with how much I love her.

Shit, I love her. I mean, of course I do. She's mine. But I hadn't let myself think those words until this moment. It's a little terrifying, but so is everything else that's worthwhile in life.

She turns away again and lets her head fall back on my shoulder, reaching up with one hand to caress my horn. The intimacy of that gesture and her trust makes my head swim with heady desire. "I knew that monsters have different needs after helping Doug with his change, but I didn't consider what that meant for a relationship. I didn't realize you weren't just trying to be nice—that it went deeper. I want you to get what you need. That's all I wanted when I... when I mentioned breaking up. Now I get how utterly wrong that was. I'm sorry, Wesley."

"It's okay, sweetheart. I didn't tell you it went beyond being your boyfriend or your daddy, so you didn't know." I stroke her face and she leans her cheek into my palm, her eyelids fluttering closed. The way she sinks into my touch warms me to the core of my being.

She takes a deep breath before continuing. "I haven't let anyone take care of me. It's easier to not ask for anything than to be let down when someone decides I'm not worth the effort."

My hand roaming her stomach creeps up higher to tease the underside of her breasts, and I bring my other down to tug her up so my cock rests firmly against her ass cheeks. "You're worth it. Fuck anyone who told you otherwise. Including that mean voice in your head."

She laughs, the sound breathy and intoxicating. I wish I could bottle it up and keep that effervescent magic that is pure Ariana with me at all times. "Okay, okay."

I slide my hand up to cup her breast possessively. "Say it."

She ducks her head toward her shoulder with a groan of protest.

"*Say it.*" This time, the command comes out as a rough growl.

"I... I'm w-worth it."

The hesitance in her voice makes my heart ache for her, but it's not good enough. Releasing her breast, I slide my hand up and rest it against her throat, cupping her chin. "You can do better than that."

"W-Wes," she half-protests, half-moans. She squirms against my hold, but there's no way in hell she's getting out of this.

I grab her hip with my free hand, fingers kneading into her softness as I put a hint of pressure on her throat. I barely resist the urge to grind against her ass when she lets out a breathy whimper.

"I'm worth it." It's slightly less tentative this time.

Sliding the hand on her hip across her belly, I dip it between her thighs. She parts them for me, allowing my seeking fingers better access to her pussy. Fuck, she's so hot and silky. My dick jerks futilely at the feel of her, desperate to experience it too.

"Again," I command, circling her clit with a teasing stroke.

Her hips buck against my hand, legs parting further as she silently begs me for more, but I don't move my fingers, cupping her pussy instead, like it belongs to me.

She frowns as she realizes my game. "I'm worth it." She says the words with a hint of petulance and frustration.

Gods, that tone has me growing even harder for her. "Good girl," I rasp. "Now tell me what you're going to let daddy do."

She bites her lip as I continue to play with her, too teasing to be enough to get her off. "I'm going to let you fuck me?"

"Hah! Only good girls who've earned it get their daddy's cock, Ari. What are you going to let me do?" The thumb on my hand spanning her throat presses into her lower lip. Having her in my tub, wet, desperate, and completely at my mercy, is clouding my mind with lust, but I won't give in to it. I need her to know how serious I am about this.

That doesn't stop my cock from throbbing and leaking pre-cum as she swallows heavily against my palm. "I'm going to let you help me." Her voice is quiet, but sincere.

I want to shout in triumph and carry her out of the tub, throw her down on the bed, and fuck her again and again. Instead, needing to reward her vulnerability, I settle for stroking her clit and watching the delicious tension on her face over her shoulder as she gets closer to release. Water splashes against the side of the tub as she rocks her hips into my touch and I can tell she's close when she gasps my name.

Fuck, I don't have enough hands to touch and hold her the way I want to. I reluctantly release her throat to grasp her breast. She cries out as I roll her nipple. "That's it, baby girl. You're so perfect for me. Let daddy give you what you need. Take what you deserve."

Her chest rises and falls with rapid breaths as she nears her peak. "I want you to fuck me. Please, daddy. I need you inside me."

My stomach clenches as I hold back the sudden surge of arousal at her words. I've waited all damn week for her, and I'm not about to come before she even touches me.

"Be a good girl and come for me first."

She shudders and tenses, and I want to slip a finger inside her and feel her coming on it, but it's too difficult at this angle, so I settle for continuing my firm pressure as I rub her clit until she breaks, coming with a soft cry as she grabs onto my forearm.

Her urgency fades as her orgasm subsides, and as much as my aching cock begs to be inside her, I can sense fatigue overtaking her arousal. I let her rest against my chest and stroke a hand up and down her stomach and chest, scooping up water to let it sluice over her as her breathing evens out. I don't bother actually soaping her up since neither of us were dirty to begin with, just letting the warm water and the path of my touch continue to soothe her.

I'm content to stay here indefinitely, secure and blissful in the knowledge that I've satisfied Ariana, but after a minute, her stomach growls, breaking the comfortable silence.

"Thought you weren't hungry," I say, chuckling at the loud sound. "You stay here and relax while I get dinner ready."

Ariana pushes herself up and turns in the tub to frown at me. "But what about... don't you want to..." Her eyes drop to my unflagging erection poking up out of the water, then back to my face, her cheeks flushing.

Gods, she's adorable. Even after everything, looking at my dick makes her blush. "Sweetheart, I've waited all week to fuck you. Another hour or two won't make a difference."

She places her hand on my thigh and starts to slide it slowly upwards. "What if I don't want to wait? I've been good, haven't I?"

Her pinky brushes against my balls, and I suck in a sharp breath as my cock bobs with interest. "You have. I don't like you being hungry, though, so it'd make me feel a lot better to get dinner ready for you."

"I don't want food," she says, her tongue darting out to wet her lips.

Fuck, I can't resist her. I know once I get inside her, that's all I'll want to do for the rest of the night, but I can think of a compromise. "Hmm, you're hungry for daddy's cock?"

She nods, a hint of a smile forming on her lips at the cheesiness of my words, but her pupils still dilate. I love that I can say these silly, filthy things to her without shame.

I shift back, spreading my legs to make room for her and pushing my hips up so my cock juts farther out of the water. "Then put it in your mouth, dirty girl. If you do a good job, daddy will give you a special treat."

18

ARIANA

Something remarkable happens to my brain whenever Wesley calls himself daddy, like there's a dimmer on the switch that controls my shame and anxiety. Each time it happens, the bliss of being unencumbered by my mental litany of self-doubt surprises me. My desire to please him rises in its place, morphing into something so hot and potent it makes me squirm.

I would give anything to always feel the freedom I do as I slip between Wesley's thighs and lower my mouth to his cock. I'm not the stressed, messy Ariana who almost broke up with the best thing that's ever happened to her. I'm Wes' baby girl. His to command and cherish. When I belong to my daddy, I finally feel safe to just *be*.

The feeling is only made more potent in the aftermath of our conversation about his nature. This isn't just a kinky power exchange game for him—it's who he is at his core. And I'm starting to wonder if this version of me, the one on my knees letting go of control, is the truest one. I'm terrified that giving him the chance to help me will only lead to heartache and disaster, but there's an inherent part of me that trusts Wesley like no one else.

With past partners, I was always self-conscious when giving head. Too nervous about not doing the right thing to explore any aspect of it beyond sucking them into my mouth and trying to get them off as quickly as possible. A shiver of pleasure and excitement runs down my spine as I lick a stripe from the base of Wesley's cock to the flushed tip. He strokes a hand through my hair and makes a pleased hum, but doesn't press me for more. The indulgence of getting to take my time with him thrills me and makes my clit spark, begging me to slip a hand between my legs despite my recent orgasm. Too bad I'd probably slip in the tub and fall face first into the water if I tried to hold myself up with only one arm.

The ache that builds between my thighs makes my slow exploration all the more enjoyable. I circle my tongue around his piercing, the cool metal a stark contrast to the flushed heat of his skin, teasing the underside before I close my lips around it to give a testing suck. Wesley hisses and bucks his hips, sending a ripple through the water that splashes over my breasts and my straining nipples. His grip on the edge of the tub tightens, and he sucks in a ragged breath.

Knowing he's barely restraining himself to allow me all the time I need makes my head swim with a powerful mixture of lust and affection. He's so good to me. How did I end up between the thighs of this magnificent minotaur? I return to the base of his cock and lick him from root to tip, savoring this gift.

Wesley strokes my cheek with his thumb as I reach the head of his cock again. Most guys would be pushing my head down and taking what they need, but he just smiles indulgently at me as I look up at him. "That's it, angel. Get daddy's dick nice and wet. Make sure you taste all of it."

"Yes, daddy," I murmur, holding his gaze as I continue to lavish every inch of his straining erection with my tongue. He tastes clean, with an underlying musk that makes me ache for him. When I swipe a bead of pre-cum that's gathered at the tip of his cock, I treat it like a delicacy and a gift, letting it coat my tongue with a soft moan. Because that's what every moment with Wesley feels like. It doesn't hurt that it tastes faintly sweet, rather than the bitter salt of most cum I've encountered.

He groans, his pupils blown wide and his chest rising and falling in shallow breaths as I continue to explore his cock with kisses up the shaft and testing licks along the thick veins and leaking head. We're both squirming when he finally breaks and fists his hand in my hair. "Wrap those pretty lips around it, baby girl. Daddy needs your mouth."

I nod as best I can in his grip. "Please... fuck my mouth, daddy," I murmur, feeling shy about asking something so crude but wanting him to take whatever he needs from me. I know from last time he worried about choking me with his monster cock, but right now I crave the feeling of him using me. When he lets go, I accept that I deserve his attention and affection, secure in the knowledge that I really am his pretty, perfect girl.

"Gods, Ari" he rasps, his eyes screwing shut like the sight of me begging between his thighs is too much for him to bear. When he opens them, his expression is tortured and burning with lust. "You sure you want that? Daddy's been aching for your mouth since the last time. I don't know if I'll be able to control myself."

My stomach clenches with an aching pleasure. Yes, that's *exactly* what I want. I grip his thighs and give him a soft smile. "I trust you. Please."

"Fuck," he groans, tightening his grip on my hair. "Pinch my thigh if you need me to stop."

"I will," I say, my breath speeding up in anticipation. He's going to choke me with his monster cock, and I've never been more turned on. "Thank you, daddy," I add, relishing the look of wonder and hunger in my minotaur's dark eyes.

"Such a naughty girl, begging daddy to fuck your mouth. Gods-damn, how did I get so lucky?" He guides the head of his cock between my lips with his free hand. "Open wide."

I obey and he doesn't wait any longer than it takes for me to part my lips before feeding the slick, blunt head into my mouth. It's a struggle to accommodate even that much, the girth of his cock stretching my lips to their limit. With a cock his size, there're no thoughts of finesse—there's only surrender and a feeble attempt not to scrape him with my teeth.

He observes my face with intense focus as he guides my head down on his dick, not putting any pressure on me beyond the natural weight of his hand. I gaze up at him in return, already feeling dizzy and a little drunk on the role I've taken on. I gag a little when he reaches the back of my tongue and he frowns and attempts to guide me back off of him, but I resist and take him down even further on my own.

"*Shit.*" His hips press up to meet my mouth in an involuntary thrust. "You want it bad, don't you? Such a dirty girl," Wesley rumbles, his voice hoarse with lust.

I moan around his cock as he eases back, then thrusts in again, sliding his length inside and holding my head in place as I fight to take him. While I'd love to be able to deepthroat him, we both know that his size makes that almost impossible and definitely not something I can do without training.

He builds up a slow rhythm, pumping his cock into the well of my mouth while I cling to his thighs. “Look at you, Ari. Fuck, you’re amazing. So beautiful, sucking me down. Daddy’s gonna give you your reward soon. You’re too good for me to last.”

I can’t tell if my eyes are tearing from his dick choking me or from the wave of emotion when looks at me like I’m the best damn thing in the universe, but either way, I blink them back and beg him with my eyes to give it to me.

His chest heaves, hips stuttering as he gets closer to the edge. I try to flick his piercing with my tongue each time he pulls back and hollow my cheeks as much as I can, but the way I suck him ends up much more sloppy than skilled. The wet sound of him shuttling inside my mouth is filthy, and I have to hold back a moan as I imagine the picture we make right now—this powerful, massive minotaur using my mouth for his pleasure as water splashes against the edge of the tub.

Wes curses and gives one last thrust before holding me in place. “Here it comes, baby girl. Take daddy’s cum. Oh fuck, it’s coming.” Wes lets out a primal grunt that echoes off the bathroom walls and then he’s unloading into my mouth with rope after rope of his release. “Fuck, that’s it. Swallow it all down.”

I do my very best to listen, but there’s so much that I can’t accomplish the task, his cum dripping out the sides of my mouth and down my chin. His cock gives one last twitch before he eases it out of my lips with a slick pop. I barely have time to take in a gasping breath before he’s hauling me up and crushing his mouth against mine. He groans at the taste of himself on my tongue, and when our mouths part, his eyes drop to my messy chin.

“Don’t waste a drop of your reward, sweetheart.” Using his

fingers to gather up the cum painting my face, he feeds it to me. I lick his fingers clean, loving the flare of his nostrils as I do. "That's my girl," he murmurs, before leaning down to kiss me again.

I'm so turned on that I want to beg him to fuck me, but once again my annoying stomach growls, much more insistent this time.

Wesley gives me a dirty grin. "Thought you'd be full after that. If you give me a couple of minutes, I can give you more."

I laugh and shake my head at him, the spell of our kink melting into the comfort of the friendship our relationship was built on. "Your cum doesn't count as a meal."

"A pity," he chuckles. "Why don't you relax while I make you some actual food? Oh, wait! I got you some stuff." He slides up and hops out of the tub before I can protest. He rummages through a drawer under his sink and comes back with a trio of colorful bath bombs, which he presents to me with an excited grin.

"A friend introduced me to a witch who specializes in fancy magic soaps and shit for all kinds of things. This one's for mental clarity, this one is for stress relief, and this one..." He waggles his eyebrows at me, "is supposed to help you relax in other ways."

"Other ways?" I ask, intrigued by the seemingly innocuous light pink and orange bath bomb in his hand.

"*Sexy* ways. I got some magic lube, but this will make it even easier for you to take my cock inside that tight little human cunt."

My breath hitches at the idea, and Wesley gives me a knowing smirk. "Refill the tub and soak it up for me, baby girl. Because after dinner, nothing is going to keep me from fucking your pretty pussy all night long."

19

WESLEY

Leaving Ariana all wet and flushed in my tub is a special kind of torture, but I'll be damned if I don't feed her before having marathon sex. She needs the sustenance, and once we start I doubt I'll be able to stop until dawn. Plus, I'm not letting the pan of prepped lasagna in my fridge go to waste. That shit is too delicious, and it fills me with pride to know I'm making an awesome meal for my woman.

Once the oven is preheated and I stick the glass pan inside, I consider heading back into the bathroom to spend the next fifty minutes with my face between Ari's legs, but decide against it. I doubt she's let herself rest for an hour in months. She could use a respite, and I'm more than happy to facilitate.

Being alone with my thoughts while she's naked in the other room is definitely a challenge, though. Despite her sucking out my soul through my dick, it's as hard and eager as ever. Not bad for a guy on the other side of forty. One of the perks of my minotaur blood—a cock that's perpetually primed for breeding.

Fuck, now I'm thinking about filling Ariana up. She'll look so good with a few of my loads dripping out of her pussy. It's way too soon to even think about kids, and honestly, I'm ambivalent about the idea of being a dad, but unloading inside her is a primal urge. A wet spot forms on my sweatpants and I grip my dick firmly, trying to get it to behave until after dinner.

I consider sending a third thank you text to Caleb for hooking me up with Tomas' witch friend and the fancy lube that will make that fantasy of breeding Ari over and over a reality tonight. *Probably shouldn't.* I've messaged him a few times already with follow-up questions about best use practices for the lube since he offered to help, so I'm sure he regrets giving me his number.

Swiping away from my conversation with Caleb, I see a series of texts that make my pulse spike.

Doug (6:58): Dude, you would not believe the day I've had. I could really use some company tonight before I do something stupid.

Doug (7:01): Are you home? I don't think I should be alone right now and Ari's not answering my texts. Even if she did, she's probably in admin hell, and I don't want to add to her stress.

Doug (7:02): Tomas isn't working tonight, or I'd go to Nightlight and bug him.

Doug (7:08): Shit, man. I think I'm just gonna head over in case you're home. I feel like I'm crawling out of my skin. Be there in ten.

Doug (7:08): If you're not there, I'll just let myself in. You can yell at me later for stealing all your snacks.

Fuck. I check the time—7:14. *Fuck!*

Ari and I haven't had time to have a more serious discussion about telling Doug we're together. I'd planned on bringing the subject up tomorrow morning, once the urgency of our shared lust had diminished. Just because I decided at the monster support meeting that we need to tell him sooner rather than later doesn't mean we don't have to finesse our approach. If he's having a monumentally shitty day, this isn't the time for him to find out that I'm screwing his little sister.

I race into the bathroom, and Ari gasps in surprise as the door smacks against the wall in my haste. "Jesus, you scared me! What's up?" She pushes herself up from her reclined position and gives me a coy smile. "Couldn't stand being away from me for fifteen minutes?"

The water sloughing off her tits pulls my focus for a second, but I shake that distraction away. "No. I mean, yeah, but uh, we have a problem. An urgent one."

Her sexy grin fades. "What? What kind of urgent?" She sees the panic on my face and her voice grows more high pitched. "Is there a fire? Shit!" She grabs the edge of the tub and almost slips in her haste to hoist herself out.

I grab a towel and race over to help her. "No, not a fire. Slow down, baby. We're safe. It's... Doug is coming over."

Her brow furrows. "Why? Did you have plans you forgot about? Oh god, this is bad."

"No plans, but he texted saying he was having a rough day and needed to come over. I didn't see it until now and he said he'd be here in 10 minutes." I glance at my phone again. "That was 7 minutes ago."

"Call him and tell him he can't come!"

I shake my head. "You know he doesn't answer his phone while he's driving. I can't stop him. Stay in here, and I'll get rid of him as fast as I can. Unless..." I give her a weak smile. "Unless you just want to rip the bandage off. Maybe it's a sign."

"Yeah, it's a sign. A sign that Doug is determined to be a pain in my ass," she grumbles as she wraps the towel around her body. She sighs. "I... It's a terrible way for him to find out. If he's already mad, then stumbling upon us will only make things worse. I don't want him to hurt you."

I snort in derision, and she narrows her eyes at me. "You're beefy, but not invulnerable! I care about both of you too much to see either of you get hurt because of wolfy rage we could've prevented. I'll hide in here, even if he wants to stay the whole damn night."

She's right, but I don't like it. Ariana isn't a dirty secret meant to hide out of sight. She's someone to be shared proudly, showing the world how lucky I am to be with her. I pinch the bridge of my snout. "Alright. I'll figure it out." I press a hasty kiss to her lips and head into the bedroom, but she calls out to me.

"My car!"

I curse. "I'll figure it out," I say again, though I have no clue how.

I grab the car keys from her purse, then scoop up both the purse and her overnight bag and shove them into my closet. I almost forget to put my glamor back in place as I race out the door, letting out a string of expletives as I run to her car and scramble inside.

When I turn the key, the engine gives a pathetic choked noise, and the car doesn't start.

"You've got to be fucking kidding me!" I attempt to start the car again and this time, nothing at all happens.

I slam my fists against the steering wheel in frustration. My mind races to come up with a solution. If my garage was empty, I could try pushing her car in there, but it's currently housing my home gym and a bunch of boxes of random crap I keep meaning to donate.

Doug is going to be here any second. If I can't get rid of the car, I'll have to figure out an excuse for why it's sitting in my driveway that doesn't include his sister being here for dinner and a night of dirty sex.

I pop the hood of her car, then hurry to grab my toolbox from the garage. In an attempt to sell the lie better, I smear some engine grease on my shirt. I only know the basics of car maintenance, but luckily Doug knows even less, so he won't be able to call my bluff.

I'm bent over, pretending to check something under the hood, when I hear Doug's car pull into my driveway. I stand up and give him a perplexed wave, grabbing a rag and pointlessly wiping my clean hands on it.

He gets out of his car with a similarly confused frown and I swallow down my nerves, attempting to keep my voice even as I approach him. "Hey! What are you doing here? Did I forget plans?"

Doug rakes a hand through his mussed brown hair and shakes his head. "Nah. Sorry for dropping in randomly, I just... I'm having a rough time, man. I thought you'd see my messages by the time I got here."

I pat my pockets and give him an apologetic look. "Must've left my phone inside. I've been out here for a while."

Doug glances over my shoulder at Ari's car. There's no chance of him not recognizing it as hers with her unfortunate license plate number of A55 F4N. When she got her new plate in the mail after transferring her registration to this state, Doug teased her about it for months.

His head cocks in an almost canine way. "Why is Ari's car here?"

"Oh, you know..." Panic makes my insides squirm as I attempt to lie on the spot. Dammit, I *hate* this. "She's having trouble with her engine but is too busy to bring it to a mechanic, so I offered to take a look. I feel bad, though, because now that I've gotten under the hood, I think the issue is too complex for me."

"Oh!" The frown fades from his face as he accepts my words without question. I don't think I've ever lied to Doug before I started trying to conceal what's going on with Arianna, so why wouldn't he believe me? The knot in my stomach twists tighter at his implicit trust.

He flashes me a rueful smile. "I really appreciate you looking out for her, dude. I wish I knew about cars, but I'm hopeless with that stuff. Sometimes I think I'm the worst brother in existence."

"What? No! Ariana loves you."

Doug sighs, and darkness clouds his expression. "I know she loves me. That doesn't mean that I'm a good brother. I'm a self-centered jerk who can't even get my shit together enough to help her when she needs it. I bet even if I knew how to fix cars, she wouldn't bother asking me to look at it."

Now that he's standing closer, I notice the deep dark circles etched under his eyes and the tense way he's holding his body. He said he was in a bad mood, but I figured it was because of something that made him angry, not that he was sinking into grim self-hatred. What kind of friend would I be if I tried to get him to leave when he's feeling so low?

I mentally scramble to figure out how to save this situation before Ari ends up trapped in my bathroom all night. There's no way I'm letting that happen.

I clap a hand on his shoulder in reassurance. "Of course she would. If you don't believe me, you can ask her when we go inside. Just give me a second to put this stuff away."

His dark brows raise. "Ari's here?"

"Well, yeah. Where else would she be?" It takes all of my feeble acting skills to not betray my skyrocketing anxiety. Ariana's going to kill me. I've just committed her to a night of hanging out with her brother and pretending that there's nothing between us.

"You don't look happy about that." Doug crosses his arms with an assessing look.

Dammit, he can sense something is off. Will he be able to tell the second he sees Ariana and I together that she had my cock in her mouth less than an hour ago?

I laugh, the sound coming out a little choked. "No! She's fine. She's great. Annoying as always, but..."

He's totally going to know. *Get it together!*

I clear my throat. "I've been avoiding going inside because I don't want to give her the bad news about her car."

"Hah, fair. Do you want me to go in first and help soften the blow?"

"No!" I say, almost shouting in my panic.

Doug's brows knit together at my bark of protest.

Crap, I'm screwing this up so bad. I try to backpedal. "I mean, yeah, that'd be nice, but you said you're having a rough day. I don't want to make it any worse."

"Uh, okay. Sure." He gives me a funny look, his golden eyes assessing me. It takes all of my willpower not to crack and confess everything.

I close the hood of the car and put the tools away, surreptitiously wiping away the sweat beading on my brow. I know Ari told me that this was the wrong time to let Doug find out about us, but if my sloppy lies are any indication, trying to keep it hidden tonight is an even worse idea. Gods, give me strength not to fuck this up.

20

ARIANA

Just when I was starting to think today wasn't a total disaster, my damn brother has to show up uninvited. I know it must be something bad if Doug is coming over with barely any warning, and I shouldn't be upset, but that doesn't stop the flash of anger when Wesley leaves to go head him off.

I silently grumble to myself as I dry off and get dressed. All the languid arousal that built while I soaked in the magic bath water and the pulses of heat from anticipating what would come later tonight has been doused. Now I'm on edge and frustrated for a decidedly unsexy reason.

I'm not proud of my pissy reaction. It makes me feel like the world's worst sister to hope that Doug will be persuaded to leave quickly. I shouldn't care more about an intimate night with my new boyfriend than making sure his mental state won't cause him to lose control.

It's just... I've put his needs over mine for so long. Taking care of Doug after he was bitten meant leaving behind my old life and starting over in Moonvale, all while adjusting to the fact that monsters are real. There was over a year where I spent every moment I wasn't around my brother worried that he'd lose control and attack someone if they looked at him wrong. Doug was mild-mannered and non-confrontational before turning into a werewolf, so at the beginning he had no coping mechanisms for the bursts of rage that overtook him at the smallest provocation. I was the only person he never threatened, because according to him, I smell "safe" and his beast knows that I'm family.

I don't regret the decision to take care of him and I'd do it all over again if I had to. But sometimes I wish things were different. That he hadn't gone camping during that full moon and that damn irresponsible werewolf who bit him hadn't assumed she was far enough away from civilization to fully unleash her wolf. I still love Doug with my whole heart, and in many ways, his personality has blossomed since becoming a werewolf. He's more confident and outgoing, and he's doing a lot more with his life now that he's gotten through most of the adjustment period for his new monster side. But I miss the brother who didn't get upset easily. The old Doug wouldn't bat an eye if I told him I was dating his best friend. Though I doubt he and Wesley would've ever met if it weren't for Doug joining their monster support group.

Hiding my new relationship with Wesley sucks, but I don't want anyone to get hurt, and I definitely can't risk ruining their friendship by breaking the news when Doug is already stressed. When the two of them grew close, I could breathe a little again. Wesley offers Doug something I can't—a monster's perspective and lifetime of experience reconciling his beastly urges with living as part of human society. As exhausted as I was being my brother's only source of security for so long, I was upset when the beefy minotaur gym bro insisted Doug hang out with him instead of me. Looking back on that now, I realize that even before we knew each other, Wes was helping me out. He wasn't pushing me out of Doug's life, he was giving me a chance to live my own.

My heart squeezes and I'm filled with overwhelming affection for Wesley. A feeling that could easily be mistaken for love. *Oh god, I love him, don't I?* The thought simultaneously has me panicking and giddy, and I let out a squeal of shock that echoes against the tiled shower wall.

Crap. I hold perfectly still for a long moment, expecting Doug to come barging in here at any moment, having heard my noise and found out my deceit. At least a minute passes before I unclench and sink down to sit on the fluffy bathmat with a weak, soundless laugh.

Get it together, girl. He's not going to find you in here. Just settle in and wait.

"Ari, are you alive in there?"

I startle, eyes flying open at the voice on the other side of the bathroom door followed by two loud raps. I'd been attempting to meditate to soothe my nerves and must've dozed off. I'm wide awake now.

"Doug!" I call back, scrambling up to my feet in a panic. Shit, did

I lock the door after Wes left? Will that even matter? He knows I'm here! What the hell did Wes say to him? Is Wes okay?!

"On a scale of one to ten, how bad is it?" my brother asks from the other side of the door, sounding far more calm than I'd expect from someone with anger issues who found out his best friend is banging his little sister.

"Wh-what?"

"You've been in there for like thirty minutes. Are you coming out soon or is it like that time at Grandpa's funeral? I can steal a pair of Wes' sweatpants for you. He won't care."

It takes my brain a moment to catch up with what the hell he's talking about, but I groan once I do. Wes must've made up something to explain me being here and hiding in his bathroom. Dammit, why couldn't he have just not told him I'm here? I consider pretending I'm in intestinal distress until he leaves, but knowing Doug, he'll wait around until I'm feeling better out of some sense of sibling solidarity.

"Not like that. Leave me alone, weirdo! I'll be out in a minute or two."

Doug huffs out a laugh at my affronted tone. "Excuse me for wanting to make sure you didn't pass out on the toilet and crack your skull open."

"Go away!"

He laughs again and I breathe a momentary sigh of relief as I hear him retreat, but it doesn't last for more than a second. I have to go out there and interact with him, with no idea of what kind of excuse Wesley came up with for me being here. I wait a minute and flush the toilet a few times, then attempt to put on my poker face as I wash my hands, wincing as I rub against the raw scrapes on my palms. At least the nervous sweat beading on my brow will help sell the fake stomach troubles. Maybe I'll be able to get away with a quick greeting, then claim that I need to head home while I feel up to it. I really don't want to go home, but what other option is there?

My pulse races as I exit the bathroom and leave the safety of Wesley's bedroom, heading downstairs to the kitchen and living area.

"There she is! And still wearing her own clothes." Doug gives me a teasing smile that doesn't quite reach his eyes when he sees me enter the room. He really must be having a rough time if his amusement at my pretend predicament doesn't pierce through his distress.

"Ariana!" Wesley says my name like he's surprised to see me here. He clears his throat in an attempt to cover his weird reaction. "Uh, you feeling better?" His worried, nervous expression has nothing to do with my fake bathroom troubles. He's freaking out about lying to Doug. If I wasn't so worried myself, I'd be angry at him, but we both need to keep ourselves together before this night spirals completely out of control.

"Yeah, a little better." I give him a weak smile. "I should probably head home though...thanks for your...uh, your..."

Wes shakes his head and steps in to help me out. "Don't thank me yet. I couldn't fix your car. It still won't start." He gives me a meaningful look.

Ugh, that's why Doug knew I was here. My stupid piece of shit car. I cross my arms and frown back at him. "Oh. Damn. Thank's for trying. Well...I guess..."

"I can drive you home now if you're not up to staying for dinner." Wes sounds so dejected as he makes the offer, and I'm barely able to disguise my own sadness at the thought. I wanted to stay with him. I was ready to accept his help in figuring my messy life out, and then lose myself in him all night.

"What about your lasagna?" I ask weakly, glancing over at the oven timer, which is only a few minutes away from buzzing. It smells incredible in here already. Yet another thing I won't get to enjoy tonight if I go home.

"Dude, I can take you home." Doug sounds almost affronted, like he's upset I didn't assume he'd be the one to help me out.

"N-no, that's okay!" I squeak in protest, and Doug's expression twists into a scowl.

"What did I tell you? I'm such a shitty brother that she doesn't even trust me to drive her home." His words are directed at Wesley, but they pierce into me like a knife.

"What are you talking about? You're not a bad brother."

"Yeah, I am. I don't do shit for you. I can't fix your car, you're slammed with your business stuff and I don't help because I'm too wrapped up in my own drama, and apparently I can't even be trusted to give you a ride. I ruined your life just like I ruin everything." Anguish is written across Doug's face as his despairing words flow out of him.

Shame about my earlier anger knots my stomach. I'm over at his side in an instant, pulling him into a hug. "Shut up. You didn't ruin anything. Whatever is going on with you, we'll figure it out."

Wes joins us, placing a hand on Doug's shoulder. "Yeah, man. You've got us. So quit listening to that asshole in your head that's catastrophizing things."

I squeeze my brother tighter, willing some of the tension radiating from his bulky form to ease. "You suck at a lot of things, but being a brother isn't one of them."

Doug lets out a shuddering sound that's a mix of a laugh and a heavy exhale, then squeezes me back before releasing the hug and stepping back. He scrubs a hand across his face and gives a tired sigh. "You're right. I'm just... today has been a fucking disaster."

"Then it's a good thing your best friend and I are both here to talk you through it." I say, giving him a reassuring smile.

"Yeah, if anyone can help your mopey ass, it's Ari. She can do anything." Wesley's tone is laced with far too much affection, and my breath stutters as he turns his warm gaze on me, looking at me with what can only be described as adoration.

I quickly turn away so Doug doesn't catch the flush rising in my cheeks, heading over to the fridge under the pretense of getting something to drink. This is going to be tough, but I can't go home now that I know how much Doug is struggling. If Wesley keeps looking at me like that and saying things that definitely aren't normal for us, he'll give us away.

When I return with a can of seltzer, I make sure not to look at Wesley again. I can't see his besotted looks and not make what's going on between us patently obvious to Doug. "It must be bad if you're dropping in on dinner rather than spending time with your hot girlfriend," I say teasingly, attempting to bring my focus back to my brother.

My heart sinks when Doug visibly flinches at my words.

"Oh shit, man. What happened with Margaret?" Wes asks with a frown.

"She cheated on me." Doug says it so matter-of-fact, like it was a foregone conclusion.

"What?! I'll kill her!" I blurt, and Wesley's eyebrows shoot up in surprise. I don't care that my reaction is extreme. Doug has given all of his time and energy to this woman, seeming truly happy and at ease for the first time in a long time. She always rubbed me the wrong way, and now I know why. She's a cheating asshole.

Doug snorts in amusement. "Thought I was the one in the family with anger issues."

"I don't have anger issues! I just... shit, Doug. I'm so sorry."

"It's okay," he says, though his worn out, pained expression says otherwise. "I should've expected it. A woman like her wouldn't want anything serious with a loser like me."

Wesley huffs, dismissing Doug's words. "Nope. We're not doing that. She cheated on you. That means she's the loser." He grabs him by the shoulders to steer him to the dining table and pushing him down into a chair. "Now sit here while I get the lasagna out of the oven."

"Damn, dude, you made your lasagna? What is this, some kind of date?" Doug laughs and shakes his head, thankfully not catching the panicked look I exchange with Wesley.

This would be the moment to come clean. It'd be a disaster, but we could say something. I don't though.

What kind of asshole would I be to bring up our new relationship when Doug's just imploded? *Sorry for your awful girlfriend, but guess what? Wesley and I are dating and I think I'm in love with him!* No way I could do that. No, we'll just have to get through dinner.

Wesley lets out a humorless chuckle. "I had the ingredients in the house and Ari looks like she needs a decent home-cooked meal."

The tender concern in his voice makes my chest ache. He doesn't deny that it's a date, but Doug doesn't notice. My discomfort with hiding the truth amplifies, but I swallow it down. We'll tell Doug soon. As for our ruined date night, I guess that's what we get for keeping it a secret at all.

21

WESLEY

Sitting next to Ariana at my dining table and pretending like there's nothing between us as Doug details his woes is torture. Between trying to maintain the lie and Ariana squirming in her seat every time I look over at her, I'm doing a terrible job of keeping track of what he's saying.

The bath bomb must've worked its magic, because Ari is flushed and I swear I smell a hint of her arousal whenever she shifts. It'll be a miracle if Doug doesn't notice with his keen sense of smell. Gods, that would turn this mess into a full-blown nightmare. Poor Ariana would probably die from embarrassment and I'd die from being disemboweled.

That's an exaggeration. The more Doug talks, the more I realize that he's not at risk of bursting into a rage. Instead, he's... defeated. That makes me worry about him more than any anger would. I push away thoughts of our deception and will myself to focus on his distress. Not being there for him properly right now is worse than any guilt I feel for not confessing the truth about Ariana's presence here tonight.

"So then she told me, 'you're good for some fun, but not serious relationship material.' Like we didn't spend the last month looking at apartments to move in together. I was putting aside money to buy her a goddamn ring. How could I be so blind?" Doug rests his face in his hands with a heavy groan.

"Say the word and I'll go over there right now and give her a piece of my mind," Ariana says, her eyes blazing with indignance.

"With what car? I'm not driving you over to go yell at my girlfri—" His expression grows even more pained. "Ex-girlfriend. I doubt Wesley condones that, either. Better to let it go and pretend she never existed."

Gods, the way his girlfriend treated him is abhorrent. Cheating is awful, but making it seem like it was your partner's fault... I have to suppress a growl of anger. My thirst for vengeance is as high as Ariana's, but I need to be a grounding presence in this conversation, so I don't voice my wishes that she gets tortured for eternity in the demon realms when she dies.

I'm also worried about his veneer of calm and the utter defeat in his words. "I don't think Ari should go yell at her, no. But dude, you have every right to be furious and hurt. This is the time to feel those feelings."

Doug's eyes are glassy when he looks up at us again. His hand shakes a little as he reaches out for his fork, and he grips it so hard his knuckles turn white. "I can't."

Ariana reaches from her side of the table and places her hand over his clenched one. "Doug... it's natural for you to be upset."

"No, it's not! If I let myself be angry, I'll... I'll break." A tear slides down his cheek, and he furiously swipes it away with his free hand.

I shake my head. "I know you've worked so hard at controlling your wolf's rage, but maybe you've gone too far." He opens his mouth to argue, but I hold up a hand. "If Nik were here, you know what he'd say. It's not about removing all traces of the monster in you. It's about finding a balance between the monster and the man."

"That's a lot easier said than done." Doug laughs humorlessly, but lets Ariana continue to hold his hand. "Thanks, Ari," he murmurs, giving her a soft, slightly pained look. One I recognize from the very first time I met the two of them.

The love and concern bleeding out of her is palpable, and my chest aches when I dare to glance over at her.

This wonderful woman. She'd do anything for her brother. Hell, she's already done it. I didn't realize it at the time, but I think I fell for her when she hauled her brother to his first monster support group meeting. Sure, I thought she was gorgeous, all decadent, soft curves that begged for me to sink my fingers into them. But it was more than that. Doug was worried about getting too emotional, so Ariana sat outside the meeting room the whole time, waiting in case he needed her. A few times he got up and left the room, excusing himself to grab water or go to the bathroom, and though I didn't intend to, I overheard her whispered reassurances. He made it through the meeting because of her. She gave him the courage and support to ask for help.

Now more than ever, I swear to myself that I'll give her that same level of care. She deserves everything. Doug will be able to return her support someday, but he needs to find stable ground and ease with his wolf first. So I'll be Ariana's rock.

She holds my gaze for a moment, looking confused by my sudden intensity, before flushing even more and snapping her eyes back to her brother. She squeezes his hand tighter. "You're not going to lose control. You're so much stronger than you think you are, and I'm here with you." She looks back over at me and there's so much trust and affection in her eyes that it makes my heart skip a beat. "*We're* here with you."

Ariana is right. Doug's anger spills out of him like a dam has broken. There are a few moments as he gives voice to his hurt that he starts to snarl, his eyes flashing gold, but he pushes it back down. Not for the first time, I wish for a pack in Moonvale that he could spend time with. I do my best to support the monster side of him, but I'm not a werewolf. I've always been a minotaur, so the monstrous parts of me feel as natural as breathing. He was ripped from his human life and forced to be something that terrifies and confuses him. He needs a safe space to shift and get used to his wolf, so it's not a constant sword hanging over his head.

By the time he's released all his tangled thoughts, hours have passed and his voice is so hoarse it's barely more than a whisper. Both siblings' cheeks are ruddy and chapped from tears. I shed my fair share too, and I'm pretty sure I'll have bruises from when he crushed me in a hug and sobbed about how he was sorry he'd missed so many workout sessions because of prioritizing his ex over our friendship.

Weathering the storm of Doug's emotions leaves us all battered, but in the aftermath there's also a sense of calm. The release is cathartic, and while he's going to be angry and devastated for a while, there's a lightness in Doug's eyes that gives me hope.

He agrees that it'd be better for me to drive Ariana home instead of him, since he's so drained. We both give Doug a huge hug, and there's a pang of guilt that I'll be causing him more pain when I tell him about my lies. I almost break and blurt it out as he gives a weak smile and heads out the door.

Despite my guilt, when the door closes behind him, I breathe a sigh of relief. The second I turn around, Ariana is on me, wrapping her arms around my waist as far as she can reach, and pressing her cheek to my chest. "Thank you. I don't know what we did to deserve you in our lives, but thank you."

I squeeze her back, then stroke a hand through her hair. "You don't need to thank me, Ari. You two are the best part of my life. I'd do anything for you." I want to tell her that my monster side has claimed both of them—Doug as the brother I never had, and her as the woman I want to cherish and worship for the rest of our lives. That I *love* her.

"I don't want to hide anymore. Doug deserves to know about us. It was wrong of me to think he couldn't handle finding out." She sighs heavily. "My brain is still stuck on how he was after the attack, not who he is now. I told him that he wouldn't lose control, but inside there was a part of me that doubted my own words. I'm ashamed that I didn't realize how much he'd changed until tonight."

I pull back a little so I can look down into her eyes. "You spent a year of your life worrying about Doug non-stop. Of course you were concerned. Shit, I was worried and I've directly seen his progress in our group. What matters is you were here for him, even though you weren't sure what would happen."

I stroke her cheek, attempting to soothe away her shame. Her eyes well with tears, but she nods and gives me a soft smile. "What would I do without you?"

"Oh, you'd be fine," I say with a grin. "Me, on the other hand? I'd wither away without you in my life."

She laughs. "Well, we can't have that, so I guess I'm stuck with you."

"Damn right you are. That's what you get for dating a minotaur. We don't let the ones we... cherish go." Once again, I want to say love, but after everything that's happened today, I think it's better to save that weighty proclamation for a calmer moment.

"Now that that's settled, when do you want to tell Doug? I can text him to come back now if you want." I chuckle as her warm expression shifts into alarm.

"Don't you dare! I've had enough drama for one evening. Let's tell him tomorrow. I'll want to check in on him, anyway. Maybe we could go together in the morning?"

I pull her closer and press a kiss to her hair. "Anything you want, baby girl."

Ariana's eyelashes flutter at the pet name, and she wets her lips. She's clearly exhausted, but there's still a spark of arousal in her reaction that makes my dick perk up.

Even after this rollercoaster of a night, I want her. It's late and I really shouldn't, but when I stroke my hand over her hip and her breath hitches, I can't stop the words from coming out of my mouth. "Tell daddy what you need, sweetheart."

She takes a moment to reply, worrying her lower lip between her teeth. I want to tug that lip into my mouth and soothe away the indents she's making with my tongue. I don't rush her, because I don't want to pressure her, and chances are she won't want to do anything tonight.

"I know I should get some sleep... I shouldn't want..."

"Want what?" I prompt when she doesn't continue.

She wets her lips. "Maybe it's still the effects of the bath, but I *ache*."

My arousal flares to life, and my voice thickens with desire. "Mmm, we can't have that. What kind of ache, baby? Where do you feel it?"

She presses in closer, and I feel how hard her nipples are as her breasts brush against my chest. "Somewhere naughty," she whispers.

Fuck me. My cock surges fully to life. "No secrets between us. How can daddy take care of you if he doesn't know what's wrong?"

"It's..." She looks down, then back up at me through her lashes. Gods damn, she's sexy. I love that we can indulge in this play together and that she wants it as much as I do. "It's... my pussy. I feel so empty. I need..."

I groan at her shy words and rock my hips so she can feel my erection against her stomach. "You need daddy's cock. You need it to stretch you open and fill you up like no one else can."

"*Yes*," she says in a breathy exhale.

I echo the enthusiastic sentiment in my mind, and I bend down to kiss her, but stop when she stiffens.

"Shit, should we wait until after we tell Doug?"

Screw Doug. I care about him, but he's kept me from Ariana long enough today. "There's no fucking way I'm leaving you wanting, baby girl. Now, let's go to the bedroom before I lose control and try to fuck you against the wall."

She rubs herself against my thigh with a little whimper that makes my dick jerk. "That doesn't sound too bad to me."

"I want to fill that needy pussy up until you pass out from pleasure, which means we need that magic lube. Get in the damn bedroom, Ari. *Now.*"

22

ARIANA

It's amazing how being turned on can give me a second wind, especially considering how many times I've cried today. By all accounts, I should be a puddle on the floor, but one rumbling "baby girl" from Wes and I'm ready to go. Well, that and whatever was in that magic bath bomb. I thought for sure I was going to soak through my panties sitting at the dinner table, despite the very unsexy topic of conversation. Next time we try any kind of sex magic, we need to lock ourselves away where we can't be disturbed. I don't ever want to be that horny while in the same room as my brother again.

I shudder mid-dress removal, and Wes raises a brow at me in

concern. "I'm good. Just...glad Doug is gone. The magic from the bath bomb is really, uh, potent." Even mentioning it makes my clit give a needy pulse.

He chuckles and palms my ass as soon as I get the dress off, tugging me against him. "I could tell. I'd say I'm sorry for the torture, but you looked so pretty, all flushed and squirming in your seat."

I scowl and pretend to shove away from him, but he grips my ass and holds me tighter. "You should apologize! You're the reason I was there with you two to begin with. I would've been perfectly happy in my hiding place, but no, you had to tell Doug I was there."

"Only because your car wouldn't start!" he huffs, rolling his eyes at me. "Besides, it turned out for the best that you didn't stay in hiding, didn't it? Horny awkwardness aside."

"Ugh, quit being logical! It's annoying." I try to sound frustrated, but can't stop my lips from curving into a smile.

"It's almost like you want to mouth off to me so you can get in trouble, but it won't work tonight, sweetheart. I've waited too long to fuck you and nothing is keeping me from being inside your little human cunt. Even bratty behavior." Wes lowers his voice to a low rumble tinged with something dark and hungry. "Get on the bed."

I scramble to obey, our silly banter evaporating with the heat of his words. I feel oddly small as I climb up onto his enormous bed, and I almost groan in pleasure when I lie back and feel how comfortable his mattress is. Lost in momentary comfort, I squeak in shock when Wesley grabs my ankles and tugs me further down the mattress. I bounce a little before settling again, and I immediately imagine how that will feel when he's pounding inside me. My memory foam mattress is good for my back, but makes sex feel like I'm sinking into quicksand.

"What's going on in that pretty head of yours, angel?" Wesley asks, stroking his hands up and down my thighs.

I flush in embarrassment at being caught in the midst of my wandering thoughts. "Uh, your mattress."

He doesn't miss a beat, despite the weird tangent I've taken us on. "Mmm, it's made to handle everything I want to do to you. Be a good girl and spread your legs for daddy so he can get you ready for his cock."

All thoughts of mattresses fly out the window. "Y-yes, daddy." I bend my knees and spread my legs, heat coursing through me as he watches, drinking in the sight of my pussy. I'm already so wet that my thighs are coated and I'm probably making a wet spot on the bed.

"Fuck, baby girl. You're soaked." Wesley strokes two fingers across my pussy, and I gasp at the teasing touch. "I'm not gonna need much of this lube, am I? Your needy pussy knows to get ready for daddy's cock."

Heat washes over me at his words, and I nod. "Please, daddy. It aches. I need you inside me."

I watch with rapt attention as Wesley slides one of his huge palms along the massive bulge in his pants, then gives it a squeeze. "You don't have to beg, baby girl. Daddy's going to take care of you."

He retreats for a moment to grab a small jar from the top of his dresser. My breath hitches as he turns and slips off his sweatpants, bearing himself to me, cock swollen with a shining trail of pre-cum dripping from the tip that draws my eye to his piercing.

Despite my arousal, there's a flutter of nerves in my stomach. His size doesn't get any less shocking each time I see it. If anything, now that I've experienced it inside me—and the aftermath—I'm even more concerned. Yes, I want the thrill of taking such an enormous cock inside me, filling me like no one else can, but I also want to be able to walk tomorrow.

"Y-you're sure that lube is going to work?" I'm embarrassed by how wobbly my voice comes out. I don't want to make things less hot by questioning him, but I can't help it. My sense of pussy preservation is heightened in the aftermath of our last attempt.

Wesley steps out of the pants pooled around his hooves and moves to stand between my legs. He runs his hand along my outer thigh and lets out a soft, rumbling sound that helps soothe me a little. "I have it on good authority that it works. But if it doesn't, we'll stop and I'll spend the rest of the night making you come with my fingers and tongue." He grips my hip and gives me a solemn look. "I promise I won't hurt you again—outside of when we agree to that sort of play. You're mine to take care of, and I take that responsibility seriously."

My insides go molten at his words, because I believe him. I know with absolute certainly that he's going to take care of me, and I can let go.

I release a shuddering exhale and nod. "Okay. I trust you." He beams down at me and I suddenly realize that I've missed telling him a crucial part of my feelings. "You're mine, too. You know that, right?"

Wesley goes still, his lube-slicked fingers hovering over my pussy. "Oh? Are you claiming me, sweetheart?"

I squirm as I wait to feel his touch where I crave it. "Yes! You're mine. Now please, touch me!"

He lets out a bark of laughter and unfreezes. "I'm yours, angel." His fingers circle around my entrance, making me gasp. "Gonna get you ready so I can give us both what we need."

"Yes, d-daddy—*oh*." I sigh as he slips two fingers inside me with no resistance. I'm so wet already that I take them with ease. He pumps them inside me slowly, each time spreading them apart a bit more to press against my inner walls. He works a third finger in, and I brace myself for the stretch, but it's not painful at all. No, it's *amazing*. I'm full and hot, impossibly slick around his fingers, and everything in my body screams to have his cock inside me. "Please, I need more," I groan in desperation.

Wes chuckles and continues to move his fingers inside me. "I'll give you more, baby girl. Patience." He tilts his hand and uses his thumb to circle my clit as he slides a *fourth* finger in. My body resists it, but the stretch as he makes me take him feels unreal. I can't stop myself from tilting my hips into his touch and when he focuses on my g-spot, the pressure becomes too intense.

"Wes!" I cry out as all of that building arousal and strange full pressure breaks, and I come, gushing all over his hands. "Oh fuck, oh *fuck*." I buck against his insistent touch, overwhelmed by the sensation and astonishment at what happened. I can't believe he made me squirt. Again!

My minotaur rumbles in approval, his fingers inside me and his thumb on my clit wringing the remains of my explosive orgasm from me. "That's it, baby. Such a good girl, coming so hard for me."

As I come back to my senses, embarrassment at the puddle I've created beneath my hips creeps in. I open my mouth to tell him I'm sorry, but Wes shakes his head at me.

"Don't you fucking dare apologize," he growls, grabbing my thighs possessively and groaning as he stares at my pussy and the wet bedspread. "Fuck Ari, you soaking my bed as you came on my hand is one of the hottest things I've ever witnessed. If you're worried, I'll go grab a towel and put it down for next time, but I don't give a shit about my comforter. Not when you're so gods-damned sexy and wet for me."

I appreciate the reassurance, but the thought of squirting again makes my stomach do a flip in a mix of embarrassment and excitement. "N-next time?"

He raises a brow at my question. "You squirted the last time my cock was inside you. You squirted from my fingers. Maybe it won't be as much, but that sweet cunt of yours sure does seem to want to gush for me, baby girl." Wesley pauses, considering my reaction more closely. "Does that not normally happen to you?"

I shake my head, face flushing furiously. "No! I've never done that before! I'm so embarrassed. It's... messy."

He snorts, and I can tell he's resisting the urge to roll his eyes at me. "The woman that begged me to come all over her tits is worried about making a mess?"

"That's different!" As soon as the protest leaves my mouth, I realize how ridiculous I'm being. But there's that nagging worry that society programs into people with pussies—the one that tells us our genitals are somehow shameful or gross, even though our worth is so often reduced to what's between our legs.

A hungry look washes over Wes' face and he presses a kiss to my inner thigh. "Baby girl, I'm going to flood your little cunt with so much of my cum that we won't even notice the wet spot you made. I want to fuck you until my bed is covered in our release and I smell the mix of us on my sheets even after I wash them."

I flush, my clit sparking at the filthy picture he paints. "When you put it that way... it's not so bad."

"No. It's fucking perfect." He nuzzles into my other thigh and gives a pleased groan.

The blend of my arousal and affection for Wesley crash over me in a blissful wave, washing away my worries. I wrap a hand around his horn and tug on it, so he'll bring his attention back to my face. "Come up on the bed with me so we can make that mess you're so eager for. I don't want to wait any longer to feel you inside me again."

23

WESLEY

Ariana on my bed, legs spread and cunt glistening from where she soaked my fingers, is the prettiest vision I've ever had the pleasure of seeing. She's *finally* here. The woman that holds my heart is in my bed, and she's begging for my cock. Something I've spent an inordinate number of times fantasizing about late at night. Fuck, how did I get to be so lucky?

I groan as I give my dick a rough stroke, loving the way her breath hitches as she watches me. I've thought about fucking her so many ways on this bed. On her hands and knees while I stood behind her. Spread underneath me as I leisurely stroked inside her.

On my back, letting her ride me. When given the choice of how to have her now, I'm almost paralyzed by indecision on what to try first.

She lets out a little whine and lifts a leg to poke me in the chest with her toe. "Quit staring at me and do something!"

I snatch her foot before she pokes me again. "So impatient. Maybe I should make you wait longer." We both know it's a hollow threat. I'm even more eager to be inside her than she is to take me.

I release her foot and take a step back, surveying the position and appreciating her intoxicating desperation.

Ariana's eyes go wide and she pushes herself up onto her arms. "No, daddy, please! I can't wait any longer."

I huff and shake my head at her, moving to grab a pillow before returning to the foot of the bed. She watches me in confusion, with a frustrated gleam in her eyes that makes my dick throb. Her shallow breaths make her tits rise and fall, jiggling enticingly.

Without preamble, I grab her under her hips and shove the pillow beneath them, then snag her ankles and place her feet as close to my shoulders as they'll reach, given our height difference.

"Oh!" Ariana's arms splay out to the sides to balance herself in this new position.

I love how soft and decadent her body looks beneath me, and I can't resist reaching down to palm one of her breasts. "So beautiful. My perfect baby girl. You ready for daddy's cock?" I practically growl the words, overcome with emotion and lust.

She nods, pupils blown wide as I swipe my fingers across her pussy and smear my cock with the mixture of her release and the lube. "Yes, daddy. *Yes*. Please put it inside me."

We both gasp as the head of my cock presses against her entrance. Unlike the previous time, it starts to slide in right away.

Her channel feels as tight as before, but it's amazingly slick and gives way to my giant cock with an ease that's truly magical.

Remind me to thank Caleb, because, *fuck*, this is better than I could've imagined. I regret my choice of position because I can't see past her thick thighs to watch as I sink my cock into her. Good thing I have plans to take her every way possible before the night ends.

"Oh god, daddy! *Wes*. Fuck, you're so big!" She fists the bedding beneath her, her voice sounding almost pained, but the way she tilts her hips up to meet my slow press into her tells me to keep going. Her pussy clenches against me as my piercing rubs against her inner wall and she moans.

"You like daddy's fat bull cock don't you? Feel how greedy your little cunt is, squeezing me and sucking me in. No one can fill you like daddy can."

I grunt as I push my cock inside as far as I can go. Sparks of intense pleasure dance behind my eyes and I have to grit my teeth to not come right then at the sensation of being sheathed inside her.

I hold myself still as I let the intense feeling pass and reach down to stroke her soft belly. I'm so deep and stretching her so wide, I swear I can feel a faint bulge from my minotaur cock inside her small human pussy, though I know that's just my horny imagination.

I marvel as I look down at her flushed face. "Look at you, angel. You're taking me so well. Such a good girl."

"I need...please..." Ariana sounds almost delirious as she brokenly begs me for more.

"Shh, baby girl. Daddy's got you." I pull my hips back, both of us shuddering at the sensation of her pussy clinging to me as I retreat. Her mouth falls open as I begin to piston inside her in slow, deep strokes, silently gasping as her eyes lock on mine. Heat crackles between us as a tether forms, not just where our bodies meet, but from somewhere much deeper inside. It feels like my soul is calling out to hers, telling her that she's mine and that I'll always take care of her.

Sex with Ariana in the escape room was amazing, but it was rushed and tinged with desperation. This is... there are no words. Just the two of us and every yearning hope we've shared for almost a year finally manifesting.

"*Ari*," I groan, nuzzling my snout against her ankle, since I can't kiss her in this position.

"*Wes*." Her voice echoes my awe-filled tone. She feels the connection, too.

Pleasure crackles again at the base of my spine. Shit, I'm not going to last long at all. With such a goddess taking me inside her, how could I?

"Rub your clit for me, sweetheart. I want you coming on my cock before I lose control," I rasp.

She attempts to follow my instructions, but the angle and the lack of space between her thighs make it hard for her to touch herself. I let out a frustrated exhale, once again displeased with my choice of positions. Next time, I'll have her bring over one of her small vibrators. Or better yet, see if that sex magic witch knows how I can get a vibrating cock ring in my size.

There's no scenario where I'm letting myself come before she does, so I release her legs and pull out. Both my cock and Ariana protest at the sudden lack of stimulation.

"Turn over. On your hands and knees. Daddy wants to go deeper and see how good that pussy looks taking his cock."

Ari nods, eyes wide at the prospect of me somehow getting even deeper inside her. My impatient dick twitches and I grab more of the lube and rub it over my length for good measure while I wait for her to get into position.

When her luscious ass and glistening pussy are presented to me, I let out a deep groan and knead my fingers into her hips, tugging them back toward me. "Fuck, baby girl. You look so good, I could blow my load all over your pretty ass."

"Daddy," she whines, pressing her hips back toward me. "I've been a good girl. *Please*. Put it inside me. Give me your cum."

My grip on her hips tightens at her begging, her words just as filthy as my own thoughts. "Mmm, you're right. You've been very good. Daddy will give you his cum, but first you have to come for him."

"Y-yes, daddy." Ariana slides a hand down between her legs to circle her clit, letting her weight rest on her chest and further present her cunt to me.

I line my cock up with her entrance and thrust inside in a slow, fluid motion, letting her get used to the size of me again. It looks even better than I imagined, her flushed wet pussy stretched obscenely around my cock, gripping me as tight as a fist.

"Shit, you feel even bigger," Ariana curses once I'm as deep inside her as I can go. I pull back and pump inside again, still marveling at the easy glide the lube provides but testing to make sure it's as pleasurable for her. She gasps each time my piercing strikes against her g-spot, and I wonder if I can make her squirt again like this. She was embarrassed about it last time, so I don't need it to happen, but damn, it was sexy.

After a few testing pumps with no sign of discomfort, I set a steady pace. Ari matches my strokes with her fingers on her clit, and I release my grip on one of her hips to reach forward and grab her breast. She moans as I tease her nipple, her pussy fluttering around me. I hope she's close, because holding back is blissful torture.

Time melts away as I thrust inside her, finding the angle and rhythm that has her crying out with each pump of my hips. I murmur praise to her, telling her how gorgeous she looks, how good she feels, how she's my perfect baby girl, each word full of sincere reverence. Sweat beads at the base of my horns, but I keep myself steady and hold back my orgasm. I have to give her what she needs.

She pants and gasps, fingers tirelessly working her clit until her orgasm rolls over her in a deep wave. Her cunt pulses around my cock, and it almost forces me over the edge despite my attempt at restraint. "*Gods.* That's it. You're doing so well. Come on daddy's cock."

When her release fades, Ariana lets out a deep exhale, followed by a slightly dazed giggle. "Thank you, daddy. That felt so good."

I lean forward and press a kiss to the nape of her neck, savoring the taste of her skin. Ari hums in pleasure, sounding drowsy and sated, but after a moment, I stand back up and slide my cock out of her, still hard and throbbing with need.

She doesn't move to close her legs, her cunt flushed and dripping with her arousal. Something primal unlocks inside me, seeing her like this—her body still on offer for me like the human sacrifices made to the ancient minotaurs. Contrary to legend, the humans came willingly, desperate to be fucked and bred by a massive beast until they were delirious with pleasure.

Now it's my turn to do the same.

"You ready for it, baby girl? Once I start, I'm not gonna be able to stop using you until you're dripping with my cum."

She turns to look back at me over her shoulder with a slight frown. "What do you mean? You've been fucking me."

A dark laugh erupts from deep in my chest. I press back inside her, moving slowly so she feels every inch of my cock dragging against her channel as I speak. "That wasn't fucking, angel. Fucking is when I'm slamming into you so hard that you don't know where your body ends and mine begins. I'm not a man, Ari. I'm a monster. I'm going to rut inside you like a beast and breed your tight human pussy. It's time for daddy to take what he needs. So, I'll ask you again. Are you ready for it?"

24

ARIANA

A*re you ready for it?*

Such a simple question, but hearing the full extent of what Wesley wants to do with me makes my whole body erupt in goosebumps. It's more than the primal picture he paints. It's the dark, hungry edge to his voice that tells me this goes beyond rough sex. No, it's a claiming. He's going to own me, body and soul, stripping away everything until the only thing that's left is my need for him.

I should be scared to give myself to a monster. The brush of his tail against my thigh as I attempt to come up with words for a reply further emphasizes the fact that we really aren't the same. I'm a human, small and fragile compared to his hulking minotaur self. It would take nothing for him to break me.

But this is *Wesley*. How could I ever worry with him? He's the best person I know. If anything, his minotaur strength and instincts only reinforce my certainty that I'm safe with him.

No, I'm not scared. I'm just as ravenous for his claiming as he is.

"Yes. I'm ready. I want it, Wes. I want my monster daddy to fuck me. I want *all* of you."

A deep, rumbling groan is the only warning I get before he slams inside me in a brutal thrust that slides me up the bed a few inches. He growls and yanks my hips back to him, fingers kneading into the flesh of my hips in a bruising grip.

Stars burst behind my eyes each time his piercing strikes inside me, and I gasp into the pillow my face is pressed against. "Oh f-fuck."

The way he spears me with his cock with goes far beyond anything I've experienced before. It's like he knows the exact angle to work inside me to make me cry out, tirelessly slamming into me with bestial grunts and groans. It's all I can do to hold on, fisting the sheets beneath me to brace myself as I take what he gives me.

"Take it," he rasps, sliding a hand down my spine, his weighty palm holding me in place possessively. "Daddy's needed your sweet cunt all week. A *week* without you, cock hard and balls ready to burst." He says "week" like it was a lifetime, sounding desperate and almost pained. "Never again. I'm not going a day without my baby girl's pussy milking my cock dry."

It's a promise and a threat that sends a hot pulse of pleasure through me. I know I should protest, but *fuck*, I want that, too. Now that I know we can do it without splitting me in two, I want this every day for the rest of my life. More than that, I want him in my life every day. How can I live like I did before, knowing that *this* is an option? Not just the amazing sex, but the even more incredible monster who adores me.

"Yes, daddy. I want you every day."

"Fuck." He groans, his hips stuttering for a moment and his tail wrapping around my ankle like he needs every part of himself touching me. Secure in his hold, Wesley resumes his rapid, deep thrusts that almost knock the air out of my lungs.

An orgasm sneaks up on me, and I'm barely able to gasp out his name before I come apart. Tears well in my eyes at the intense pleasure and the rush of emotions that follow in its wake.

It feels like he's torn my chest open and branded his name on my heart. Or maybe it's always been written there, hidden behind layers of protection that he's stripped away with his touch and care. All I know is that I'm utterly his.

"Godsdamn, that's it. Choke my cock. *Shit.*" He fucks me through my release, his rhythm faltering. "Can't wait any longer. It's coming. Time for daddy to fuck his cum into you."

"Please, daddy," I whine, feeling drunk on him and his mastery of my body, eager to return the pleasure he so expertly gives. "I want it."

"Here it comes, angel... *Fuck*, here it comes..." He slams into me two more times and lets out a thunderous shout as his cock unloads inside me. I gasp as he fills me with his hot cum in a seemingly never-ending stream. He holds me on him, grunting and cursing through his orgasm, and I let out a pleased sigh as I receive my reward for being my daddy's good girl.

When his cock gives a final weak jerk, Wesley exhales heavily and his grip on my hips loosens. I know I'll have marks where he held me, and the thought makes me shiver with strange excitement. He soothes his hands across my ass, hips and back, then roves them up and down my belly and up to cup my breasts.

Touching me everywhere he can reach, both possessive and soothing.

"Such a good girl. Gods, so perfect. More than I could've ever dreamed of." His sweet cinnamon-apple scent envelops me as his chest folds over my back and he rains kisses over my neck and shoulders.

"Thank you, daddy," I sigh, savoring the weight of him over me and his reverent touches. When his breathing evens and the fever that took hold while he rutted me subsides, he pulls out slowly, my pussy clinging to him like it doesn't want him to leave. A gush of his release pours down my thighs and I can only imagine how much of a mess we've made.

I roll over onto my side as Wesley climbs up to lie beside me. His arm snakes around my waist to tug me in tight against his warm bulk, and our mouths meet in a soft, sated kiss. I grin at him when our lips part, a reflection of the dazzling smile on his face.

"You're incredible, Ari," Wesley murmurs, smoothing back my mussed hair and running his hand down to cup my cheek.

I lean into the touch and place my hand over his, closing my eyes for a moment to sink into it. This tender embrace feels just as good as the frenzy of him fucking me.

When I open my eyes, he's watching me intently. I lean forward and kiss his snout, bringing one of my hands to stroke his horn. He nudges his horn into my touch, and my heart flutters. "You're okay, I guess," I say, shooting him a teasing grin.

Wesley huffs in disbelief and swats my ass with his tail. I giggle and shake my head in surrender. "Okay, fine, you're amazing." My voice grows softer. "If you're not careful, I'll never want to leave."

His dark eyes flare with interest. "Don't tease me, sweetheart. You say something like that to a minotaur and the next thing you know you end up with all your shit moved into his lair and your ass up in the air like this at least twice a day."

I shiver at the image of him taking me like that again, and my pussy gives a weak pulse. "What if I want that?" I ask, not realizing what I'm saying until the words come out. I can't breathe for a moment as their veracity hits me.

I've been working so damn hard, and my business is going well, but if I take a moment to really examine things, I'm... I'm *miserable.* The times I've spent with Wes in the last week were the only moments I've felt happy in months. Things have to change. Not out of any obligation I feel to be there for Wes as much as he is for me, but out of an obligation to myself. To my happiness. What the fuck is the point of all this hustle and stress if I never let myself live?

I didn't realize how bad it had gotten until Wes bull rushed into my life and showed me what I was missing. It's probably nuts to consider moving in together after less than a week of dating, but fuck it. Nothing about us has been conventional. It's time to take a leap of faith and trust that he'll be there to catch me.

"You want to move in with me, baby girl?" Wesley attempts to ask me in an even tone, but he's practically vibrating with poorly concealed excitement at the idea.

"Yeah, I'm sick of living without a tub," I say with feigned nonchalance.

His deep laugh rumbles against my chest where we're pressed together. "Even if you're only in this relationship for a tub and my cock, I'll take it. Speaking of both..." His hand slides down to my ass and I gasp as he swipes his fingers through the mess on my thighs. "I made a mess of you, baby girl. I should clean you up."

He sounds proud of that, and like he's thinking about making me even messier. "I don't mind being a little dirty," I murmur, hooking my leg over his to allow his hand better access to my pussy.

"Mmm, is that so?" His cock is already hard again against my hip, and he makes a pleased sound as his fingers glide between my thighs to stroke my clit. "Does my dirty girl need daddy's cock again? Or does she want me to clean her up with my tongue first?"

The thought of Wesley licking his own cum off of me sends a filthy thrill through me. "You'd do that?"

He rolls me onto my back and slides down my body to rest between my spread legs. His eyes gleam with wicked heat. "How else did you think I was going to clean you up?"

25

WESLEY

It takes until 3am for the fever in my blood to die down enough to let Ariana rest. Every time I think I'm sated, she makes a little breathy sigh or whispers something that makes my chest expand with warmth and my cock surge back to life. Somewhere around my third time claiming her sweet pussy, we transition from our roleplay to our raw selves. Ari chants my name, calling out for me to give her what she needs, and I groan hers in return as my movements inside her become less hurried. I could keep going until the sun comes up, but I know she's exhausted and can't let myself deprive her of any more sleep.

I guide Ariana to my shower, and her eyes droop as she stands under the hot water. A strange, primal pride surges in me when she relaxes fully into my hold, trusting me to keep her standing and allowing me to take over cleaning her off. I reluctantly wash the trails of my release from where I coated her breasts, stomach, thighs, and ass in my beast's attempt to mark her as mine thoroughly.

When we're both clean, she reaches out to stroke my cock, stiff from the pleasure of touching her lush body and caring for her the way I crave, but I shake my head. "That's enough for tonight."

A cute little wrinkle forms between her brows as she looks up at me. "You're still hard. I want to take care of you, too."

I suppress a groan at the thought, but stand my ground. "If we used my cock as a guide, we'd never stop fucking. My dick being hard is not nearly as important as you getting some rest."

"It's just..." Ari wets her lips as she thinks, drawing my eyes to her mouth and reminding me of all the ways she used it tonight.

I stroke her arm, forcing myself not to dip in to caress the side of her breast. My voice is a little hoarse when I prompt her to continue. "Just what, sweetheart?"

Her eyes flutter closed, and she releases a deep sigh. When she looks back at me, she smiles weakly. "Once we stop, I'll have to face reality."

That's not at all what I was expecting, though I can't say I don't understand. Nothing outside of us matters when our bodies are joined. Still, I'd hoped she wouldn't worry quite as much now that she knows I'm by her side. Does that mean that she wasn't serious about moving in? Shit, maybe it was just idle talk spurred on by post-coital bliss.

I must not keep my worries off my face because Ariana frowns and shakes her head. "Not face reality about you! About my business. About Doug."

I breathe a sigh of relief. "Had me worried there for a moment, baby girl. I know it's daunting, but you don't have to conquer either of those things alone. Get some rest and we'll take them on when you're not about to fall asleep on your feet."

She opens her mouth to say something, maybe a protest, but all that comes out is an enormous yawn that backs up my point. Ariana giggles and nods. "Alright, alright."

She smiles softly at me and goes up onto her toes, and I dip my head down to meet her, but she doesn't put her lips on mine. Instead, she reaches up and cradles my snout in her hands and kisses the side of it in an achingly sweet, affectionate gesture that makes my eyes fall closed in contentment. I bask in her small, loving touch, and once again, the urge to tell her I love her swells inside me.

It's not the right time. I want to tell her when she's fully relaxed and rested, not after such a harrowing day. I open my eyes and she pulls back after placing one more gentle kiss just to the side of my wide lips.

Shaking away my reverie from her tenderness, I quickly strip the bed and put on sheets that aren't coated in cum. Ariana wrinkles her nose at how much of a mess we made of my bedding. "You're going to need some industrial strength laundry detergent to deal with those."

"Eh, I can always buy more sheets if I can't get them clean. You're worth it."

Ariana laughs and rolls her eyes. "Oh wow, I'm worth a new set of sheets? You really know how to make a girl feel valued."

"What can I say? I'm a sucker for a beautiful woman who takes my cock so well."

She scowls at me, but I know that there's no genuine anger behind it. "That's all I am to you? A pretty cocksleeve?"

I shrug. "Not *just* that. Hmm... Oh! I know. You helped me solve those puzzles in the escape room. So you're good for that too."

Ariana smacks my chest with her towel and I cackle in delight. Fuck, I love how we can go from the most intense sex of my life, to tender emotion, to silliness so seamlessly. It reinforces what I already know in my heart—we were made for each other.

I tug her closer and laugh even harder as she pretends to struggle against me. After a moment, she sighs and relaxes into my arms, the burst of playfulness overtaken by fatigue. I press a kiss to her hair and squeeze her tighter. "You're everything to me, baby girl," I murmur.

"Mmm, so are you. Everything. To me." Ari's voice is slightly slurred, letting me know it's past time for her to sleep.

I guide her over to the bed and wrap myself around her back, savoring the way she fits there perfectly. Sure, I have to lie further up on the bed than her to make sure that my horns don't poke her in the eye if she rolls over in her sleep, but who cares?

Hmm, I should look into getting horn cozies. Max knits and crochets, so maybe he'd be willing to make something for them. Maybe put a pom pom on the ends to look extra cute...

As I sleepily ponder horn protection, Ariana's breathing evens out to a slow rise and fall. She's already asleep, and it doesn't take me long to follow. Right before I drift off, I kiss her shoulder and sigh in contentment, then let out the words I've been holding in, whispering them into her skin.

"I love you, baby girl."

Ariana's soft form is still tucked up against mine when I wake up the next morning, exactly as she was when we fell asleep. Harsh sunlight hits me right in the face when I open my eyes, and I hiss in distress.

"Not yet...just a few more minutes," Ariana groans, tugging the arm I have draped over her in closer so it rests beneath her breasts.

I glance over her shoulder to check the clock on the bedside table, surprised that it's almost 11. I never sleep in late, even on the weekends. Guess fucking for hours really knocked me out. Good thing Doug and I don't meet to work out on Sundays, or he'd be wondering where the hell I am. The last thing we need is for him to come back again and find Ariana naked in my bed.

"As much as I don't want to, we should probably get up. Need to check and make sure Doug's doing okay and..."

"Tell him about us," Ariana finishes for me with a tired sigh.

"Trust me, I'd much rather stay here snuggling with you than go tell a heartbroken werewolf that we've been sneaking around behind his back."

Ariana groans again and rolls over. My breath stutters at the sight of her beautiful face, her cheek pillow-creased and sleep flushed in a way that utterly charms me. Though, I feel a bit of guilt seeing the dark circles still present under her eyes. Dammit, I've gotta get my girl some rest.

"How about I go meet up with him while you sleep more?" I ask, stroking a strand of hair away from her eyes.

Her forehead crinkles as she frowns at my words. "What? No. I'm awake, and I want to be there. Doug needs to see us together if he's going to believe it's more than a sex thing. Besides, I want to make sure he's still doing okay. Shit, I should've already checked on him."

She pushes up on her arms and reaches to grab her phone from the bedside table, but I take her hand in mine and bring it to my lips. "He's okay. You don't need to be there for him 24/7, and no one expects you to except you."

"I know, it's just...I feel bad that I didn't check in and—"

I kiss her to stop her from spiraling. She lets out a little huff when our mouths part, but doesn't continue. "You're allowed to prioritize your own needs, Ari. In fact, I insist on it. So be a good girl and go do your morning routine. I'll check in with Doug and make you some coffee."

She laughs and shakes her head at my order. "Alright, *daddy*."

It takes all my willpower not to roll her onto her stomach and discipline her for her bratty tone, but if we start that, we'll never get out of bed. I'll file it away for later. My dick perks up as she slips out from under the covers, and I watch her ass jiggle as she walks to the bathroom. Hopefully not too much later. Gods, please let this conversation with Doug go alright so we can spend more time in my bed together before the weekend is over.

I know Ariana said she wants to move in together, and we'll have plenty of time together in bed then, but I'm greedy for more of her after months of hiding my feelings. My monster instincts tell me to barricade the doors and never let her leave. She thought I was kidding about keeping her trapped in my lair, but there's a not so insignificant part of me that screams at me to do just that.

Not that I ever would, despite the very selfish part of me that wishes she'd scale back her business and let me provide for her so I can have as much of her time as I want. So much more of me wants her to thrive and have the success she's dreamed of. My covetous, greedy beast will just have to be content with caring for her and supporting her as much as she'll allow.

Yes, I'm going to take care of my baby girl and give her everything she needs to shine. Starting with today's conversation with

Doug, then with finding her a godsdamned personal assistant, so she has some time to breathe.

Doug agrees to meet up with us for a late brunch at a diner owned by sisters who apparently are also part of the recently formed Moonvale coven. Their mega meat breakfast platter is one of Doug's favorite cheat day meals—partially because his wolf craves the protein and partially because he likes to joke that he's eating my distant cousins when he digs into the steak. I can only hope that he won't want to sub in minotaur for beef after he hears about me and Ariana.

While Ari gets ready to go out, I call a tow truck to take her car in for maintenance. She barely fights me on doing that for her, so she's either beginning to learn how to release her guilt about getting help or she's just too exhausted to argue. Either way, I'll take it.

She emerges from my bedroom as I'm pouring coffee into travel mugs, looking like a vision in an adorable light pink dress that hugs the curves of her belly and hips more than her usual baggy outfits. Her hair is pulled up into a ponytail, showing off her neck and the line of her cleavage peeking out from the neckline, and she's put on some makeup that highlights her sparkling green eyes and her plush lips.

"Godsdamn, baby girl," I say, letting my eyes drag up and down her body. I love all versions of Ariana, but this dress is especially nice. Makes me want to lift her up on the counter and bury my face between those juicy thighs.

"Don't look at me like that!" Ariana says, her pale cheeks flushing in a way that makes her even more enticing.

"Why not?" I ask with a grin, tugging her closer so I can run my hands across her hips and thighs.

She squeaks when I grab a handful of her ass. "Because I don't want to be a mess when we meet up with Doug!"

I release her and take a step back, grinning and holding my hands up in appeasement. "Okay, okay. I'll do my best to keep myself under control until we get back here."

"Good." Ariana shakes her head with a soft laugh and murmurs "horny monster" under her breath. I file that comment away to the list for her discipline later.

Before we head out the door, I put up my human glamor. Ariana practically pouts at the sight. "Am I really that ugly as a human?" I ask with a chuckle.

"No. You're super hot and you know it. But you're *too* pretty—it makes you look almost like you're fake. Which I mean, I guess you are, since that's not the real you."

"Hah! Never had anyone complain about me being too good looking. I don't control what I look like as a human—the glamor takes my minotaur appearance and translates it as best it can to a human. Not my fault I'm 'too pretty'." I strike a pose and give her my best smoulder, laughing when she rolls her eyes at me.

"Part of it is my annoying worry that I don't belong with someone that's model handsome. When you look like a minotaur, you're still gorgeous, but it's more approachable because you're not human. Plus, I really like your horns, and how soft and nice you are to touch. And how, uh... *big* you are."

"Oh, I know how much you like my impressive girth." I cup my cock through my jeans and give her a wink. "Still, there are perks to my human glamor. For one thing, I can kiss you a hell of a lot better like this."

"I like your kisses!" Ariana protests, but she sighs and melts in my arms when I bend down and press my lips to hers. Kissing feels good either way, but in my glamor I can slip my tongue deeper into her mouth without threatening to choke her, and there's a lot more finesse.

She whines softly when I pull away, clinging to my arms. "That *is* pretty nice, but I think I need to test it more to be sure."

I laugh and shake my head. "Later. We're going to be late if we keep going, and I thought you didn't want to be a mess when you see Doug. Grab your coffee and get in the car. If you behave, I'll show you how well I can kiss you other places like this."

26

ARIANA

As hot and bothered as I was right before we left for lunch, by the time we get to the restaurant, I'm sweating from nerves instead of arousal. Wesley gives me a hand to help me out of his absurdly fancy sports car that sits so low to the ground that I have to be careful not to flash people as I step out. He squeezes my hand reassuringly, and when he tries to let go, I cling to him. I know I'm being ridiculous, but the only thing keeping me from running away from the disastrous conversation heading our way is this tether to him.

"You alright, baby girl?" Wesley asks, cocking an eyebrow at me in concern. "If you're not ready to tell Doug, I can figure out how to deal with waiting longer. Or I can go in and tell him alone."

He's already offered that option, but I can't let him shoulder the responsibility and I certainly can't stomach keeping a secret from Doug after everything he's gone through lately.

"No. I'm okay. Maybe..." I look down at our joined hands, then back at his face. "Maybe we hold hands as we go in? Show him right away what's going on. Or is that stupid?"

He considers my proposal for a second, then nods. "We hold hands. I want everyone to see what you are to me. Not just Doug."

The thought sends a pleased thrill through me, followed by a reflexive gut clench of anxiety. I wasn't exaggerating when I said his human glamor intimidates me with how handsome it is. Having everyone at the restaurant see that we're together, that someone like me was able to bag such a hot guy, is a little terrifying.

Will they judge me? Will they judge him? Ugh, why the fuck do I even care?

Wesley doesn't give me any more time to spiral, bending down to kiss me on the cheek, then leading me by the hand toward the entrance. The door swings open and I immediately see Doug by the host stand. I almost yank away from Wes in the moment before my brother turns back toward us, but I shove the instinct down. Wes needs to know that I claim him as much as he claims me, and that means facing this head on.

My stomach lurches, but Doug smiles as he sees us. Fatigue is written across his features, but there's no sign of the distress he felt last night. "Hey! I put in my name. It should only be a minute or two." If he notices our joined hands, he doesn't react at all.

"Perfect. Uh, how you holding up, man?" Wesley sounds trepidatious as he asks the question, no doubt wondering why the hell Doug isn't commenting on us holding hands.

"Eh." Doug shrugs and lets out a heavy sigh. "Not great, but sure as fuck better than last night. I was so drained that I fell asleep as soon as I got back to my place. Means a lot to me that you both wanted to check in though even though you were up so late last night."

"It wasn't *that* late," I sputter, this time unable to stop myself from letting go of Wesley's hand. Shit, I need to get myself together.

Doug gives me a confused look, but the host saves me from explaining my weird protest. Wesley slides a hand onto my lower back as we walk and my skin burns, knowing that if Doug turned around, he could see the possessive way his best friend is touching me.

My brother slides into one side of the booth and I have a moment of panic trying to decide where to sit. Wes makes the decision for me, subtly guiding me with the hand still resting on my back to go to the side across from Doug. He scoots in next to me and grabs my thigh under the table, giving it a soft, reassuring squeeze. It doesn't make me feel any better, because it's all I can do not to blush thinking about that hand touching me other nearby places.

"Did Wes give you a ride?" Doug asks casually.

Is that suspicion in his voice or some kind of euphemism? Because technically I didn't ride Wesley's dick last night, but that was only because I was too weak and overcome with pleasure to do much more than take him. *God, stop thinking about his dick!*

Wesley's fingers dig into my thigh, attempting to get me to chill out. "Yeah. Got her car towed to the shop this morning, but I'm not sure when it'll be fixed, so I'll probably be giving her a ride for a while."

Now I know I'm turning red. I kick Wesley's leg under the table to get him to stop it with the innuendos, but smiles innocently at me.

"I can also drive you around if you need," Doug offers, and I'm infinitely grateful for his different choice of words. Was that intentional? Does he know that we were up all night fucking? *Oh god.*

I suck in a shallow breath and attempt a calm smile. "You both are sweet. I'll be okay. I'm usually holed up at my place, anyway. The only place I go regularly is the post office and I can have them do a mail pickup instead."

"Ooo, that'd give you an excuse to flirt with the cute mail guy." Doug waggles his eyebrows at me.

Wesley frowns at Doug, then turns to look at me. "What cute mail guy? You have a cute mail guy?"

"She's never told you about hot mail guy? Dude totally has a crush on her, but she doesn't believe me. I mean, the guy brings her mail directly to her doorstep rather than leaving it in the mailbox, and he gives her homemade cookies at least once a month. No one does that shit unless they're flirting."

"He doesn't like me! He's just nice." I protest, squirming as Wes pins me with his gaze and Doug chuckles at my denial.

Is Doug right? I thought my mailman Raf was bringing me the cookies because he had extra from his home baking experiments. Sure, he smiles at me and takes a moment to chat when he drops off the mail, but that's just because he can tell how much of a hermit I am. Right? Oh god, he does have a crush on me and I'm just oblivious. No wonder it took me so long to find out Wesley was interested in me.

"You have a hot mail guy who brings you cookies?" Wesley's frown deepens. "Not surprised he'd be interested, but he should ask you out if he's into you."

"You're one to talk!" I blurt. Horror sinks in a second later.

Doug's brow furrows in confusion. "What do you mean? Wesley asks people out all the time."

Wesley stiffens beside me and now he's the one that's panicking, judging by his rough tone when he replies. "Asking someone out and wanting a deeper connection isn't the same thing."

He's looking at Doug, but I can tell he's trying to reassure me. I'd be lying if I said the insecure part of me isn't cringing at the reminder of how many people Wesley's dated. It'll take time for me to not have that knee-jerk fear that he'll drop me for someone better, but I trust him when he says he's serious about us. Everything he's done over the past week has proven that again and again.

I'm a little surprised when Wesley turns his focus back on me instead of moving the conversation away from our dating lives. "Do you like him?"

I blink back at him, flustered. "Do I like who?"

"*Hot mail guy.*" Wesley sounds like he'll fight my mailman to eliminate any competition.

It's kind of hot in a caveman possessive way, but it's also so absurd that I have to hold back a laugh. "What? No!"

Doug holds his hands up appeasingly and shakes his head at us with a chuckle. "Relax! We don't have to talk about the hot mail guy. But that means you'll have to entertain us pathetic and lonely people with your exploits, Wes. Are you seeing anyone?"

The minotaur beside me and I freeze. *Fuck. This is it.*

"Yeah." Wes gives me a soft smile and holds my thigh in a tight grip.

"Dude, I need more details than that! What're they like? Are they a..." Doug looks around to make sure no one is listening. "Are they a monster? Oh! Is it that changeling who was flirting with you at the gym? Or maybe the barista that's always giving you drinks for free. What's their name?"

Not wanting to hear more about Wesley's list of romantic possibilities, I break. "It's me! He's seeing me!"

Doug blinks once. Twice. Then shakes his head with a low chuckle. "Man, you almost had me there. You two would never—"

"It's not a joke. Ariana and I are together." Wesley releases his grip on my thigh to bring his arm up and drapes it over my shoulders, pulling me in closer to his side.

Doug shakes his head in disbelief again. "There's no way." His eyes widen when Wesley leans down and kisses my cheek. My heart races and my face flames as I wait for Doug to say something. But he doesn't. Instead, he rests his elbows on the table and buries his face in his hands. His chest starts to shake.

Fuck, he's upset. A stream of words spill from my mouth in an attempt to placate my brother and calm him down. "It's only been for a week! That night at the escape room when you didn't show up...we realized some things." I keep my tone as even and soothing as possible, but Doug shakes even harder. "We wanted to make sure it wasn't just a fling before we told you. I know this is terrible timing with what happened with Margaret yesterday, but we didn't want to keep it from you any longer. Please don't be upset. I care about you both so much... I *love* you both so much."

"Upset?" Doug finally looks up at us, and I'm shocked to see that his face is twisted in amusement, not anger. He's laughing!

I scowl at my brother, my anxiety shifting to hurt. "We told you it's not a joke! Is it really that unbelievable that Wesley would want to be with me? God, I thought you of all people would be able to set fatphobic bullshit aside and see that I'm good enough for your best friend, but I guess not."

Wesley's brow furrows in concern. "Baby girl, you're a total catch. You're more than I ever dreamed of finding."

Doug's grin falters, his eyes wide with shock at how upset I am. "Whoa, whoa! That's not why I was laughing. Jesus, Ari, if anything, you're way out of this meathead's league."

My minotaur snorts at that comment and nods. "Got that right."

Doug's mouth twists as he takes in the adoring way Wesley's looking at me. "I was laughing because I've waited for the past six months for you two idiots to get your heads out of your asses and tell each other how you feel! I was worried it would never happen. You're both so stubborn and self-sacrificing." He lets out an amused sigh. "When Kelly had the idea to flake on the escape room and set you up on Valentine's Day, I went along with it even though I didn't think it'd work. Damn, I owe her fifty bucks."

I look back at my brother, mouth agape. We were so worried about telling him and he *knew* we were into each other? "What the hell, Doug? If you knew how much I liked Wesley and that he wanted me too, why didn't you say something?"

"I didn't know for sure. It seemed obvious, but I didn't want to make things weird on the off-chance that I was wrong. You guys are way too important to me to risk making things awkward." Doug pauses, narrowing his eyes at Wesley. "This isn't going to make things awkward, is it? If this is just a hookup for you, and you hurt my baby sister, you're dead to me. Ariana said she loves you, but you didn't—"

My stomach lurches. Oh god, I did tell him I love Wesley. I wasn't going to say anything because it felt crazy to confess after only being together a week, but I needed Doug to know how serious we are about our relationship.

Wesley cuts off Doug and my panicked thoughts. "Of course I fucking love her! I've loved her since that very first monster meeting you came to. She's everything to me." He turns and looks at me. "I love you, Ari."

Everything melts away at his proclamation and the fevered devotion shining in his eyes. My heart swells with so much love and appreciation for the glorious minotaur sitting next to me. "I love you too, Wes."

Uncaring about our surroundings or Doug watching us, Wesley claims my lips in a passionate kiss. I'm about to open my mouth to let his tongue inside, clinging to him and pressing closer, when Doug clears his throat.

"It's great that you love each other, but if this is going to work, I'm going to need you to put a limit on your makeout sessions in front of me. I'm happy for you, but I don't need to see my sister all breathless and ready to climb into your lap." Doug's face crinkles in disgust.

"Sorry!" I squeak, pulling away from Wesley as my cheeks burn from the call out. "We'll keep it to a minimum around you. But you... you mean it? You're okay with us being together?"

"Yeah, why wouldn't I be? You're perfect for each other. Wesley will force you to rest and have fun, and you'll keep his ego from getting too damn big."

"Too late for that," I say, giggling at the indignant huff Wesley lets out. It almost turns into a gasp when he pinches my thigh and gives me a look that says I'll pay for that comment later.

Wesley's expression sobers, and he focuses on Doug. "We really are perfect together. I promise you, I'll do everything in my power to make Ari happy. I'll cherish her and keep her safe."

Doug nods. "Good. You both deserve to be happy and loved." His face falls, and I reach out across the table to put my hand over his.

"You deserve that too, Doug. You'll find it."

He gives me a weak smile. "Yeah. You're right. I just hope it doesn't take me a whole damn year after meeting them to figure it out."

My chest squeezes at his forlorn tone that he tries to mask with humor. I hope it doesn't take a year for him either, but if it does, Wes and I are proof that amazing things are worth the wait.

27

WESLEY

The rest of our lunch goes by in a happy blur. Doug spends half of it making fun of us for how oblivious we'd been to each other's attraction. We all crack up when he reminds us of when we went to the beach and I almost had a heart attack helping Ariana put sunscreen on her back. Running my hands over her back and shoulders was one of my favorite memories to jerk off to. Thinking about the goosebumps that rose on her delicate skin and the way her breathing sped up was enough to make me come every time. I always felt like such a damn creep afterwards, but now I know that Ari was having the same thoughts.

Ariana and I take the jokes in stride, both too relieved that Doug is happy about our relationship to tell him to shut up. It doesn't hurt that discussing our cluelessness distracts Doug from thoughts of his breakup.

I can tell that he's worried about what will happen if Ari and I break up. We all are. Replacing a friendship with a romantic partnership is tricky, but in my soul, I know Ariana is it for me. Maybe it's foolish by human standards to invest my whole heart into this relationship so fast, but it's not for a minotaur. Hell, I've held off my instincts to claim Ariana for almost a year. We aren't moving too fast. I would've waited a lifetime for her, and now that she's mine, there would have to be a cataclysmic event to tear us apart.

I get Doug's promise not to skip our morning workouts this week, because I know this is going to be a rough time for him, despite his easy jokes and smiles right now. He needs something to keep him going each day while he works through his heartbreak. On his own, Doug offers to come help Ari on his lunch breaks, which to both his and my surprise, she accepts. Looks like both siblings are learning to lean into the support system we've created between the three of us, and I couldn't be happier.

Ariana almost nods off on the car ride back to my place, so I guide her to the bedroom as soon as we get inside. She licks her lips and gives me a sleepy, seductive smile. "Mmm, back in bed already?"

I laugh as she reaches out toward the fly of my jeans and dodge out of the way. "Yeah. My baby girl needs to take a nap."

Ariana's face scrunches in displeasure. "I'm not an actual baby that needs to be told to take a nap." She immediately follows her words with an enormous yawn.

I raise a brow at her. "Could have fooled me." My cock twitches to life at her bratty tone, but she's way too tired for me to give her the punishment that's been brewing. Not before she gets some rest.

She sits up and scrubs her face with her hands. "Fine, if you don't want to fuck me, then I'll work on some stuff." Tension suffuses her body and her eyes widen. "*Shit.* I haven't checked my emails at all today. I need to follow up with that vendor and check on my shop orders."

Placing my hand in the center of her chest, I gently push her back onto the bed. "No. You need to rest."

She glares up at me in exasperation. "I can't take a nap! I'm all for the daddy roleplay, but I'm an adult woman with adult shit that needs to get done."

This is a turning point for us. Do I let it go and allow her to exhaust herself even more because she's too stubborn to let herself take a break? Or do I dig my hooves in?

The dark circles under her eyes make the decision for me. I snatch her phone away from where it sits next to her on the bed and shove it into my pocket. "Take. A. Nap. Your business can wait a few more hours and if you don't rest, you're going to burn out. You're setting boundaries with your work, starting now."

"You can't just proclaim that! I decide when that starts," she protests.

"Not anymore. We agreed that I'm your daddy, Ari. That means that it's my job to take care of you. Not just during sex." I increase the pressure of my palm on her chest, observing her expression to see if I've pushed too far. She lets out a shuddering sigh and some of her indignant tension releases under the weight of my palm.

Good.

Ariana's submissive side needs this as much as I do. I don't pretend to know everything that's best for her, but I sure as hell can figure out when she needs to rest before she completely collapses. I lock my eyes on hers and deepen my voice. "That's better. I already have a list of things to discipline you for. Do you want to make your punishment worse? Or will you be a good girl and get some sleep?"

She furrows her brow in a weak show of frustration, but the fight has already bled out of her. "I..."

When she doesn't say anything else, I continue. "Use your safeword and I'll let it go. Whatever you decide is okay with me." The second part of that is a bit of a stretch. I won't be upset with her, but I don't think there's any way I can stop myself from worrying about Ari. That worry has no bearing on my respect for her decision. What matters most to me is that she gets to choose. She's the one that's in control, no matter how much I command her.

Ariana's pupils expand at the mention of her safeword, and I watch her silently as she grapples with the decision. After a minute, she nods. "Okay."

My hand moves from her chest to stroke up her neck and then up to her ponytail, where I ease the elastic off. She groans when I sink my fingers into her loose waves, massaging her scalp. At first, her breathing speeds up, and she squirms a little as my other hand digs into her hair. I file away the knowledge that this turns her on with a smile.

Eventually, she relaxes further and my heart squeezes with love and pride when she falls asleep. I reluctantly remove my hands from her hair and ease myself off the bed. I'd love to lie here with her while she sleeps, but there's more I need to do today. Ariana rolls over onto her side and the sound of gentle snoring fills the room, so I have a feeling she'll be out for a while.

Once I've left her peacefully sleeping in my bedroom, I head to the living room and pull up the monster support group chat on my phone. There's a chance Ari isn't going to be happy with me for taking the initiative on something for her business without asking her, but she's needed an assistant for months and hasn't found the time to look for one. She can be mad at me all she wants, as long as it ends with her being able to manage her workload better.

Wesley: This may be a long shot, but do any of you know someone looking for part-time work?

Susan: Where at? Your office? There's no way I'm asking someone I know to become a corporate stooge. I don't care how much they pay you.

I chuckle at the harpy's hypocritical distaste for my job. Susan works at a company even bigger than mine, but she loves to rant about how corporate culture is destroying our lives.

Wesley: No, it's for my girlfriend. Her online shop is taking off, and she needs a personal assistant. Figured I'd check with you first since some of the work will be at her place, and there's no way I want some rando in her home alone with her.

Nik: Your girlfriend?

I can't tell if Nik forgot my confession about being with Ariana at our meeting, or if he's pretending not to know.

Wesley: Ariana. Doug's sister.

Sage: Oh, she's such a sweetheart! I wish I knew someone to help her out. I just ordered one of her cat hoodies for my partner. She's so talented. Please tell her I'm a fan of her art. Or I can tell her myself. We should have a party to celebrate you getting together!

Susan: Why? It's not like they're engaged.

Nik: A party sounds like a great idea.

I can easily imagine the bear shifter's chipper tone as he completely ignores Susan's negativity. He's a pro at trying to keep a conversation going despite her jibes.

Sage: Yay! Look at your calendar and let me know what dates work for you.

Ren: Will there be any other humans at this party?

Susan: Ugh, dude, you've got to chill. You're so thirsty for humans, it's getting weird.

Ren: There's nothing weird about looking for a mate. Tomas and Max found humans, and now Wesley too.

Max: What's this about a party?

Sage: We're throwing a party for Wesley and his new girlfriend, Ariana.

Sage: Wait. Does Doug know you're together?

Susan: @Doug you know Wesley banging your sister, right?

Gods, really Susan? I wish she could feel my glare through the phone.

Doug: Yes. Please stop talking about them banging. I know they're together and I'm cool with it.

Doug: A party would be nice.

As sweet as the offer to throw us a new relationship party is, I let out a frustrated sigh. A party isn't going to help Ariana be any less busy.

A few minutes pass as Sage and Nik discuss options for party themes, while Susan interjects with snarky comments. I don't want to seem like an ungrateful jerk, so I hold off from directing the conversation back to finding a personal assistant. Thankfully, Tomas pops in and does it for me.

Tomas: I'll ask Caleb about helping Ariana. His job is freelance and very flexible, and he mentioned wanting to find something else to do with his time. Does she need any help with accounting, too?

Wesley: I'll check, but I think she needs help anywhere she can get it. Her business exploded in popularity and she's doing her best to keep her head above water, but it's too much for one person. Thank you for checking with Caleb. He'd be perfect if he's available!

A minute later, I get a separate text from Tomas.

Tomas: Hey! I didn't want to mention this with the group, but Caleb working with Ariana would be great. It's not that he needs the money—though he wouldn't say no to some kind of compensation. It's just, he's anxious around new people, and is having a really hard time making connections with other humans in the area. I mentioned spending time with Max's partner, Mona, but he felt too awkward about "bothering" her. Having a job to do while he's spending time with Ariana might make it easier for him to connect. Please don't tell Caleb I brought this up. I'd selfishly keep him all to myself, but I know he wants more friends.

Oh man, I knew Caleb was shy, but I didn't realize it was that bad. No wonder my texting him so much freaked him out. Caleb is such a nice guy. I know Ariana would love him.

I try not to get too excited about the prospect, but he could be exactly what Ariana needs.

Wesley: I won't say anything to him. I think it'd be great for Ariana, too. Have Caleb text me if he's interested. That is, if he hasn't blocked my number after my questions about the magic lube.

Tomas: Haha he was definitely flustered, but I think it made him happy to have someone new to talk to. Fingers crossed, he likes the idea of working for Ariana as much as we do.

Only fifteen minutes pass before I get a message from Caleb letting me know he's interested in the job and to have Ariana text him with details so they can see if he's a good fit. I already know he is, but I pretend that she'll want to vet him.

I set my phone down with an excited grin plastered on my face. My chest swells with pride at finding a potential solution to some of Ariana's stress. Now I just have to tell her the good news and hope she doesn't get mad I asked around without checking with her first. If words won't appease her, maybe I can coax her to an understanding in another way.

28

ARIANA

When I rouse from my nap, it takes me a second to get my bearings, wondering if I've slept into the night by how dark the room is. The headache from lack of sleep that was brewing before Wesley compelled me to rest is gone, and something warm and solid is pressed against my back.

"Mmm, you're awake," Wesley purrs. The minotaur lying behind me strokes his fingers idly along my thighs. He plays with the hem of my dress, dipping his fingertips underneath but not straying any higher. "How do you feel?"

There's a part of me that wants to make a snarky complaint about my forced nap, but I feel too good. He must've been touching me for a while before I woke, because when I shift, I notice how wet I am. A fantasy of him sneaking into bed with me, and using my body while I sleep floods my mind. Why is that so hot? I flush, wondering if he can read my dirty thoughts and if he'd be interested in that kind of play. Being with Wes has awoken a number of strange and exhilarating needs that I didn't even know I had.

My skin prickles as he moves his hand up to caress my stomach. His lazy touch isn't inherently sexual, but it makes me want him all the same.

"G-good," I say, the word a breathy sigh as he skims his hand just underneath my breasts. I attempt to push away my horny thoughts as the sleep fog fades, but in their wake comes harsh reality.

My stomach sinks. I took a nap when I should've been catching up on work, and now I have to pay the price. "What time is it?"

"A little after 7. I checked on you a few times, but you were out cold."

Anxiety surges through me, and I push myself up and out of his hold. "What?! You let me sleep for *three* hours?" I shouldn't have let him talk me into this. It felt so nice to let him take charge, but that was obviously a mistake. "Next time, wake me up! Shit, I need to go home."

Wesley sits up next to me and rests his hand on the back of my neck. "Breathe, baby girl. You needed the rest. Let's have some dinner and discuss a plan of action for the week." He massages my neck, and the even, deep rumble of his voice helps diminish some of my panic. "I promise you didn't make things worse by getting much needed sleep. I wouldn't do that to you."

I turn myself around to face him with a slight frown. "A plan of action?"

"Yeah. I do a lot of project management in my job. So consider me not only your stunningly handsome and amazing sex god boyfriend, but your new business consultant. Don't worry. My services will be completely free of charge. Unless you want to add in some roleplay where you get on your knees in exchange for—"

I shove against his chest with a scoff, and he laughs, grabbing my hand and bringing it up to his snout for a kiss.

"Here's the deal. I know I can be domineering—it's part of my nature and general personality. But I'm not arrogant enough to think that I'm always right or I can jump in and be the hero."

"You're not?"

He nips at my finger with his blunt teeth, and I giggle in surprise. "Nope. Let me finish, I'm trying to be serious."

"Wow, there's a first time for everything," I say, unable to keep my snark at bay.

"Careful, baby girl. What did I tell you about being a brat?"

"Sorry, I couldn't help it." I take a deep breath and sober my expression. "No more jokes. I'm listening."

Wesley narrows his eyes at me like he doesn't quite believe me, but continues. "I have ideas for how I can help you balance your business and personal life, but say the word at any time and I'll back off. You don't want me involved with your work, I won't be. You don't want me to set boundaries to help you rest, I won't. You're in charge, Ari. Yeah, I'll be really fucking happy if you give me the chance to try to help make your life easier. But I'll also be happy just being by your side at all."

His tone is so earnest and loving that I can't resist wrapping my arms around him and pulling him into a hug. His apple spice scent envelops me as he holds me against his chest and lets out a soft sigh.

"Thank you," I murmur. "I want you to help. I just don't want to be a burden."

Wesley huffs, ruffling my hair, and holds me tighter. "You will *never* be a burden. I've waited my whole life to have someone to spoil and take care of."

I pull back a bit to search his face. "You sound like you want a trophy wife or a pet. You know that's not me, right?"

"Oh, I know." Wes chuckles and squeezes my arm. "That's why this thing between us works—we both know that you don't need saving. I may pretend to be your daddy, but you're enough on your own to do anything you set your mind to. You're *brilliant,* Ari. So when I say I want to spoil you, it's because I want to help you shine even brighter."

Tears well in my eyes at my magnificent minotaur's unwavering confidence in me. I swallow down the lump of emotion in my throat, and grin at him even as a tear slides down my cheek. "The fact that helping me makes your dick hard doesn't factor in at all?"

Wesley reaches up and swipes the tear away, and heat pools in my belly as a wicked smile stretches across his lips. "I never said that."

My eyes fall to his lap where his cock strains against his jeans. I lick my lips. "Want me to help you out with that?"

He laughs and shakes his head. "Not yet. Get me even more worked up by letting me run some ideas by you during dinner."

Turns out, Wesley's help is less brainstorming and more concrete steps he's taken to help me. I bristle when he tells me that he asked his friends about finding me an assistant, but when he explains that Tomas' mate is interested, I can't stay too mad at him. Yes, he should've asked first—I tell him he's not allowed to do that again.

But having an assistant who we already know is trustworthy and nice would be an incredible help, and it's exhilarating to have a problem that I've avoided for months potentially resolved. The perpetual knot of stress in my stomach eases at the prospect of *finally* having help.

While I'm embarrassed at first to divulge all of the things that I'm falling behind on or unable to tackle, along with my neverending to-do list, it also feels like a weight is lifted off my chest just by letting someone else know what's going on. I've tried to hide how much I'm struggling, but I guess I wasn't doing a great job because Wesley doesn't balk at anything I mention.

Talking business with Wes is surprisingly easy. I knew he was smart, but he has a lot more business acumen than I realized. I wrongly assumed his success was due more to his charisma and good looks than practical skills. But my minotaur isn't just a beef-cake bro, he's a wealth of knowledge. By the time we're done with dinner, I have action plans for a few of my biggest pain points, broken into steps that are manageable for even my overloaded schedule.

For the first time since starting my shop, I accept that I can't be perfect at every aspect of my business. I'm creative and intelligent, but I'm mediocre at best when it comes to strategic planning and time management. Not to mention that I'm complete shit at separating work from my personal life. It'll take a while for me to not feel like any shortcomings are a reflection of my worth, but at least I see that I'm hurting myself and my business by stubbornly clinging to the idea that I can do it all without help.

Wesley pulls me into a hug after we finish clearing the dishes, and I sink into his embrace, tucking my chin against his chest. "I'm so proud of you, baby girl," he murmurs against my hair.

I feel lighter than I can ever remember. Hopeful and excited about my business in a way I haven't been since I first started it. All thanks to him. Happy, relieved tears well in my eyes. "Thank you. I love you so much. I… I don't know if I've said it yet, but I'm here for you for whatever you need, too. I know you have your shit together, and I'm a mess, but I take care of the people I love."

"I know, angel. I saw everything you did for your brother, and I have no doubt that when I need your support, you'll be there for me." Wesley rubs his snout against my hair, letting out a contented sigh. After a few more seconds he releases the hug, and levels his steady, slightly stern gaze on me. "You're not a mess. You're in a huge transition in your life. Don't compare yourself to me. In case you forgot, I'm almost ten years older than you. I've had a lot more time than you to find my footing."

Warmth suffuses me at his reassurance, but I can't help teasing him. "True, you are pretty damn old…"

"That's it. Time for daddy to teach you some manners after how bratty you've been today. "

I squeal as he scoops me up and throws me over his shoulder. "Wait!" I flail against his hold feebly, but he laughs and grips me tighter. God, I'll never get over how *strong* he is. There's no escaping Wesley as he strides to the bedroom and deposits me on the edge of the bed.

The dark intensity in his gaze has my pulse racing. "Daddy, I was good! I took a nap and talked through stuff for my business."

"True, but you've also been a snarky little brat all day. You don't think I should let you get away with such rude behavior, do you?"

I reach forward and grab his thighs, attempting to beseech him for lenience. He's hard, the girth of his cock looking even more erotic framed by my small hands. "I was just teasing, daddy. I can make it up to you." I slide one of my hands in to palm his length, fluttering my eyelashes as I gaze up at him.

His stern expression shows no sign of my touch or begging affecting him, but his cock jerks in my hold. "I don't want to encourage bad behavior, sweetheart. Now, because you were good, I'll only give you ten."

I open my mouth to protest, but he cuts me off with a shake of his head. "If you argue, I'll give you twenty."

Though I'm nervous about his discipline, I'm secretly thrilled at the thought of Wes spanking me again. I never knew I was into any kind of pain, but last time it made me needy and desperate to come. I'm sure Wesley knows that—he's only doing this because we'll both enjoy it, not as an actual punishment. At least that's what I assumed until he continues.

"I'll give you twenty, and when I'm done you'll have to suck daddy's cock and drink down his cum, but you won't be allowed to touch yourself or come."

"What? Daddy, that's not fair!"

Wesley gives me a cruel smile that makes me shiver, then sits beside me on the bed.. "Last warning. You're going to lie across daddy's lap and take your punishment without argument. If you don't, you know the consequences."

Part of me that wants to push him and take this game between us somewhere unexplored, reveling in the thought of him using me and leaving me wanting. But at my core, pleasing him is a much stronger urge. I *want* to be my daddy's good girl.

"Yes, daddy," I say softly, then maneuver myself so that I'm lying over his legs. Wes grunts as I wriggle my way into position, my hips raised up slightly by the bulk of his body. Heat suffuses me at the press of his stiff cock against my low belly.

"That's better." Wesley tugs the hem of my dress up to expose my panties. He rubs a hand in large circles around each globe of my ass, his fingertips dipping in ever so briefly to stroke the gusset of my panties. I do my best not to squirm or spread my legs, knowing that he might take that as me misbehaving.

When his fingers hook under the elastic of my panties and he tugs them down to my thighs, my stomach clenches in anticipation. He removes his touch and I wait for what feels like ages, cheeks burning at the thought of him staring down at my huge, cellulite dimpled ass. I know Wesley likes my body, but he's never spent so much time examining it.

"D-daddy," I whimper, when I can't stand the wait any longer.

"So fucking beautiful," Wesley groans, finally returning his hand to my ass, giving it an appreciative squeeze. "Are you ready, baby girl?"

I nod into the blanket my cheek is resting on. "Yes, daddy."

He lets out a rumble of approval. "Count for me."

29

WESLEY

Ariana lets out another breathy "yes, daddy," her body tensing as she waits for my first strike. I can't help torturing her a bit longer, stretching out her anticipation as I stare down at her luscious pale ass, ready to be marked by me. Her breathing speeds up, and when it seems she's about to beg me to do something, I bring my hand down onto the center of one cheek. The flesh of her ass jiggles beautifully at the impact, and Ari sucks in a sharp breath, her hips instinctively trying to pull away.

"O-one," she says, her voice already shaky. The second my hand connected with her body, it frayed her already strained composure.

I'm not sure she'll be able to handle ten, judging by how wrecked she sounds.

"Good girl," I murmur, soothing the red spot with my palm for a moment, before pulling back and spanking her other ass cheek.

Ariana gasps and attempts to wriggle away, but I hold her in place with an arm banded over her lower back. I take a moment to admire the twin red marks as she counts the second strike, suppressing a groan when I lift my hand to give a third and she flinches, pressing her stomach against my aching cock.

Shit, I'm not sure if *I'll* be able to handle ten.

My balls are ready to burst after spending the evening helping her. She's absolutely right—caring for Ariana is an extreme turn-on for me. There's something incredibly sexy about a woman so capable and hardworking allowing me in. It strokes my ego and makes my dick hard to know that she trusts me.

I do the next two spanks in quick succession, rushing a little in my eagerness. I'll stretch things out and savor it next time, but tonight I'm too worked up to wait much longer.

Ariana whimpers as I dig my fingers into the supple flesh of her ass, pressing into the marks I've made, then quickly blurts out the count before I chide her for forgetting. Her thighs are already glistening with her wetness, and her heady arousal perfumes the air, fogging my mind with lust.

"Did you learn your lesson?" I ask, my voice strained with need.

Ari squirms in my lap, her ass pressing subtly up into my touch as I skirt my hand along her inner thighs. "Y-yes. I did. P-please daddy, I need—ah!"

She cries out in shock as my next spank lands on her pussy. I keep the impact light, but she still jolts beneath me like my hand is electrified. I grip her hips to hold her in place, but it's not necessary. She's spreading her legs and presenting herself to me for another.

"Five," she gasps. Her body tenses for more, but I don't spank her again. Instead, I press two fingers to her sopping cunt and thrust them inside, sliding my other hand under her belly to stroke her clit.

Her moan sends a thrill through me. I love that I can make her desperate with just a few spanks. "Such a good girl. Your little pussy needs daddy too much for him to ignore it any longer."

"Th-thank you, daddy." Ariana gasps as I fuck her hard and fast with my fingers, rubbing rough circles on her clit with my thumb. She starts to shake as I assault her g-spot, and tries to squirm away even as her channel flutters around my fingers.

"Don't fight it. Soak me, baby girl."

Ariana cries out my name, and her tension breaks as she comes on my fingers, wetness gushing out of her and onto my hands and lap. There's something so primal and erotic about Ariana squirting all over me. It infuses me with pride that she trusts me enough to let go of her inhibitions. Pride that makes my cock so hard against the fly of my jeans, I worry I'm going to have a permanent indent from the zipper if I don't release it.

When she's come down from her orgasm, I slide Ariana off my lap and make quick work of removing my clothes. She follows suit, tugging her dress off over her head and tossing her bra to the floor. She goes to the bedside drawer and pulls out the jar of magic lube without my prompting, unceremoniously scooping some out and pressing her slick fingers into her entrance.

I raise a brow at her, stroking my dick as I watch her prepare herself for me. "So certain you're getting daddy's cock."

"No, daddy," Ariana says, shaking her head but not stopping her fingers as she coats herself with lube. "I just wanted to make sure I was ready. Your cock looks so hard, it must hurt. I want to be your good girl and make my hole ready whenever you need it."

Gods, I'm going to bust my load if she keeps saying such filthy things. I squeeze my cock tight in my grip and take a deep breath. "Hmm, it is such a pretty pussy. Such a nice, tight human hole for daddy's bull cock."

I adore the way the mention of our size difference makes her breath stutter. "Y-yes. My pussy belongs to you, daddy." Ariana moves her fingers to toy with her clit, her other hand pinching her nipple as she watches me fist my cock.

"On your back, sweetheart. Spread your legs for daddy," I command.

She obeys, giving me enough space to kneel between her thighs. Ariana keeps rubbing her clit, gasping as I grab her legs and press them toward her chest.

Fuck, she looks incredible like this—her glistening pussy spread wide and the folds and curves of her stomach painting a lush, sinful picture. It only gets better when I line my cock up with her entrance and the tip sinks in with little resistance.

"Mmm, this little hole was made for daddy's cock." We both moan as I press in slowly, and I monitor her expression for any sign of discomfort. She rubs her clit, eyes wide as she watches my cock stretch her obscenely. "You see how good you look taking me, don't you, dirty girl?"

"Oh god, yes. Yes, daddy. You're so big, you feel...oh!" Ariana's words break off with a cry as my piercing rubs against her front wall, her pussy clamping down hard around my cock. She's so tight and slick that I know it won't be long before I lose myself inside her.

I set a slow pace, thrusting down into the overwhelming pleasure of her gripping wet heat, then pulling back out in a long drag as her cunt clings to my cock. Ariana's eyes stay locked on where we're joined, and she moans over and over as I pump inside her. My gaze bounces between her pleasure-twisted face, her stomach and breasts, and my length disappearing inside her, a visual feast that's pushing me rapidly toward the edge.

My grip on her thighs tightens as I pick up the pace, pumping into her with more force. It's not long before Ariana's pussy flutters around me and she cries out. "Y-you're going to make me come, d-daddy."

"Good girl. Come for me," I rasp, futilely attempting to ride out her orgasm before succumbing to my own.

It's too late. I'm too far gone. My balls draw up, ready to unload at any second. "Time for daddy to fill you up. Put his cum where it belongs."

"Please, daddy, *yes*," Ariana begs, and I give myself over to her, coming with a bellowing shout. Pleasure boils from my balls up the shaft of my cock as I press myself as deep inside her as I can, and hot jets of my cum splash inside her as she moans filthy encouragement.

I stroke her clit while I unload, and she tenses and comes around my cock again, her cunt squeezing the rest of my load out until she's so full that some of it seeps out. I'm suddenly envious of shifters with knots—a primal part of me doesn't want any drop of my cum escaping her sweet pussy.

Though, I do love the glorious mess I make of her when I pull out and my still hard cock slaps onto the cushion of her belly. My hand on her thigh keeps her body folded, and my excess release trails down her belly and pools between her breasts. Yes, coated with my cum is as good as plugged up with it. Maybe even better.

I place a kiss on her calf and finally release my grip on her, letting her relax into a more comfortable position. "Don't move," I command, getting up and grabbing my phone from the dresser behind me.

She smiles up at me with languid satisfaction as I return,

trailing one hand through the mess I've made on her stomach and tits.

I swipe open the camera app on my phone. "Can I take a picture of you, sweetheart?"

Her eyes widen. "What? Why?"

"Because I need you to see how fucking gorgeous you look right now, and I want something for when you're too busy to come over and let to do this to you again."

Ariana flushes and bites her lower lip, inadvertently making herself look even sexier. "I… Okay. But if I don't like how I look, promise to delete it."

I hold my phone up and center my beautiful, debauched Ariana in the frame. "I promise. Spread your pussy open with your fingers so we can see how well you stretched for me, baby girl."

Ariana's flush deepens, but she obeys. I groan at the sight of her stretched cunt dripping with my cum, then snap a few photos. The pictures don't hold a candle to reality, but they're pretty fucking hot.

I join her on the bed and hold my phone out for her to inspect them, but she covers her eyes with her hand and groans. "I'm not sure I want to see."

"You don't have to look. If it makes you uncomfortable, I'll delete them right now and you never have to see them. Though I have to say…it would be a damn shame."

With a heavy exhale, Ariana drops the hand from her eyes and looks at my phone screen. "Oh."

I worry that I've made a mistake, but she takes the phone from my hand to get a closer look. "I look so…*dirty*." She chuckles weakly. "You really wrecked me, didn't you?"

"You look like daddy's perfect girl," I say, gripping the back of her neck possessively. "Do you like it?"

"I...I can't believe I'm saying this, but yeah. I look like a filthy slut covered in your cum, but it's hot. Really hot."

"Told you." I'm unable to keep my smugness out of my tone.

She shakes her head at my self-satisfaction and hands the phone back. "You can keep it. Might be useful when I need a reminder that I'm not a total gremlin."

Immediately, I think of all the ways I can tease her with these photos, and my dick twitches with interest. I know she loves when I praise her, but I wonder, given her choice of words when she looked at the photo...

"Do you like being degraded, Ari? Do you want to be daddy's slut sometimes, and not just his good girl?"

"Maybe..." Her breath hitches as I thumb her nipple. "Is that weird?"

"Not at all, baby girl. We're two consenting adults and as long as we both enjoy it, that's all that matters." I'm partial to praising and spoiling her, but some degradation would also be fun if she's into it.

I lean over and bring my lips to her ear. "You said you want me to use you whenever I need. Do you want to be my little cumslut?"

"Y-yes, daddy," Ariana whispers.

"Such a naughty girl. You're a mess." I scoop up some of the cum on her chest with my fingers and bring them to her lips. "Clean it up. Be a good little slut and show daddy how much you love his cum, and maybe he'll give you some more."

Her pupils dilate as she opens her mouth and sucks my fingers inside, her tongue laving them until they're clean. I pull them out with a wet pop and tug her lower lip down with my thumb. She opens for me and sticks her tongue out without my prompting, and fuck me, it's so sexy I want to come all over her eager tongue and pouty lips. I feed her more of my cum, groaning as she swallows and licks her lips.

"Thank you, daddy," she says coyly, batting her eyelashes as she looks at me.

I'd thought I'd be responsible and drive her home after her punishment, but there's no fucking way that's happening now. Not when she looks at me like *that*. I need to learn better restraint so I can be the daddy she needs, but tonight, all I care about is giving my dirty girl what we both want.

30

ARIANA

"You're a menace," Wesley huffs, attempting to catch his breath after his latest round of rutting into me, as I tease his semi-hard cock with a playful stroke.

I laugh and move my hand away. "Are you tired already, daddy?"

"How are you *not* tired?" he asks with a raspy laugh, bringing his hand down to grab my ass and tug me against his chest. I wince as my sticky skin presses against his short fur, hoping we won't get glued together like this, but as I've learned, Wes doesn't give a shit about bodily fluids or mess. In fact, he probably loves the feel of my sweat and cum soaked skin.

You'd think he'd be equally gross, with how he exerted himself fucking me, but pressed up against him and my face dangerously close to his armpits, he smells good. A little more musk in the spice of his normal scent, but it screams sex in the best way to my lizard brain.

No wonder I used to get turned on when I saw Wesley after he'd been working out with Doug. It's some kind of damn minotaur pheromones. "You smell too good. It keeps making me horny," I mumble into his chest.

He laughs even harder, his chest reverberating against my cheek. "Then I guess it's time to take a shower. Actually, I'll take a shower and you take a bath. Don't want you to tempt me again."He groans dramatically. "I thought it would be impossible, but I think you drained me dry."

I did go pretty hard on earning my role as his cumslut, going down on him after he called me that, then begging for him to fill me up twice more. Now that we're coming down from the rush of sex, I feel like I should be embarrassed, but instead I'm oddly proud of myself. Who knew kinky roleplay could help me appreciate myself more?

"Fine, but only because I think I might pass out if I come again," I say, realizing how drained and sore I am now that the high of multiple orgasms is fading.

Wesley gives me a sheepish smile. "I wasn't the best daddy tonight, but I couldn't help it. You're too damn sexy."

"Dude, we're making up for a year of suppressing our attraction to each other. It's okay that you wanted to fuck me instead of being 'responsible'. We'll figure out the balance."

He cocks a brow at me. "Dude?"

"Yeah. Anything else I call you right now will sound too hot." I giggle when he gives me an even more incredulous look.

"Alright, *dude*, get your ass in the tub," Wesley says, rolling his eyes at me.

"Eww, it sounds weird when you say it to me!" I scrunch my nose in exaggerated displeasure.

Wesley huffs and pinches my ass, causing me to squeal and pull away from him. His eyes fill with heat as I stand and move out of reach, and I watch as his cock begins to swell. "On second thought, maybe I'm not completely drained."

"Now who's the menace?" I ask, eyebrows raising in surprise.

He reaches out to grab my hip, but I dart away toward the bathroom. I laugh in delight as he lets out a low growl and stands to give chase. I run into the shower, but before I can close the glass door behind me, he's there, pressing me inside and against the cool tile.

"Wes," I gasp as he turns on the water and drops his mouth to my breast as his other hand palms the other.

He pulls off my nipple and sinks to his knees in front of me, water cascading over his shoulders. "You're right. We're making up for lost time. There'll be time for temperance and self-discipline later. Right now, I need you again."

I grab onto his horns to steady myself and sigh as his wide tongue swipes against my clit. I'm not sure we'll ever stop needing each other, but I couldn't care less right now.

Over the next few months, we learn through trial and error how to strike a balance between desire and responsibility. It's tempting to allow myself to sink into the bliss of being with Wesley and ignore everything else. I never thought I'd be the kind of girl who'd throw away her goals because of some good dick and the general excitement of a new relationship. But the joy of spending time with him is a stark enough contrast to the stress of my daily life that part of me wants to say fuck it, close my shop, and be his baby girl around the clock.

I don't do that, of course. I've worked too hard to give up on what I've built, and it means too much to me. No, I don't quit. Instead, I adjust.

It's hard and exhausting, but slowly I start to see the light at the end of the tunnel. Partially because of my own work, partially because of Wesley's help with planning and setting boundaries, but mostly because of Caleb.

Wesley jokes that I love Caleb more than him, and I don't argue. Sure, I love my minotaur more than I can even express, but Caleb? He's a miracle in a steadfast, hilarious package. I think we might be friend soul mates, if such a thing exists. That first day he showed up at my place with a box of donuts and a nervous smile on his face, acting like I was doing him a favor by having him help me with my shop, I knew he was perfect. And for some weird reason, he likes me just as much. Yes, he works for me, and does a damn good job, but he's also quickly become one of my best friends.

It doesn't hurt that we can swap stories about how weird our monster mates are. We're chatting on a rainy afternoon after we've finished our work for the day, when we finally address one of the few topics we haven't broached.

"So...we're friends, right?" Caleb asks, then takes a sip of his coffee. He sounds casual, but there's tension in his posture.

My stomach clenches with sudden nerves. "Yeah. I mean, I think so. Unless you secretly hate me and pretend to enjoy talking to me so you can get mediocre pay as my shop assistant and accountant."

He laughs, some of his messy brown hair falling into his eyes as he shakes his head. "Yes. We're friends. Unless *you* secretly hate me and are only putting up with me because I'm good at doing your accounting."

My eyes widen and I grab his hand. "No! You're the best! I would die without you." I'm not sure if we're at the point in our friendship where I can break his personal bubble, so quickly pull my hand back with a sheepish smile. "Sorry, not to be dramatic. But yeah, friends."

Caleb pretends to wipe sweat from his brow, but there's some genuine relief in his eyes. "Whew, okay."

A few awkward moments pass as we quietly sip our coffee. Usually silence between us is comfortable, but I get the sense he was going somewhere with his question other than confirming our friendship.

"Is that all you were going to ask?" I prompt.

"Oh! Yeah. Does..." A flush peeks out from beneath Caleb's cropped beard, and he takes a long time before he continues, like he's debating whether he should say something or not. "Does Wesley have a thing for, uh, coming on you?"

That's not at all what I was expecting. My eyebrows shoot up. "Uh, what?"

"I'm not asking to be a perv!" Caleb's flush spreads down his neck as he tries to explain the strange question. "It's just... I don't know anyone else with a monster partner, and I was curious if it was just a mothman thing or..."

Now that the initial shock has worn off, I laugh. We've never talked about sex, and I never brought it up because I'm his employer, but I've been very curious. "No, uh, it's not." I decide to venture a bit more information because I'm dying to know more. "I swear Wes would make me walk around covered in his jizz if he could."

Caleb lets out a choked laugh. “Oh my god, why is that? Not that I mind when Tomas... but like... I can’t go around like that!”

“I tried to get Wes to explain, but all he could say is he ‘needs’ to do it.” I roll my eyes, and Caleb laughs harder.

“There seem to be a lot of things monsters ‘need’ to do. Sometimes I wonder if they don’t play it up, so us gullible humans go along with it. Not that I’m complaining about my sex life. Uh, that’s...” Caleb rubs the back of his neck. “Sorry, is this weird to talk about? I don’t want you to feel uncomfortable.”

“Dude, I didn’t ever bring up monster sex because I thought it’d be weird for me to ask! Please talk to me about this. My friend Kelly is a witch, so she knows about monsters, but she’s a lesbian with a strong aversion to any conversations that involve dicks.”

“Oh damn, yeah, that’d be a problem, given how, uh, prominent our monsters’ dicks are.” Caleb makes a circle with his hands and then snorts.

“Wait, *really*?” My eyes threaten to pop out of my head as I look at the circumference he’s demonstrating. Caleb nods. “Holy shit. I mean, I knew Wes got the magic lube from you but, Tomas is *that* big?”

“Yeah, apparently one of the things mothmen share with actual moths is that their dicks are enormous proportional to the rest of their body.” He clears his throat. “Thankfully, they don’t, uh, deposit eggs like moths do.”

“Oh god, I’d never even thought about that. I wonder if any monsters do have eggs...” I can’t decide if the idea grosses me out or turns me on. “I wish I knew some other humans dating monsters so I could ask, but we seem to be rare, what with the whole ‘monsters hiding in the shadows’ thing.”

Caleb thinks for a moment. “There’s Mona, Max’s partner. I’ve talked to her a few times, but she seemed way too cool and hot for me to attempt being her friend."

"Uh, are you saying I'm not cool and hot? Rude."

His eyes go wide. "No!! You are! But I had an excuse to worm my way into your life."

I giggle. "I'm kidding. I know I put off more feral raccoon energy than hot bitch energy."

"I love raccoons!" Caleb exclaims earnestly, and I laugh even harder. "Wait, do you think raccoon shifters exist?"

I shrug. "Maybe? Don't raccoons have bones in their dicks?"

"I'm not sure if that would be a good or a bad thing," Caleb says, his face scrunching.

"Guess we might not have it too bad as far as monster weirdness goes. Maybe together we can befriend Mona and ask her what weird shit she deals with."

"Yeah," Caleb says with a chuckle. "Though I don't mind Tomas' weirdness...it's actually pretty great. I know Tomas and I are fated mates and we'll never break up, but he's ruined me for all other men."

My chest squeezes at the lovestruck look in Caleb's eyes as he talks about his mothman mate, knowing I look the same way whenever I think about Wes. "Same. Wesley is amazing. Better than anything I could've ever dreamed of for a partner."

"We're really lucky, aren't we?" Caleb asks, his voice growing soft.

My own is hoarse from emotion when I answer. "Yeah."

As if summoned by my swooning, I hear the front door opening.

"Hey baby girl!" Wesley calls out from the entryway. I turn to see him in his human glamor, laden with an absurd amount of groceries. He makes a beeline toward where I'm sitting in his living room—no, *our* living room. I keep forgetting that this is my home, because it still feels surreal. I unofficially moved in two weeks after we started dating, and a month later, Wesley hired movers to bring all my shit over from my house and helped me set up the basement as my official office and design studio.

Wesley bends down to kiss my cheek, then exchanges pleasantries with Caleb before heading over to the kitchen to set the bags down. "Got some stuff to make that stir fry you like. Also, they had a deal in the bakery, so I picked up a pie. Well, two pies, but we can freeze one of them if that's too much."

Caleb suppresses a laugh as I roll my eyes behind Wesley's back. I've given up on arguing with Wesley about him overestimating how much food we need. Mostly because he claims that it's an instinctual thing for him as a monster to provide an abundance of options to his partner.

"Do you want to stay for dinner, Caleb? We've got more than enough food!" Wes has a twinkle in his eyes, like he's goading me into complaining about the ridiculous amount of food, but I don't take the bait. My ass is still a little sore from last night's discipline.

"I shouldn't. Thank you though! I, uh, I have some stuff to do for the party on Saturday. Speaking of which, I'm going to head out." Caleb stands and I walk with him to the door.

We talk for a minute about the party before I bid Caleb good night, and he heads home. When I return to the kitchen, Wesley's removed his glamor and is putting the groceries away, but he pauses when I join him. His tail wraps around my waist as soon as I'm within reach, and he pulls me in against his chest, nuzzling his snout against my hair.

"You done with work for the day?" he asks, hands roving down my back.

"Yep, finished a bit ago."

"Mmm, good," he murmurs. "Such a good girl. I think you deserve a reward after dinner."

I frown up at him. "After dinner? Why not now?"

His hands drop further to squeeze my ass, and I gasp as he sinks his fingers into the sensitive marks he left there in a delicious reminder of what happens when I decide to be a brat. I press closer to him to try to escape his wicked fingers and feel his cock already thickening against my belly.

"Okay, okay, after dinner," I say, though I'm unable to stop myself from grinding my hips against his leg to see if he'll cave and take me now over the kitchen island.

Wesley laughs, far too aware of my game. "Don't worry, I'll make it worth the wait." He bends down to press his lips to mine, and I sink into the bubbly bliss of kissing him.

I know he will. Not just tonight. Wesley has, and always will be, worth the wait.

31

WESLEY

Ariana is uncharacteristically quiet as we drive to Caleb and Tomas' house for the "new relationship" party the monster support group is throwing for us tonight. It took them months to pick a date, so the strange celebration is even odder since we've been together for three months now.

The best godsdamn three months of my life.

We park on the street behind Nik's car, and I reach over to squeeze Ariana's thigh. "You okay, sweetheart?"

"What?" She looks up at me like I startled her. "Oh. I'm fine. Well, actually...I'm nervous. I've met the people from your monster support group, but I don't really know most of them. What if they don't like me?"

I blink at her in confusion. "Doug and Caleb are going to be there, and you've spent plenty of time with Tomas. Plus, Kelly is coming, right?"

She sighs. "I know it's ridiculous. I'll be fine after like five minutes, but that doesn't make me any less anxious about tonight."

My poor sweet ball of nerves. I take her hand in mine and bring it to my lips. "I'll stay with you the whole time. You have me, always."

Her eyes grow a little glassy at my words, and after a moment she nods. "Thank you." She steels herself with a deep inhale. "Okay. Let's go in."

We hold hands as we make our way around the side of the house toward Tomas and Caleb's backyard. They've gone all out with the decorations tonight, with votives lining the cobblestone path, and flower-shaped lanterns on poles swaying gently in the evening breeze.

I didn't think that it would be so fancy, but I guess Ariana's beautiful blue cocktail dress and heels should've been an indicator that this wasn't just a backyard barbeque. "Damn, did Caleb set all this up?" I ask as we approach the tall wooden fence that blocks the backyard from prying eyes so monsters can shift or drop their glamors.

"I'm not sure, I think so—oh!" Ariana lets out a little cry as her heel gets stuck between two of the stones in the path, and I curse, my lumbering body too slow to catch her before she falls.

"Shit, are you okay?"

She doesn't look like she landed hard, but she's clutching her hip. "I'm fine! Just give me a second while I die from embarrassment."

I glance around. "Don't worry, no one saw. Even if they did, I'll say it was my fault." I reach a hand out to help her up, but she doesn't take it. "Are you sure you're okay? What's wrong with your hip?"

"I'm okay," she says dismissively, but then mutters, "at least I hope so," under her breath. She gives me a weak smile and attempts to get up on her own, but can't seem to do more than get on one knee.

"You don't look okay!" I go to bend down to hoist her up, but she scowls at me and bats my hands away. "What the hell, Ari? Why are you being so stubb—?"

"Wesley, just shut up for *one second*. Jesus, you're so dense sometimes!"

My brow furrows in confusion and I open my mouth to ask her why she's being so damn weird when everything clicks into place. Ariana looks up at me from one knee, the hand down by her hip pulling something out of the pocket in her dress.

Not something—a ring box.

"Yes," I say, my voice suddenly hoarse.

She rolls her eyes at me and scoffs. "You didn't even let me ask you!"

A huge grin spreads across my face as I beam down at her. "Yes."

"How do you know that I'm not about to show you a cursed gem and ask you for your blood to bind its power to me?"

"My answer is still yes, baby girl. Anything I have, it's yours. Yes, I will give you my blood. Yes, I will find a way to break the curse and save you when the binding inevitably fails."

Ariana laughs as tears spill down her cheeks. I offer my hand to help her up and this time she takes it. Once we're on even ground again, I clasp her hand and the ring box with both of mine. "Most importantly, yes, I'll marry you."

She sniffles and gives me a watery grin, her jade eyes sparkling with hesitant excitement. "Really? Are you sure?"

I snort. "Give me the damn ring, Ari." She laughs and allows me to take the simple, elegant metal band and put it on. "'Am I sure?' Like you even have to ask. I was sure from the moment I met you."

Our mouths meet, and the empty ring box tumbles from her hand as I haul her up against me and she wraps her arms around my neck. I pour all my love and reassurance into each swipe of my tongue against hers, and she moans softly as my hands knead into her ass.

She's breathless when we part, but I know if we keep kissing like that, we'll never make it to the other side of the fence, where everyone is waiting for us.

"Wait, so does anyone else know?" I ask. She nods sheepishly, and I frown down at her bare hand. "Dammit, why didn't Doug tell me? I've had a ring picked out for you since the first week we started dating. I could have brought it!"

Ariana's eyes widen. "You've had a ring for *that* long?" She swats my arm. "What the hell, Wes? Why didn't you ask me? I've been nervous for weeks psyching myself up about this. I'm going to kill Doug! He never said anything to me about you having a ring."

I catch her hand and bring it to my lips, pressing a kiss to her finger where my ring should be. "Don't murder your brother. I made him promise not to tell you when I mentioned it to him. I was worried you'd think I'm nuts for wanting to get hitched so fast."

"Ugh. Fine." Ariana wipes her tears away and smooths a hand through her light pink tresses. "All that matters is that you said yes. If you said no, this engagement party would've been really fucking awkward."

I help pick a leaf off of the hem of her skirt from when she "fell", then register her words, my mouth falling open in surprise. "This is an engagement party?"

"Yeah, of course it is. You think I'd just randomly propose to you at Caleb's house? I was going to do it at home before we came over, but I was freaking out too much. Then you said such sweet things in the car, and I knew I had to be brave."

She's so damn sweet, but I can't resist teasing her a bit. It's truly absurd that she'd have any doubts about my willingness to be with her forever. "Can you really call it brave if it's obvious to anyone with a pulse that I'm crazy about you?"

"I know, but anxiety isn't logical! Just let me have this, okay?" She crosses her arms over her chest with a huff.

"Yes, baby girl." I tug her back into my arms, my chest swelling with so much love I worry I might burst. "You're brave and smart and beautiful, and I can't wait to spend the rest of my life with you."

ARIANA

I BARELY GET through the gate into Caleb's backyard before I'm bursting into tears again. Doug gives Wesley a death glare when he sees me, but I wave him off. "H-happy te-ears," I manage to get out through my ugly sobs. I'm embarrassed to have everyone see me like this, but I can't stop. The relief, excitement, and love flooding my system is too much for my body to handle without being a blubbering mess.

Wesley cradles me against his chest, dropping his glamor as

soon as we're within the privacy of the backyard, so there's more of him to hide me from the concerned view of the partygoers. I wasn't actually nervous about hanging out with Wesley's friends, but now I am.

Caleb hesitantly approaches after a minute, and I force myself away from the safety of my minotaur's chest to give him a wobbly smile. "W-we're engaged. Thank you s-so much for your help. This place looks b-beautiful."

"Aww Ari, of course. Congratulations!" Caleb hesitates for a moment, then pulls me into a hug, and it takes all my willpower to not start crying again.

I'm not as successful when Doug crushes me against his chest, but if anyone can deal with me getting tears and snot on his shirt, it's him. After a moment, he releases one of his arms and gestures for Wes to join us. Then we're both being squeezed by my surprisingly strong brother, who doesn't let go for a solid minute.

His eyes are wet when he finally releases us. "I'm so happy for you both," Doug says, swiping at his tears.

Soon there's a parade of people coming up to congratulate us. Kelly teases Doug about the bet he lost with her, while tearfully proclaiming that my love with Wesley was written in the stars. The monster group leader, Nik, gives Wes an enormous hug that leaves both of them misty-eyed.

Things go by in a blur, but eventually I find myself standing alone in the quieter corner of the yard. Wesley wanted to stay by my side, but his friends were eager to talk to him, and I don't mind a moment alone to breathe.

I watch as Wes throws his head back in laughter at something a confused-looking cyclops says, while Doug pats the cyclops' shoulder in what looks like reassurance. I can only guess what they're talking about, but whatever it is, it warms my heart to see my family looking so happy and relaxed.

A soft voice pulls me from my observations. "Mind if I join you?"

I look up to see Mona, Max's partner. Damn, she's *so* pretty. Caleb was right. She introduced herself when we first arrived, but I was too weepy to notice. Her deep purple dress hugs the ample curves of her body, looking like it was made with her form in mind. She's holding two glasses of champagne, and reaches out with one as an offering.

"Oh! Not at all." I take the champagne flute from her with a smile. "Thank you!"

"Of course." Mona smiles, momentarily dazzling me with how that makes her look even prettier. "Sorry for interrupting your solitude, but I wanted to say 'hi' again now that things have calmed down a bit."

"That's so sweet of you. It's wonderful to meet you. Caleb has sung your praises many times."

Mona lifts a dark brow. "He has? I thought he didn't like me. He always finds an excuse to go somewhere else when I've tried talking to him."

I laugh, then take a sip of the champagne. "He's anxious around you because you're so hot and cool."

"Wait, *what*?" Mona's eyes widen comically, and she snort laughs. "That's ridiculous! I'm so far from cool it's not even funny."

"I don't know...you seem pretty cool," I reply with a shrug.

This makes her snort again, and she covers her mouth with her hand as she flushes at the sound she made. "See. Not cool. But, thank you. You also seem pretty cool," Mona says with a genuine smile.

I like her. Caleb would get along great with her too, if I can help him get past his nerves with Mona. I catch his eye from across the yard and wave him over. Caleb's brows shoot up when he notices who I'm talking to, but he joins us and gives Mona a shy smile.

"Hey Caleb!" Mona says brightly, and Caleb looks surprised by her excitement to see him.

"H-hey Mona," he says back, already looking anxious.

"I think we should induct her into our monster fucker society," I blurt out, trying to cut through the nerves hanging in the air.

"Monster fucker society?" Mona asks, raising a bemused brow.

"It's not a society!" Caleb clarifies quickly. "We just... We were talking about some of the stuff that happens with our monster partners and if it's, uh, normal or not."

"Oh hell yeah, I'm in." Mona claps her hands together in excitement. "Though I don't know if Max is quite as...different as Wesley and Tomas are. I mean, he knows a little sex magic and has a tail that he can use for stuff. But no two dicks or anything."

"Are there monsters that have two dicks? I ask in a shocked whisper.

Mona shrugs. "I don't know for sure, but I think so. Max's sister has mentioned some really wild stuff, but I can't tell if she's telling the truth or not."

"So does Max... does he like to mark you with his...?" I trail off, suddenly feeling nervous about asking a stranger such a personal question.

Luckily, she doesn't seem weirded out or offended. "Hmm, not that I've noticed, really. We, uh, a lot of the stuff we do is...unconventional. But that doesn't have to do with the fact that he's a monster."

"Oh! Yeah, Wes and I have, um, an.... unconventional dynamic, too."

"Unconventional?" Caleb asks hesitantly, his face flushed from the risque topic of conversation.

"We're going to need a lot more champagne before I tell you details," Mona says with a laugh, her cheeks darkening as she toys with her gold necklace.

"Same." I'm dying to know if she means kink, and if so, what kind. I've never met someone besides Wes who I could talk to about that sort of thing, but there's no way I'm prying.

Caleb looks between the two of us, coming to a similar conclusion as me. "Ah. Okay. Got it." He rubs the back of his neck with a sheepish smile. "I'm pretty vanilla, so the wildest thing I've done is sex while Tomas is flying."

Mona and I turn in unison to look at Caleb in surprise.

"Whoa! Is that safe?" I ask.

He blushes. "Probably not, but it's worth it."

"Damn," Mona says with a laugh. "You're a lot braver than I am. I wouldn't trust Max not to drop me. Alright, fuck it. If you both promise not to divulge any information revealed to the society of monster fuckers, I'll grab more champagne and we can swap some stories."

Caleb grins, looking much more relaxed now that the ice is thoroughly broken with Mona. "Sure."

I should probably say no, but screw that. This is a rare chance to bond with people who understand what it's like having a monster partner. "Alright. I'm in."

"Hey sweetheart, sorry that took so long. Ren wouldn't stop asking for human dating advice, and Susan made Kelly cry, and then Nik kept wanting to give me advice for a happy marriage. I think I may need a full memory wipe after some of the things he described."

I look up to see the slightly blurry, but always glorious, sight of my handsome minotaur. Who's so big and beefy, I want to lick him all over. "That's okay, daddy," I say with a bright smile.

Mona and Caleb erupt into a fit of giggles and I turn to shush them, but end up laughing too as Wesley raises an amused brow. "Having fun over here?"

I wrap my arms around his thick waist and lean in to inhale his intoxicating scent that makes me wet every time I smell it. God, he's the best. I love him *so much*. "Mmm, yes. But maybe we can go home and have some more fun," I murmur.

"Alright, baby girl. Let's put some food and water into you to help balance out the..." he glances over at the table littered with champagne flutes, "four glasses of champagne?" He chuckles and squeezes my hip, warm affection pouring from every inch of him. "Then I'll take you home."

"I know something else he can put in you," Caleb stage whispers, and Mona snort-giggles before covering her mouth with her hands.

Wesley laughs, undisturbed by Caleb's uncharacteristic remark. "I think I should get Max and Tomas to check on you two."

We bid the pair goodnight, and Wesley loops his arm around my waist, guiding me over to the snack table. I appreciate his help, because it's become a lot harder to walk in my heels. He points out the giggling pair we left behind to their monster mates, but I don't pay attention to what happens after that. All I care about is the minotaur holding me up and passing me a cup of water, which I gratefully drink down.

Everything feels fizzy and soft, and my heart surges with so much love for Wesley that I tug him down into a kiss as soon as I've finished my water. A few people nearby laugh and let out a whoop for us. And why shouldn't they? We've found love that most people will never have a chance to experience. We're together and we're getting married and...

"Wes, I love you. So, so much," I murmur between kisses.

"I love you too, Ari. So damn much."

Everything fades around us into nothing as we share this moment. I go up on my toes to kiss him even harder, but the bubble pops when Doug groans and yells at us to get a room. I flip Doug off and pull Wesley down so I can whisper in his ear. "You heard him. Take me home, daddy."

Wes lets out a soft groan. "Alright, baby girl. Let me just say goodbye to everyone."

By the time Wesley gives our thanks and farewells to the rest of the partygoers, and he's coaxed me to eat a bit, the buzz from the champagne fades into a gentle warmth. I nod off for a moment in the car ride home, awakening to Wesley scooping me up into his arms and carrying me inside.

"Mmm, I can walk. I'm fine," I mumble, still half caught in sleep, but he holds me closer and kisses my hair.

When we get to the bedroom, he sets me down with a soft smile. "How are you feeling, sweetheart?"

"Perfect. Sorry, I had a bit too much to drink... I wanted to induct Mona to the society of monster fuck—" Wesley raises a brow at me and I giggle, "Whoops, that's supposed to be a secret."

He chuckles in amusement at my slip up, and begins undressing. "You don't have to apologize. Seeing you relaxing and having fun makes me happy. But what's this about a society?"

My eyes follow his fingers hungrily as he unbuttons his shirt, loving every inch of his broad chest as it's revealed. "Hmm?"

Wesley laughs harder as he tosses his shirt into the hamper. "Never mind. I'll ask you when you're less distracted." His hands drop to his belt with a dirty grin, but he pauses.

"One second." He dashes out of the room without another word.

"Where are you going?" I call out after him, but he doesn't reply. I unzip my dress and tug it off over my head as I wait for him to return, hoping he doesn't take too long doing whatever the hell he's up to.

There's a muffled sound of crashing and a curse from down the hall, and I'm about to go check on him when he returns, slightly flustered but grinning. "Sorry, had to grab something." When he sees the lacy white lingerie I've picked out for tonight, he lets out a low whistle. "Godsdamn, baby girl."

My cheeks heat as I flush with pleasure. "You like it?"

He joins me where I'm sitting on the edge of the bed and sinks to his knees, hands kneading into my hips as his snout nuzzles between my thighs. A choked giggle bubbles out of me as he takes a deep inhale and groans before pulling back to look up at me. "I fucking love it." His eyes shine with lust and adoration. "Just like I love you."

He kisses my thigh. "My sweet baby girl."

Another kiss further down my leg. "My clever, amazing Ari."

One more kiss right above my ankle, and then he dips his hands into his pocket and pulls out a small box. He opens it and gives me the most heart-melting smile. "My future wife."

I blink in surprise at the *rock* he's presented to me. I knew he had a ring, but the diamond on that thing is enormous. "Wes..."

"If you don't like it, we'll pick out a different one." He squeezes my thighs reassuringly.

I shake my head at him. "No! It's gorgeous. I'm just surprised by how...big it is."

He snorts. "I thought you liked big."

"I do! I'm a little shocked, but it's perfect" My vision blurs as he slides it onto my finger. It really is perfect.

"Looks good on you, baby girl," he murmurs.

I tug on his horns to guide his mouth to mine, sending all of my adoration into the kiss. He returns it with the same fervor, guiding me further back onto the bed and moving into the space between my spread thighs.

When we pause to catch our breath, I give him a coy smile. "It'll look even better when my hand is wrapped around your cock, daddy."

He releases a rumbling sound that's halfway between a laugh and a growl. "I bet it will. But tonight, I want to show you just how well I can take care of you."

He tugs my panties down and brings his mouth between my thighs to taste me, and my emotions threaten to overwhelm me as I think about how much the care of my monster has transformed me.

I'm remade by Wesley's touch. Reawakened by his love. I was lost before that fateful, ridiculous night in the escape room, and I can't wait to spend the rest of my life with the minotaur who helped me find myself again.

WANT MORE of Ariana and Wesley's story? **Read the Patreon-exclusive sweet and spicy epilogues to see what our favorite daddy dom minotaur and his baby girl are up to a few years in the future.**

AUTHOR NOTE

Hello monster lovers! Thank you so much for reading Escaping the Friendzone. I hope you loved Ariana and Wesley as much as I loved writing them.

I tend to write about things that are on my mind, and Escaping the Friendzone might be the book that hits the closest to home for me. Not the daddy dom part—though I wouldn't say no to my own minotaur daddy that wants to take care of me. No, I'm talking about the stress and pressure of running a creative business on your own.

There's a bizarre mix of excitement and panic when you unexpectedly start to see a little success that I didn't anticipate when I started out on my author journey. I'm humbled and a bit perplexed that anyone wants to read my books, and it's the most rewarding thing in the world to know that my stories bring people joy or help them feel seen.

Being an indie author is a *lot* though, y'all. Especially when you're an anxious, controlling gremlin who hates asking for help. Writing Ariana's struggle with finding a balance between her career and personal life has helped me see where I need to give myself more grace. I'm doing my best to be my own Wesley and learn how to set boundaries and accept that I can't do everything on my own. Now I just need to find my own Caleb.

On a much more fun note, Wesley has officially taken the top spot in my dream book partner rankings (sorry, Max). I'm a total sucker for a pairing that's based on friendship, mutual trust, and support, and Wes brings all of that to the table. Plus, he's a hot, rich minotaur daddy. What more could you ask for?

One of my favorite parts of writing Escaping the Friendzone was sprinkling in characters from other Moonvale stories. Between the monster support group, and seeing more of Caleb and Mona, my author heart was very full. I plan to keep this up with my Patreon serials. Can you guess who will show up in A Guide to Ghosting?

Many thanks to my beta readers, Kass and Jen, as well as all of my amazing patrons who helped make this book a reality with their support and encouragement. Also, thanks to everyone who read the short story in the My Monster Valentine anthology and asked me to write more about this couple.

Thanks again for reading and for your support!

ABOUT THE AUTHOR

Emily loves cozy, emotional, and spicy romances with a monstrous twist. When she isn't musing on the merits of doting, dominant monsters, she reads an obscene amount of romance novels, and cultivates her eccentric recluse persona.

Made in United States
Cleveland, OH
11 February 2025

14280295R00152